Vengeance of tl

Jacob Bower is a young author living in the small town of Towcester, in England. He attended the local secondary school after which he started working at Towcester Racecourse. While working there Jacob embraced his long passion of literature and began work on The Escape from Humanity. A fifty-page handwritten novel, that soon grew into the wider Ilmgral universe. Now four years on, The Escape from Humanity has now been released. Showing Jacob Bower's unique ability of mixing the friendship and heart of teenage years with gripping action and dark tones.

Vengeance of the Gods

The Knights of Earth Saga.

Book One: The Escape From Humanity.
Book Two: Vengeance of the Gods.

History of Ilmgral.

Vol 1: The Sundering of the Two Moons

All books available as a Kindle E-Book or paper back through the Amazon store.

Vengeance of the Gods

VENGEANCE OF THE GODS
BY JACOB BOWER

Vengeance of the Gods

Copyright © 2014 Jacob Bower

All characters in this novel are fictitious and solely from the author's imagination. Any resemblance to persons living or dead is purely coincidental.

Cover artwork by Emily Mortimer.

Vengeance of the Gods

Foreword

This universe is just one in a long line of failed universes. In those before, beings beyond our comprehension played with the fabric of reality and manipulated the lives of those they created. Learning from their creations love, jealousy and eventually a hate that sparked wars between them until they ripped the universe apart and the cycle started again.

In Besan Gretan, the realm that is, Gadrika, God of life, hearing the echoes of those before him, decided to give select mortals the powers to level the playing field so that this universe could reach its chosen path.

The Ilma, so majestic in form and spirit, were chosen custodians of the universe but greed comes often to those already with power. Dark events drove them from their righteous path and the Graul, the servant race, were gifted powers so that the Ilma did not become tyrants in their toppling of the Gods.

Empires were split at this decision and the Ilma, now spread far across the stars, battled for dominion over the universe. Peace came at a heavy price and in that ruin, the Ilma sort for a chance to turn themselves back to a proper path. They sort for a new power, one not foretold by the Gods and in their search, they

Vengeance of the Gods

found Humanity. A love for mankind came swiftly to the Ilma, who saw in humanity the true custodians of the universe. Through experiments they tried to merge their DNA with ours, to give the powers bestowed upon them to the people of Earth. Then they departed, to allow Humanity to thrive and waited for any sign of their success...

Walking as a child they found him.
The secret knight of earth
Though the humans he called kin
Their skin they hid his birth
but he was of a greater kind
A power he had within
That only tragedy could find
in the mountains heart therein

Part of the poem, The Tragic knights of Earth- Author Unknown

Chapter One- The Chamber of Scaraden

"I want to know why I was summoned?" Urgarak yelled as he stopped in the threshold of the door, his breath stolen at the vastness of the grand hall. He had been inside its white walls before but rarely enough that the hugeness of it still made him feel like a tiny speck in the universe. He looked towards the great domed roof, supported by two figures both standing far over fifty feet. He cast his eyes away from the marble, sculpted in the likeness of the first kings of Scaraden, who had formed the eternal empire.

Urgarak marched forward, a ceremonial cape billowing with every step. A couple of paces behind two of his Murka generals followed, their arms scraping the red floor tiles. As he walked, Urgarak straightened the medal on his chest. The image of the flag of his 'home' planet filled him with confidence, even if the red moon of the warrist movement would outrage the members of the council.

The chairs of the hall were empty along Urgarak's march but statues of all the high kings stared down at him from marble eyeballs but Urgarak kept his own eyes on the stage in front of him. Eight of the nine seats were occupied and the figures were sat forward watching Urgarak as intently as the statues did. Urgarak stopped at their feet and bowed at the large marble figures that stood behind the council. The king eternals, those who had led Abgdon during times of war. He wished beyond anything that they were here now, they would understand his cause. Two were out there somewhere. Prisoners of those Ilmgralite fools. Only the third had died truly, one of only a small few of the Ilma who had died after the curse had come upon them.

The council regarded Urgarak with their golden eyes and Urgarak met their stares confidently, but he could not keep his gaze from moving to the middle seat of the council that sat empty. It would seem King Crio would not entertain him. "Urgarak Mortrim." One of the figures said. He was wearing robes of pure white that seemed to match perfectly with his fully white scaled skin. That made Urgarak snarl, the perfection of the Ilma. His skin was covered in red scales and many dotted his narrow face.

"Gorin." He replied scornfully.

"Remember your place Graul." Came another voice from a far chair. Urgarak's eyes strayed towards him and black veins flared before he could control it.

Urgarak took a deep breath, he had to remember what he was. The Ilma were the chosen people after all, his power was just a gift. Urgarak turned his frustration back into the cruel determination for his cause and so turned his eyes back to Gorin, "My place." He murmured, "Is to hunt down those who hold the essence of our people captive. To bring war to a race who has aided the Ilmgralite's in their tyrannical hold on the universe."

Gorin stood swiftly, the air in the hall seemed to surround Urgarak and his eyes flicked to the floor in fear, "We called you back one season ago." The head of the council said without showing any of the anger Urgarak was sure he felt, "Yet you returned to Uralese, that was a mistake."

Urgarak's golden eyes flashed black for a second and he spoke grimly, "Uralese is still a troublesome world, our might should not be forgotten there long. I returned our fleet and came with the only ship I could spare."

An old lord stood. He looked like he was close to his rebirthing, but he still spoke with the musical power of the Ilma, "It is impressive for one of the Graul to rise so high within our ranks." Urgarak nodded but it was an insult and he knew it, "You were sent to Earth to find evidence of Cirtroug's imprisonment, not to release him." He took a deep laboured breath, "We have all seen the signs. The Gods are moving, they are planning their final strike to

crush the Ilma. Crio will avoid war at all costs."
"Crio is a coward." Urgarak said before he could stop himself.
"HOLD YOUR TONGUE." Gorin yelled and all the air was sucked from Urgarak's lungs and he stood, gasping in the vacuum that Gorin had created. Urgarak could feel the pressure swelling his eyes and his chest tightening. His legs wanted to fall but it seemed Gorin was holding him up as well. Slowly with a white smile, the Ilma released him. The first breath after the denial was like syrup.
"What do you know of Uralese?" Urgarak asked through his deep breaths, "It must seem a troublesome place, the once slave world of Ilmgral. What petty trifles did they ask for it? You should see it high council, Graul, Murka and Livet children starve in the streets while wars rage across its continents. It is a forgotten world."
The old Lord spoke again, "All Uralese is worth is the Virdact that we mine from it, the Livet's could barely write before we found them and now they live in luxury."
"Starvation is not Luxury." Urgarak said grimly, "Uralese needs a war, only in war do our people find sufficient work, only then DO YOU NOT LEAVE US TO ROT."
"YOU WERE SENT TO STUDY EARTH, NOT TO RELEASE THAT MANIAC CIRTROUG UPON THE

Vengeance of the Gods

HUMANS." Gorin yelled and thunder crackled in the sky above Scaraden.

Urgarak took a step back, "I did release him." He muttered, "On Uralese the truth of the Gods was shown to me, the true legacy of the Ilma. I harness it now and it showed me how we can defeat both the Gods and the Ilmgralites. Earth is the key, the one who defeated Cirtroug was of Ilmgral, reskinned among the humans with all their divine darkness." He saw the dark look in the councils eyes and decided to press further, "Not only did the Ilmgralites create those abominations on Earth, not only did they imprison Abgdon's great heroes on that world, but they send their people to live among them, to breed them into the army Ilmgral needs to rule this universe. I will not stand by and let that happen. You are the Ilma, the chosen people, tasked with keeping the Gods from tearing our universe apart. Well the Gods work through Ilmgral. I can see it in the stars, and they will use Earth to finally crush us."

Gorin seemed tired, his eyes fell pityingly onto Urgarak. *A sign of mortality,* he thought. Urgarak would not have much longer in the universe and his haste for war was due to that fact. The council of the Ilma of Scaraden had none of those issues. Gorin had served since the first days of Abgdon. His father, who gave his energy to terraform Abgdon, had been born just after the curse had been bestowed to the Ilma. Gorin had patience and he would not let Urgarak lead Crio into a war where only the destruction of the universe would follow. Gorin returned to his seat, "Urgarak." He paused, "You are hereby suspended from command. You will return to Uralese and surrender your fleet to Flight Marshal Cambane."

Urgarak smiled, black smoke coursed through his veins, darkening his mind. He knew it would come to this. If the council would do nothing, it was best that he was a part of no nation to fight the war his way until both Abgdon and Ilmgral had no choice but to intervene, "As you wish my Lords." He bowed low and looked at the statues of the kings, "May the eternal church never falter and the Gods tremble at the might."

The council elders nodded and watched as Urgarak and his two servants left the hall in disgrace. Gorin turned to the Lord beside him who whispered in Gorin's ear, "We should blast him out of the sky."

"No." Gorin shook his head, "Urgarak is a fool, reckless and narrowminded, blind to anything else but his goal and that will one day see him to his death but he is beloved on Uralese. The empire of the Ilma have split once already and we do not need the resource planets rising up under his dark dream." Gorin then signalled for one of the guards, who had sat silently behind, to step forward. The Ilma who stood beside Gorin was young in terms of the Ilma, he had never lost the physical form he held but he was powerful and full of youthful aggression, "You will go with Urgarak and make sure he follows our command. It would be good for the people of Uralese to see one of the Guardians of Eternity."

"As you wish my Lord." The man said and he marched quickly to follow Urgarak.

"War is upon us." The old Lord continued, "Crio will not be able to delay it. We should recall our fleet. If the foretold war is not against Ilmgral then it will be against the Gods themselves."

Gorin pointed to the hall before them, "Scaraden stands forever. We built this hall so not even Livella herself could stand within it. If it is to be war, then the darkness shall lead us to victory and neither Ilmgral nor the Gods will stop us. The time is not yet ripe, however. We are too few after the last war. Crio is desperate to learn where our kin are imprisoned."

"What of earth?" A young lord, only risen after Crio had ascended to be king, spoke then, "Urgarak is right. One of the Graul has reskinned among them, that is rare enough but then to live as a human. One like that, allied with the half breeds could bring a new power to the universe that had never been foretold by

Livella."

Gorin seemed un-moved, "Ambassador Lucast assured us he has no memory of his past." He then smiled cruelly, "Though the thought intrigues me, maybe in him the experiments of old will work. A child of Ilmgral with all of our gifts mixed with the darkness and natural brilliance of Humanity, a sight that might even make the Gods tremble."

Chapter Two- The Chase

The night air whistled through the dark alleyway and rustled the ivy against the old brickwork, buffeting a single figure dressed in black. Thomas Lita's ears tuned in to the sound of dogs barking in the nearby estate, while his golden eyes examined the moonless winter sky, watching as his breath curled up towards the stars.
It was early in the morning, maybe just passed five am and Tom could feel his heart thumping in his chest as he thought about the game he was about to play. He stepped from the shadows before throwing the hood over his head and re-adjusted his school bag over his shoulder, tightening the straps ready to run.
A few slow steps took him out of the alleyway and into a well-lit street. The light from the lamppost's reflected in the frost covered grass that crunched with every light step that he took. Tom looked to the floor, his hand raised in front of him and the white grass returned to dark green, now dewy with moisture. He was no ordinary twelve-year-old, he had discovered through dark and terrible nightmares that he had the power to control the elements; Fire, earth, water, metal, and many more had become his playthings.
What he now knew to be part of some design he had found friends in Southbrook who held

some form of these powers. His friends were not like him though, they were products of a long-abandoned experiment by the planet Ilmgral, guardians of the universe, to create soldiers for their war against Abgdon.

These powers were put to the test three months ago. It was meant to be the holiday of a lifetime, the thought made Tom's stomach tighten and the wind howled around him. He had been lured to a volcano on the Caribbean Island of Curamber and become a puppet of someone else's plot to release one of the Ilma, a chosen person but this one was corrupted, a remnant of a long dynasty who had battled for the rights of Ilmgral's army and been banished for their conflict.

Cirtroug, the name still quivered at times on Tom's lips. He had been long in the planning of his escape, stealing humans and corrupting them. All it had taken was the touch of Tom's hand to bring forth his vengeance upon the world.

Only with help had Tom survived, help from his four friends, and help from Lucast, ambassador to Earth for the planet Ilmgral. They all had scars from their battles, but his touch may have been the worst. Lucast used them for his own gain, maturing their minds and setting them as his soldiers. Minds of men in the bodies of children. If Thomas Lita dreamt anymore, he was sure the nightmares would plague him. In that dark hall, Tom's true origin had been revealed to him. He was of the Graul, the meant to be servants of the Ilma who had been gifted the powers he possessed as a way of stopping the Ilma, should their quest for eternal life corrupt them beyond their designed purpose.

Tom had won though in the end. He had defeated Cirtroug in the heart of the volcano and trapped the alien's eternal essence forever, before he had been rescued by his own government.
To his shock, the world or a select few, knew all that Thomas Lita and his friends were and with the attack they had been recruited, given an area to practise and the backing to live in peace and privacy.
The months after had been tough, especially on his friends. They had gone in circles, denying what had happened, reliving it every waking hour, to shutting down, skipping school days at a time but slowly each cycle had become less severe and they found ways to deal with their trauma.
One Tom had discovered. Lucast had tried to hide his maturing in the back of their mind. It took adrenalin, fight or flight to kick start it but when they did, they became as they were on the Island. That was how this game had begun, they were once again being hunted, well Tom hoped that he was the one hunting.
Tom turned out of his estate through a white field, a shortcut into town where the others all

lived and would be stalking. Without the streetlights and no moon, the field was almost in complete darkness. Tom's hand lifted; he felt an energy in his fingers before a bright flame erupted from his hand. He held his torch aloft and stepped gingerly across the frozen field, hearing for any sign of pursuit.

The flames extinguished as he made his way onto the main high street. It was eerily empty at that time in the morning but already signs of life were starting to emerge. Tom could see a few lights on, businesses waiting to open and the occasional car appeared further down the road. Tom passed a shop window, that was still black behind it and saw himself in the mirror. It still shocked him about what he knew. He did not look like one of the Ilmgralite's, he shared none of their white and red scales, even if he was extremely pale. His golden eyes, the only part that showed his heritage, examined his neck. Even in the darkness Tom could see the mass of burn scars, ruined white and red flesh, his biggest physical scar from the Island. A crooked nose showed another. The hoody concealed his brown gelled hair, the only thing that seemed normal now about Thomas Lita.

It was getting late, increasing Tom's frustration and unease; they were meeting at his best friend's house at six. He was sure he had left enough time to at least have some form of encounter. As he was running his eyes caught something, the sight made him stop but it was the smell that caught his attention. Tom turned to face the concealed figure standing in a house front. The Tempter was considering him with golden eyes concealed by a dirty brown hood. A cloak rustled in a wind that Tom could not feel, and white scaled but rotten skin gave off some light or reflected light from wherever the figure really was. The Tempter smiled at Tom and with a flick of his wrist he pointed his walking stick down towards the street. Tom's eyes followed and he saw there, running fast, a figure who could have been no one other than Price. His head snapped back towards the Tempter, but he had vanished, leaving no sign that he had been there at all.

"You are going mad again." Tom said to himself in a voice that was starting to break, "He died on the Island with Cirtroug, he is not here." Tom could not shake the feeling that he was wrong about that. The Tempter had led him up the mountain to release Cirtroug but then he had helped Tom ever after. He was a mysterious figure who seemed to haunt the Island. Lucast had described him as a creature of desire, governed by powers he didn't understand.

Trying to shake the Tempter out of his head, he went on the hunt, hoping Lucast's power would quell the creeping doom he felt inside of himself. Following Price, he soon found himself on a large football field. He wheeled round but there was no one to be seen. He cut to the edge to hide in the darkness, an attempt to not become the hunted.

There was a noise but Tom could do nothing as a root snagged against his ankle, sending the twelve year old crashing to the floor. Tom watched as a second root burst from the ground, it quivered in the air before charging at him and all he could do was roll out of the way just as the root collided with the frozen earth. With a quick push, the ground forced him back to his feet. Price was charging towards him, his hand held backwards towards a nearby willow while he sang almost in-audible words to it. A large willow branch suddenly seemed to grow and swing towards Tom, who only just managed to sidestep. Price went silent as a ball of fire leapt from Tom's hand in an instant, charging at his best friend. This Price ducked easily and as he went to regain control of the willow; he faced his best friend.

Tom yelled, all his warmth stolen from him as a ball of water collided with his back, drenching his hoody, and threatening to freeze him in place. His eyes went away from Price. His best friend had power only over plants, but sweet little Sophie had control only over water.

Tom was trapped between the two of them. He could control what they could but not nearly with enough potency and trapped now between the willow and the river he was outgunned with the powers he would choose to use. Just as all three were about to charge, the alarm on Price's phone blared into life, followed shortly after by Tom's and then Sophie's.

All in an instant the tension subsided and Price burst into laughter. Tom walked up to him and patted him gently on the shoulder, "I thought you had me there."

Price shrugged his broad shoulders and flicked his long hair out of his eyes, "I would have if we had more time."

Sophie approached them, she was breathing heavily, "Next time we should start earlier." She said between gasps, her voice sweet and musical like the gentle trickle of water across rocks.

Price began walking away, "We should get to mine. School will start soon."

Tom looked towards Sophie who raised her eyebrow back at him. He laughed, "Price." He deadpanned, "What about your girlfriend?"

Price looked at them both wide eyed before chuckling, "Oh yeah, where is she?"

Sophie grabbed her phone and checked it, "She was over at the railway, she is going to meet us at yours."

"Why the railway?" Price asked, his face showing his confusion.

"It's all electrical up there." Tom smiled, "She would have been able to do anything to us."

"She will do all sorts if she has to stand outside my house waiting for us." Price replied, "Let's get a move on."

Price's house was not far from the field. It was in darkness since his mother left early, much earlier than the time Price would usually crawl out of bed with only ten minutes to go before the school bell. That made it perfect for their post chase rendezvous. All the others had found excuses for why they would not be up in the morning. Tom's was the simplest, his mum, fearful and concerned of who she had adopted, left him mostly to do his own things since the Island.

Price turned on the living room light and Tom saw his friends properly for the first time that day. His eyes lingered on Sophie, causing an involuntary smile to form on his lips. He smiled because her eyes were lined and her brown hair slightly curled, a change that had only come in the last couple of weeks.

She had suffered most from the Island. Her pale white skin and blue eyes screamed of innocence and sweetness, but they were not illusions. Sophie had a big heart and it had nearly been ripped out of her on the Island, she was the one who needed the most time to recover.

Price on the other hand looked as he always did; the Island had not stripped him of his cocky personality. He was slightly shorter than Tom but much bulkier and held a strength in him that surpassed his twelve-year-old stature. His round face was always full of mischief and his quick smile showed white teeth and bright braces.

Just as Tom went to sit down, there was a knock on the door. It opened, and Kathryn Dalton stepped into the living room. Price jumped up and the pair shared their first kiss of the day, Tom knew it would not be their last. She was the opposite to Sophie, taller and more outward in her body language. Her brown eyes were lined in an Egyptian style and her power over electricity made her blonde hair wild and frizzy. When she smiled it was cruel and was usually followed by her sharp, thunderous, laugh.

"Can't believe I didn't find any of you." She moaned in her loud obnoxious voice.

"That's because we were being sensible and not trying to short circuit the whole town." Price replied right in her face. She smiled wickedly, her hand came up and a spark arced from her index finger to hit Price in his slightly chubby stomach. He yelped, his long hair sticking out wildly.

Giggles filled the room while Price kissed Kat again. They had admitted their feelings on the Island, without the disaster it might not have lasted between them but what had happened formed a bond stronger than any Tom had seen.

Kat's eyes turned away from her boyfriends and examined Sophie, "Did you get much sleep?" Sophie shrugged her shoulders, "I did last night."

Vengeance of the Gods

Kat smiled and Tom wondered why they considered what could have only been five hours sleep sufficient.

"You just need more hugs." Kat grinned, her eyes flashed onto Tom while she attempted to be subtle, something she had never mastered. Tom's stomach dropped suddenly, and he crashed into the large sofa. They all knew what he was, knew he was not human, yet they had all grown up together and it was hard to look passed the normal teenage way of living. They wanted Tom to be with Sophie, to protect her but he could not do it, he would not have the luxury of doing it.

He had learnt not long after the Island of the curse he would have to face. The Ilma were immortal, the Graul like him were not but their lives still greatly exceeded that of humanity. The power inside them healed them and gave them life until the gift was extinguished. That could range from three hundred to seven hundred earth years. He sat there, knowing that one day he would say goodbye to every one of them. This thought crushed the maturing Lucast had done and Tom became again a twelve-year-old standing on the edge of a canyon with the world begging him to jump.

Sophie's eyes strained onto Tom as his hands came and rubbed at his temple, she knew the pain he went through but maybe she did not truly understand why.

Vengeance of the Gods

She couldn't look at him any longer, so she turned to Price, "Shower's free?"
"Sure, one in the En-suite other in the main bathroom." Price replied and the girls disappeared. He eyed Tom nervously, "How many showers do you think they have a day?"
Tom lifted his eyes, clearing the dark thoughts from his mind, "Probably like Five."
He opened his backpack and pulled out his crumpled Southbrook uniform that was squashed over his textbooks. They both changed into their white shirts, black trousers, green and gold blazer, and tie before making tea and breakfast for the two of them. The only thing that was different about what Tom and Price wore, was the winter scarf that Tom wore to conceal the burns on his neck. In the time it had taken to change the girls had remained upstairs. Price stamped on the floor, "How long does it TAKE?" He yelled to gain their attention.
Tom sipped at his tea, "It takes a long time to look that good."
Price ran a hand through his hair, "Don't I know it."
Tom pointed down at his best friend's spotless shirt, "Yeah especially with that tea stain."
Price shot up, moving his blazer apart to see. When he saw nothing, he stripped his blazer off and stared at his reflection.
Tom laughed as Price's eyes scanned every inch of his shirt, "You are a vain sod."
The girls emerged in their Southbrook uniforms,

though they were the same as the boys, the girls always seemed to look smarter on them. They drank their tea and ate their breakfast in silence, but it seemed to Tom like words were spoken. There was a comfort in the room, a comfort that came just from the fact that they were all together.

The walk to school was probably the best part of the morning. The four of them were able to mess around and for a short time be the kids they were meant to be. Price and Tom teased eachother about the latest football results, while Sophie and Kat gossiped behind them. The bell rang just as they arrived. Tom and Price said goodbye to Sophie and Kat.
In the classroom, Tom left on his winter scarf. He had permission to wear it from the headmaster and most of his teachers respected his wish for privacy. The class still seemed small, only fifteen students were in this class now. Some were survivors of the Island that Tom and the others had rescued but most were new faces. The school had seen an influx of students, all a bit weird and all wanting nothing more than to be friends with the survivors of the Island. Sitting there, Tom could feel the power from some of them, those that were Halve's who had moved to Southbrook to train like Tom and his friends.
The class as always went slowly for him, the study of tectonic plates bored him greatly and

he also knew what was coming. His teacher, Mr Wood was talking about volcano's and how they were formed. He could feel eyes lingering on the back of his head, wondering how he and Price would react but they did not know the truth.
The truth that what happened on the Island was not a volcanic eruption and the pair barely connected the natural power of the volcanos with what had happened to them all.
"As you can see." Mr Wood said in his Scottish accent, "The raw power of our planet can be quite spectacular."
Price leaned over to Tom, "If Sir thinks that's powerful, we should show him what we can do."
Tom did not look up from writing notes in his book, "Yeah I'm sure he would love the flower you could give him."
Price scowled, "If I wish hard enough will the Tempter take you away?"
The mention of the Tempter bought the memory of his run from home back to his mind, "I saw him earlier." He whispered.
"What?" Price's hand tightened around his pen.
"I saw the Tempter." He could feel a tension build in the room and his nostrils smelt the air for any signs of decay.
"A dream?" Price asked.
He shook his head, "I told you I don't dream anymore, this was in the town."
Price's cocky demeanour gave way slightly but

he tried to recover it, "Can't be, we have heard nothing for months, why now?"

Tom looked at his notes nervously. They all knew Cirtroug had been released for a reason and they knew that he could still be easily freed. Fear of revenge plagued them constantly and in the back of Tom's mind he wished for it. For all of them the Tempter would be a precursor of this doom. Tom could see sweat beading on Price's head. He needed to be the anchor that grounded his friends, "I'm sure it was just my mind playing tricks on me, our part in this is over."

Tom looked up, Mr Wood was watching them, but he did not seem to be angry, instead he seemed to be weighing up what he was about to do. He looked down as his eyes caught Tom's, "I don't think we can discuss this without mentioning that for all of us these parts of nature are close to our hearts." Mr Wood had not been at Southbrook at the start of the year, he was a replacement for a teacher who had died on Curamber, a body Tom had never found.

The maturity in Tom's mind broke again but he regained it once Mr Wood pressed a button on his computer. Tom's mind kicked back into the fight. He had seen no images of the Island since he had returned home but it was etched forever in his memory and the sight of it transported him back there.

It was a news broadcast and the reporter began

immediately as the image showed the plume of smoke coming from the volcano's peak, "The volcano erupted yesterday morning and the vast smoke plume still covers the sky hampering rescue efforts. Little news has come from the island and a state of emergency has been declared. Among the missing are a group of British school children from Southbrook in the midlands."

Mr Wood pressed pause as a hand went up. It was one of the band girls, her chubby cheeks were wet with tears. She had been on the trip the week before and luckily for her no halves had been present then to release Cirtroug, but she, like many, had lost friends there, "Please sir. Can we not?"

Mr Wood looked shocked, it was not his choice to show the video but the headmaster's, a way of gauging the mood of his pupils. Mr Wood's eyes strayed to Tom, Price and Stephen, one of the survivors. They were all looking down, their knuckles were white from the strain of holding their pens.

"It's almost time to go. Why don't you all take five minutes before your next lesson." He smiled and the class noisily packed up their belongings, but no words were spoken.

"I can't believe he did that." Kat yelled, causing the other students using the library to stare at her, she quickly lowered her voice, "He shouldn't just show videos of it."

Price's hand grabbed hers, "Lucy was in tears." He deadpanned, "Her sister died, didn't she? It's not fair that we can't tell them what really happened."
Sophie looked up, her usually soft eyes hardened, showing Lucast's maturing, "They can't know about that without knowing about us and that will be worse."
"It could be better." Kat whispered, "We wouldn't have to hide for a start. You three saved the world and no one says it."
Price beamed, "We could have a holiday just dedicated to me."
Tom sighed while Sophie and Kat shook their heads at him. Usually Tom would stay quiet, this discussion occurred often and always with the same results. He only stepped in when they needed reminding of how risky their position was, "As soon as people know what we can do, they will get scared of us. We will be singled out and treated differently. The longer our existence stays as a conspiracy theory, the longer we can try and be normal."
Tom couldn't see their reactions as his world went suddenly black. He knew who was covering them, he could smell her perfume and feel the softness of her hands.
"How is my little Tommykins?" Nicole squealed and before Tom could answer, her hands came away from his eyes and she began a violent tickling spree that turned him from the composed leader to a drooling mess.

Vengeance of the Gods

"Please..." He begged, "I can't breathe."
Her attack stopped and she knelt down beside him, her eyes scanned his scarf, "Still wearing that then?"
Tom tightened the folds, "I feel better with it on." Looking at Nicole brought a smile onto his face. He had only met the fifteen-year-old on the plane over to the Island, where he had seen her gift and the pair had instantly connected. On the Island, Nicole had become one of them and without her, Tom was sure they would not have survived.
Nicole had a heart shaped face with perfect skin, her brown eyes were like deep wells and when she smiled, dimples showed below her high cheek bones. Her black hair was in a ponytail, the green tips all together. She was tall, slender but as strong as the earth, a trait of her gift. She had not seemed to have suffered as much as the others; she was already older, already more mature meaning Lucast's power had changed less about her. It seemed instead to make her more focused. Her age and her exams approaching, meant she never lingered long on what had happened to them.
"You seem overly happy this morning." Tom grunted.
He watched as Nicole flushed, a smile creeping onto her lips, "Things are going well?"
"Your mocks?" Sophie asked intently.
"That and." Hey eyes darted upwards as a boy with messy hair walked past. The pair seemed

to share a smile that Kat picked up on instantly.
"Oh I know that look." Kat beamed, "Who's the lucky feller?"
Tom's eyes widened, whether he was jealous or just protective, he felt a knot form in his stomach.
Nicole's eyes fluttered, "It's nothing, not yet anyway." Her eyes then strained to Tom, "Have you taken Sophie out yet?"
Both their mouth's fell open, but Sophie's quickly shut, her eyes lingering on him, waiting for his reaction. He was silent, saved by the end of break time bell. Molten warriors, and alien war lords he felt he could handle but teenage girls were another thing entirely.

The rest of the day passed quite easily for Tom until English, the last lesson of the day. His English teacher, Mr Laws, was an old man who could barely breathe, let alone read the complex narrative of Shakespeare yet he plodded on every day. Tom was surprised though. He was usually there to meet them but in his place was a woman, small with big round glasses. She was a substitute that Tom had seen around the school, but she had never taken one of his classes. She did the register slowly, her eyes falling on everyone who answered,
"Thomas Lita."
"Here." He said.
His hand rubbing the skin under his scarf caught

her attention.

She gave him a warm smile, "Can you take your scarf off please Tom?"

He was silent, stunned by the simple request, "I can't." he murmured in disbelief.

The Substitutes smile dropped in an instant, "What do you mean you can't? Do your hands not work?"

"Mr Laws allows me to keep it on Miss." Tom said weakly, like he was begging her for her last piece of bread.

She gave a quick but disgruntled laugh, "Of course he doesn't. You know the rules Mr Lita, just because I am not Mr Laws does not mean you cannot show me the same respect."

He could feel the eyes of the whole class rested on him, his defences were slowly crumbling as his hands moved to the folds of his scarf.

Sophie's hand shot into the air, but she did not wait before speaking, "Miss he really can't."

"Now." The substitute said sternly, ignoring Sophie.

Tom stood up, peeling back the scarf, his heart fluttering and any maturity bestowed by Lucast fell away in an instant. As the skin was revealed, a collective breath was taken by the class. They had heard rumours about the Island and had guessed that Tom had been injured but they had never seen the true extent of his wounds and it shocked them. The mumbling began at once and Tom's resolve crumbled. The Substitute had her mouth wide open, "I'm

Vengeance of the Gods

sorry." She mumbled, struggling to find anymore words.

From behind him Stephen stood up, his face flushed red and his fists trembling. Tom looked at him, his eyes welling up but with a movement of his hand, Stephen sat down. He could feel shakes and tears approaching, his mind filling with dreadful images of the Island, "Miss can I be excused?"

The teacher looked shocked but she nodded gently, unsure how to react. Tom took quivering steps out of the room. Sophie went to follow but he waved her down as well. He needed to be alone, to not have the need for strength.

As soon as he was out of the classroom, Tom began to sprint. He was sure he was back on the island, back fighting for his life trying to save his friends who were doomed to die. The air was fresh on his cheeks as he stormed outside, voices and screams filling his mind. Tom felt the pull of a large tree and the resistance of the earth underneath him and he launched into the air, coming to rest on a high branch of the tall oak. He stared at the world, darkening like a plume of smoke blanking out the sun. All this was his fault, the scars they all shared, their fear, the death of all those people, all because of his weakness, "SORRY!" He yelled to the sky in his anguish.

He could still see the coach moving away from the museum, still see the molten ball that collided with it all because he was too weak to

break the Tempter's spell, "I'M SORRY." He yelled again, his vision clouded and the words that led him up the mountain formed in his mind once again, "Come to me child, up the mountains heart, through the wind and the wild, where your journey starts. Knowledge and wisdom are my key, for that is what you seek, now come and climb the path to me, beneath the mountains peak."
Tom's eyes burst open, "LEAVE ME ALONE." A great wind rolled up and the branches creaked but as it faded Tom was alone still. He had always been alone. There was no one to hear his apology, no one to ease his guilt. They waited for him now, only in the darkness.

Through the next forty minutes Tom worked through his trauma, taking his mind through all the events, trying to form a mental barrier once again. With a deep breath his heart rate calmed. The bell for the end of school rang and he lowered himself back towards the ground. Before he knew it, Sophie was in his arms, holding him tightly. Tom looked at Price and Kat who stared at him nervously, "You left this." Price said, his hand holding up Tom's scarf. Tom released Sophie and took it gingerly, wrapping it tightly around his neck.
"Are you okay?" Sophie asked, her blue eyes glistening.
He looked down, "I will be." He tried to smile but the effort failed him.

Vengeance of the Gods

She took his hand in her delicate ones, her finger running up and down it, "Do you want to come round mine?" She asked gently and not without a hint of want in her voice.

Tom looked at her, knowing what she wanted him to be but his regression back to the island showed him that he could never be that, "I'm going to the Agency."

Sophie looked at him and nodded, knowing better than to try and dissuade him. Her hand grasped his one more time before she let go and turned to leave with Kat. Price lingered, "Are you sure you are okay?"

"I just need to let off some steam." He smiled. Price's eyes showed his disbelief, but he nodded as well and walked away with the girls, leaving Tom on his own, a fate which time would bring.

Chapter Three- The Agency.

People still stared at the high walls of the construction site as they drove passed the services on their way through Southbrook. What lay beyond was still a mystery to most people. The construction was soon to be the home of the Agency that monitored Halves. The government had spent millions on the new site, readying for the change that was soon to come to the world. Tom stared at the beginning of the vast satellite relay being constructed on the concrete roof. Tax, the director of the Agency, had told him that it was Earth's first step towards the stars.

Tom was filled with eager excitement as he stared at it. He could see it the moment he left school and it helped lift his mood slightly, he could not wait to train there. For now though, the Agency had acquisitioned an old office building and hastily adapted it for their uses while they recruited staff and began the training of their new Halve strike teams.

Tom felt sorry for his friends, who still did not understand his need for distance. He only felt complete when training at the Agency, where he could fill the void created by Lucast and Cirtroug. The office building looked like nothing spectacular. White walled and dull carpeted, it smelt like it had not been used for many years prior to the Agency. Tom said good afternoon to the outside guard and then signed in with one of the admin department who stopped Tom before he could charge off to the second floor, which had been stripped out and re-enforced, used for training the Halves, "Director Warman wants to see you." He deadpanned.

Tom gave a nervous smile. The director was never one for idle chat, if he wanted to see Tom it would not be for a good reason. Nervously Tom tugged on his scarf. He charged up a dirty staircase, ignoring the welcoming sound of those training until he reached the admin department. He passed desks that were nearly empty at that time until he came to Tax's office. The door was ajar which was rare, and his secretary was not sat beside it. Nervously Tom knocked.

"Come in." The Director said in a cheerful voice. Tom stepped through; the Director looked much different than the first time Tom had seen him. In the mountain cavern Tax had been a long haired and scruffy looking man. Now he looked completely different. His hair was short and neatly styled, flecked with silver greys. The suit he wore looked expensive, if not a little bit creased by this time of the day and he smiled like a man who truly enjoyed his work.

"Evening Tom." He said as he sat down behind his desk. He beckoned Tom to sit at the seat opposite and he took it gingerly. As soon as Tom was sat Tax continued, "I just wanted to talk to you. It has been a while since we spoke about everything." Tax stared at him and Tom wondered whether he knew about what had happened at school that afternoon.

"I'm fine." Tom muttered his downcast eyes betraying him but Tax didn't seem like he wanted to press to greatly yet.

"And the others?"

He thought back to the morning, how they had seemed so much back to themselves but there was always that edge, always that wall that Lucast had created ready to break through at any moment, "They are doing better sir. I think we are starting to get ourselves back to some form of normality."

"Are you dreaming yet?" Tax asked as he wrote some notes on a sheet of paper.

Tom looked down. Before the Island he had the most vivid dreams. Dreams of another world but that had all ended on the Island when a link to himself and the Tempter had been broken in a dream. Now if he dreamt at all they were blurred beyond any form of understanding, "No not yet." He deadpanned but suddenly he remembered the Tempter again, "But I saw the Tempter this morning."

"The figure by the mountain door?" Tax asked, his eyes rising to examine Tom more closely.

"Yeah, I was on my way to school this morning." He thought it was best to leave out the chase, "When I saw him stood in a doorway."

"Saw or thought you did?"

"I don't know." Tom mumbled trying to remember as much as he could, "It seemed real but with the Tempter it is hard to tell and sometimes when I see the Island or something that happened there, that can seem real to."
Tax stopped writing notes, "Are these visions occurring regularly, regression is dangerous Tom."
His head shook vigorously, "Only on bad days but they've never been the Tempter before." He thought back to all that happened on the Island, all the warnings of the war soon to come, "Cirtroug was released for a reason. The Tempter was part of that. If he was here, then..." His voice trailed off as he struggled to find the words.
"So you think he is a precursor?"
"A warning more like." Tom deadpanned, "I'm still not sure whose side he is on." His heart rate fluttered, and he caught the smell of mould that always accompanied him whenever he thought about the destiny laid upon him. He wanted to scream and to run away from it all but if what the Tempter said was true, there was no escaping the path chosen for him, he just had to be ready for it.
"I wish I had some answers for you." The Director said sadly, and Tom believed he meant it, "I have the military scanning everything I can think of, waiting for any sign of what might be coming. What worries me is everything is silent, like a breath before a storm. We were caught

off guard on the Island and peopled died as a result. I do not want that to happen again."
Tom laughed sadly, "Me neither."
"Are Price and Kat doing well? I don't go on Facebook often but when I do, I can't seem to escape pictures of them both."
Tax saw the corners of Tom's mouth twitch, the involuntary reaction to thinking about his friends, "They are good." He replied, "They might be extremely annoying when they are together, but I thank the world that they are. Nicole is doing great as well not that I think it has hit her yet."
"And Sophie? She was always the worry."
Now Tom's smile faltered but his jaw clenched, a more defensive response, "She's getting there, sleeping more now and she has begun to take care of herself again."
"She has a thing for you I hear." Tax said it slowly and watched Tom's reaction. His eyes dilated, his forming Adams apple rose and fell in a large gulp. He seemed afraid of it and knowing what he did about Tom, Tax understood why. The revelation that was made on the Island would have crushed most people yet Tax watched him carry on and use the knowledge to strengthen himself and he thought as he watched the minute reactions to his question's, that his strength came from the love of his friends.
Seeing Tom's discomfort, Tax changed tact, turning him back into the soldier, "What are

you training with today?"

His smile returned, "I was going to exercise in the fire room."

Tax's eyebrows raised, "And metal I hope."

"Yes and metal." Tom deadpanned but it did not sound convincing.

"I will make sure David comes and see's you. He says you are still struggling with it."

Tom went to argue but Tax's phone began to ring. Knowing that he was not meant to listen in on the Director's calls, he smiled at Tax and made his way out.

On his way down the stairs Tom thought about the Tempter and the Island but it did not work to break down his barriers now, instead it built them up, working on Lucast's maturing and spreading his natural fire through him. When he stepped into the training hall he was back as he had been on the Island, a leader, a warrior. The training room was large, with stations for different gifts. Very few Halves were training, just a few of the younger ones, who like Tom, had come after school.

Tom stepped towards a room lined with metal, blackened by the fire users who trained in there frequently. A man was stood inside, Peter Ward, member of the strike team Fox and Tom's occasional fire instructor.

"And I thought I would be left in peace today." He smiled, "Let's see if school has tired you out."

Vengeance of the Gods

Tom lifted his hand and a ball of flame appeared within, the air from his fingertips to the flame became distorted with the energy required to keep the flame alight.
Peter smiled and from his own hand a ball of flame now hung, "Ready?" He asked and Tom smiled wickedly in reply, the ball in his own hand dispersing.
Peter threw the ball towards Tom, who ducked and held out his left hand, immediately the ball came under his control. His right hand slipped into his pocket and withdrew his father's lighter as the ball circled over his head. Tom flicked the lighter and another stream of flame joined the other, doubling it in size and with a yell Tom launched it forward, not at Peter but at the blackened painted target. The flames burst apart and faded in a whimper.
Peter smiled at Tom, "Nice trick, where is the lighter?"
He held it up to his fire instructor, "I always like to keep it with me, the fuel stops me getting tired out so quickly."
Peter seemed to like the idea of that, "I will remember."
They trained together for a while until Peter's eyes strayed out of a reinforced window built into the fire box, "Uh oh, looks like David is waiting for you, you wouldn't want to keep him waiting."
Tom nodded and with a smile he left Peter. David was stood in the now nearly empty room

and when he spotted Tom, he nodded towards the metal station.

Tom jogged over, "Hey."

"Tom." David deadpanned; his metal instructor tried to seem tough. He felt he needed to with Tom's reluctance to train with metal, but he was a kind and patient teacher. His brown hair seemed to shine with silver highlights and his dark eyes were warm even if a smile rarely graced them. With frightening speed his hand came up and from the table a coin launched in Tom's direction, almost instinctively his hands lifted, the fifty pence coin halted almost immediately. David smiled, applying slightly more pressure. Tom's knuckles whitened as he tried to hold it back, then with a cruel glance David released his hold. He almost fell forward and David had to duck as the coin was launched across the room with the force of Tom's resistance. With a slight laugh Tom stared at his teacher who regarded him with what looked like pride, "Well my training seems to be working." He pointed to a heavy metal object, the size and shape of a cricket ball, "Tax is really expecting some improvement so let us work on your hold before we go onto something technical. I want you to lift this ball thirty times."

Tom stood so that the ball was at his side, his hand rested above it, palm downward. He immediately felt the connection, like strings linking his hand to the metal ball. It quivered

and his hand trembled under the weight, but the ball barely lifted an inch before the connection snapped. The thud echoed around the empty hall and Tom's shoulders sagged.
"I'm not counting that." David smiled cruelly, "Metal is interesting Tom, it is a much more physical connection than with fire and water. Turn your palm, imagine that the ball is in your hand."

Tom's palm turned the other way and he gasped. He felt as though he could feel it, the ball bearing, its weight pressed against his palm. His arm lifted again and this time the ball lifted with it; its weight made his arm ache but at least he was able to keep control. Twenty-five of these he now managed before his arm felt like it was about to fall off. With one more heave the connection broke and the ball clattered to the floor again. Tom looked nervously up at David, knowing that his tired arms could never try that again, but David was smiling, and he handed Tom a bottle of water from the table. He drunk from it greedily, the exercise had dried his throat.

"Not bad." David lifted his hand and the ball came with it, resting with ease upon the table, "Would you like a challenge?"

"What sort of challenge?" He asked, wishing he had left straight after his meeting with Tax.

David lifted from the table a small lockbox with no key. Tom knew what he wanted at once.

"You want me to open it?" He asked glumly. He

had done such a thing on the island, but he could not recall how he had done it. Then it had seemed so natural, now the memory failed him. "A power over metal won't be much use if it can't help you in everyday tasks now would it?"
"Or felony." Tom retorted dryly.
He lifted his hand and felt for the pins inside the lock. It was only a simple three pin lock for him to move but they were small and he struggled to define which was which as he searched for the correct pattern. After five minutes Tom's frustration grew, he gave up looking for the pattern and moved the pins wildly.
David seemed to notice this, "Enough." He said sternly, "You are not concentrating."
"I'm trying my best." Tom replied like the twelve-year-old he was.
"I don't believe that." David said grimly, "Now close your eyes, cut out everything else. The connection to metal is more physical, you must feel it."
Tom took a deep breath, building up his barriers to the outside world. His hand lifted and he closed his eyes. His mind sort for the pins. He connected to the table, held together by metal screws. Then they found the lockbox. The result was instantaneous, he could feel the metal pins and sense the air in the void between them. The pattern became clear and with it his fingers moved instinctively, the pins slotted into place and the box opened. When Tom opened his eyes he was smiling widely, "Did you see that?"

Vengeance of the Gods

Tom grinned, "I can't believe it worked."
David high fived him, "Well done." He checked his watch, "It's getting late and you have given me something to tell Tax. You should get home and get some rest." Tom charged away but stopped when David called his name. His hand lifted, and the lockbox hovered into the air and moved towards Tom who caught it physically. "Take it home for practise, if you struggle stick your phone in. I'm sure you will soon open it then."
Tom laughed and charged out of the training room, he felt if he made progress like that every day, then nothing would stop him.

Tom's house was not large, but it was enough for the four of them. His father's job in the city earnt them enough to be comfortable.
He stepped through the door, the stairs to his bedroom were in front of him, the kitchen to his right but he ignored these and stepped lightly into the lounge. Two sofas sat around the edge. Its yellow walls seemed incredibly bright after the darkness of the day but the mere smell and feeling of his home was a comfort. Peter, Tom's little three-year-old brother looked up at him with large round eyes. His smile filling his round face, chubby cheeks flustered from running around. Tom's adopted father sat with him. He had the same round baby face of Peter and the same wide eyes, but his dark hair was thinning. Peter's curly hair he took from Tom's mother

who was sprawled on the sofa, crying while she watched TV.

"Hey buddy." His dad said, "Good day?"

Tom thought about it, school had been difficult but they would not understand why but his time had the Agency had been great fun, they wouldn't understand that either, "It was good." He said as he placed the lockbox on the table.

"Your dinner is in the microwave." His mum said with a warming motherly smile, a smile that made Tom wish he were just a normal person. To his parents, he was just another Halve like the others, a Halve that had been abandoned by his real parents. He needed security no matter what he really was, and Tax did not want his chance of a normal life threatened.

Tom grabbed his dinner and sat beside his mother and without thinking she began playing with his hair while he ate. Tom's stomach dropped, this was the worst part of his life, this lie of humanity that he lived but what choice did he have. He had no clue about who he was and what life he could live beyond these four walls.

"Tom." His mum said nervously pulling him from his thoughts, "Me and your father have been speaking. Well Christmas is nearly here, and we know we don't let you use your umm?" She stuttered, "What do you call them?"

"Gifts." Tom finished for her, stopping eating to hear what she would say.

"Gifts yes." She continued, "We was wondering

if you and your friends would like to." She
trailed away mumbling but luckily for her Tom's
father, who seemed to understand and accept a
lot more, finished it for her, "We want you and
your friends to use your gifts to decorate the
house this year. Maybe on Christmas eve. A
good present for you all."
Tom's fork clattered onto the plate and nearly
fell to the floor. His hand reached out and his
power halted it before it hit the ground. He
never took his eyes off his dad while the fork
lifted back towards him and landed delicately
on the plate, "Really?" He screamed, "Price
could do so much and Kat with the lights."
His dad's hands shot into the air, "Don't ruin the
surprise buddy." His smile faltered and tears
glistened in his eyes, "With what happened to
you, we realised we need to help you through it
and only in understanding what you can do will
we be able to do that."
Tom felt his eyes welling up, he wanted to hug
them both and he would have done without the
plate in his lap, "Thank you." He beamed,
"That's better than anything I could ask for."
He began eating almost at once in the hope to
stop himself crying.
"Some music?" His Dad said as he stood and
moved over to his prized possession, an old
record player. He went to turn it on, but Tom
stopped him.
"Let me show you what I've learnt." He yelled
and his Dad took a step backwards, arms lifted

in surrender.

Tom used the joy to fuel him, his hand lifted up and he searched for the vinyl player. It was old and made mostly of metal components. His hand reached for the needle and moved it into position. He flicked the metal switch and the record began to turn. Delicately and not without his heart beating in his chest, Tom lowered the needle. The song started immediately; he had missed some of the intro with his needle placement, but it seemed his training was beginning to pay off.

Tom spent the night talking with his parents, talking about his training, and opening about what had happened at school, though they did not begin to understand the guilt that plagued him. As the hours ticked by the tiredness from his early morning forced him up to his bed. He read some of his old dream diary, in the hope the memory might spark some dreams that night and then he prayed for forgiveness, his mind recalling those that he had lost. His list of the dead never reached its end before another dark and dreamless sleep claimed him.

Chapter Four- The Wrong Kiss.

"Are you sure you are okay?" Nicole asked as she walked with Tom across the back of the estate where they both lived, "You seem distant."
Tom stirred from his day dreams, the weeks of school leading up to Christmas had passed by in all the normality that they had previously. Tom had gone to school, gone to the Agency and then returned home but some emptiness was creeping up on him. His nightly prayers were becoming less frequent, his regressions back to the island less potent. He was healing but he didn't feel he deserved it. Old ideas of someone coming to get revenge on him began to stir again and he sort for the Tempter, wanting the next stage to happen quickly. Waiting as tense as a spring was not what he wanted.
"Yeah." He tried to laugh but he realised he would have to give some explanation for his melancholy, "It is just going to be a weird Christmas, the things we saw, what we did? We get to enjoy Christmas but because of us lots of others won't."
Nicole's smile faltered, "They would have just found someone else and then maybe everyone died or became those things." Her arm wrapped around him, filling the sister role that had seen them grow so close, "It's good that we do carry on. We got dragged into a story a thousand

years old but we owe it to everyone that we lost to move on now our part in it is done."
The emptiness crept on Tom again, he didn't want it to be over, he had to remove the guilt. They had set events in motion and he knew he could not sit idly by while they unfolded and he knew as well that his friends would follow him in that.

They reached a park and Tom's eyes noticed a figure sat on the swing and at the sight of them he stood up and jogged over, calling Nicole's name as he did. When he stepped into the light, Tom recognised him, but he could not think of where. He was around the same age as Nicole, with messy brown hair and stubble already growing on his cheeks. His eyes were the same shade of dark brown as Nicole's and they could have been related if not for the way she greeted him. Ignoring Tom, she threw her arms around the boy's neck and began to eat his face, or that was what it seemed to Tom, who looked away his face reddening.

She released the boy with a sigh and turned back to him, "This is Daniel, my boyfriend." Tom didn't seem shocked, he had guessed that already, "Daniel this is Tom, he is my hero." The comment made him blush further but it also made him feel like a little kid.

Daniel nodded, "Don't worry I know who you are. I see you up the Agency nearly every day."

"You go up the Agency?" Tom's embarrassment fell away in an instant.

"Fast programme." He lifted his hand and some small stones rose with it, "I want to join a strike team, so they are training me quickly."
Nicole's eyes seemed to go all gooey as she stared at her boyfriend. Tom even struggled to see the steel willed girl who had fought with them on the Island and he began to understand why she healed so quickly. He wondered whether that was why Sophie and himself, being alone, lingered the longest on Curamber. The sense of duty and loneliness hit Tom in an instant.
Nicole looked at the sky, "Me and Daniel are meeting some friends but I can walk you home first if you like?"
Tom felt even more like a kid, "With everything we have done." He phrased it carefully, "You are worried about me walking home."
"I'm just being kind." Nicole gawped, her hand coming and jabbing Tom in the chest, "Stick it then."
He gave her a gentle push back, "I appreciate it but I'm meeting Sophie first, I think she is having a bad day."
Nicole gave him a raised eyebrow smile, "That's because she needs you."
His jaw clenched, "I will see you tomorrow." He said as he walked away, leaving the couple and the awkward questions behind. He stared at the stars, wondering what was happening beyond them.

Vengeance of the Gods

The morning was bright. The sun, creeping over the fields of Dragor, fell warmly upon Lucast's white skin. His eyes turned to the mountains beyond the city walls. Umoria, the moon of silver, where Morelin rested, was creeping slowly into the sky above the city. His partner Lucarnia who sat upon the dusk moon had already departed. The birds of Dragor carried Morelin's song, adding their melancholy to his own that always brought a silence to any street of Ilmgral.

The estates of neatly arranged houses on the outskirts of Dragor closed in around Lucast as he walked. The city stretched for tens of miles in every direction but Lucast was near the centre of the capital. Trains and other vehicle's passed through the city at swift and outrageous speeds while Ilma and Graul used their powers to move themselves upon designated lines. Humans, Murka's and other creatures walked the street as well but only a few Graul and Ilma, there had always been too few of them.

Lucast stepped through the Dragon gate into the old city. The worn features of the dragon, made of black stone, could only just be recognised but it had stood for millennia, built by the power of the Vassal Crio before he rose the dividing mountains.

All the streets ran one way now, towards the great keep of Dragor built of slick black rock, a temple that had never fallen in any war. Now it was the palace, the government building of the vast Ilmgralite empire. Lucast stepped inside the great metal gate and it was like passing into another world. While the outside stood as it had since Crio's day the inside was modernised. Technology was everywhere, screens littered the walls and people communicated to those light years away. It was unusually busy but Lucast expected that. It was the gathering of the planets this week and all the ambassadors would be summoned to speak of their worlds to the parliament of the empire.

Many delegates were present, seated within. Most were of the Ilma but there were also many Graul like himself and even the occasional native, speaking for their planet. Lucast sat at the back, amongst the other watchers of independent worlds. The great king Mordin sat resplendent on his throne at the far side of the hall, watching them all, his face a mass of red scales showing that he was of the Graul. Mordin was the first high king to be raised from the servant race. The sight of him made Lucast take a breath. Today he wore robes of dark red, the two towers of Cradlin were sown into it and on his head, he bore a crown. Golden, it reflected the light of the chamber and it was styled like many interlocking flames. Reminiscent of the secret crown the kings of Dragor wore in the years before the kingless times.

Though he was crowned king, he was more an elected official and a king could rule no more than three hundred years, a lifetime for a Graul, a season to the Ilma.

The reports came quickly, the events of Ilmgral itself had been discussed in the first day of the conference. The top tier planets in the days that followed and now it was the turn of the resource planets. They spoke of good harvests, mining strikes and the occasional war. The council would debate the matters, doll out the food that was stored and decide on whether to send an army to intervene should the empire be threatened. This lasted most of the day and Lucast listened patiently. He had a vote and used it when it was required but he, like all the other independent representatives, voted only with the King and his high council. Near the end of the day it was called for the independent planets to speak. All around the hall murmuring began and people went to leave. Lucast forgave them this as it nearly always signalled the end. The independent planets rarely had anything to report but all went silent when Lucast stood, "My King." His voice bellowed, automatically amplified by the stone walls.

Mordin lifted his hand and the council seated themselves again. He smiled, his eyes brightening, "A message from Earth?" He said in a delighted tone.

Earth held a mythical place in the heart of the Ilmgralites and it seemed mysterious to them. Its place had not been foretold in the stars, but the God, Thera, had spent long in its design.

Vengeance of the Gods

"I told the small council last time I was here of the release of Cirtroug upon the people of Earth and the council ordered me to aid Abgdon in their investigation for earth sits under our protection. Well." Lucast gulped as Mordin's smile faltered, "I have learnt of the orchestrator of Cirtroug's escape. Abgdon's representative Urgarak is behind it and he is not pleased. I believe he will launch an attack on Earth in the hope of releasing Cirtroug again."

Mordin's hand came to rub at his face, "It was a mistake of our council of old to use earth as a prison for Abgdon's defeated. It would always make them a target, but most remain hidden even to the humans. What would you ask of this council?"

"Send a fleet to Earth." Lucast begged, "Protect this planet so Urgarak cannot launch his vengeance."

The high councilman for the realm of Morelin stood, "Ambassador, the seers have warned us that we have intervened to much on Earth and that if we continue to do so then war will come. War with the Gods and Abgdon. We must halt our presence there; it was you as well who ordered that we leave them in peace."

"That was before they became the targets of the warrist movement."

"Urgarak is fool" Mordin began, "He switched his allegiance to remain a part of Uralese when we sold it to the Abgdonese. He is a turncoat and a coward. Earth will stand against him if the power of their Halves is to be believed but I will not risk war with Abgdon over one of their generals. If he does attack then I believe Abgdon will denounce him."

Lucast knew he was losing the argument and he worried, in fact he knew, that it would not even come to a vote. He played his last card, "But one of ours stands amongst them. I tried to unlock his mind but a power greater than mine changed him when he reskinned and became a child among them. He is strong though, stronger than most refugees who live on Earth and the Tempter has taken a keen interest in him. He may one day lead the powered humans of that planet onto the galactic stage. That will draw Abgdon into war."

Mordin was un-moved and Lucast feared that he knew more about Tom than just the reports he sent him, "He forsook this planet and his mission." Mordin grumbled, "He is now a human and let him stand as their defender. I am sorry Lucast I cannot, will not, entertain the idea of starting a war for Earth. A war that would certainly tear the universe apart."

Disappointment filled Lucast, anger for his people as well and he thought he could feel the curse that infested the Ilma for all their past crimes. That curse the Gods would ever exploit to their own aims but Lucast was of the Graul, and his gift was given to stop the Ilma from their own destruction. He would not waste it, even though it would no doubt lead to his death, "Then I must apologise my King. I cannot do my duty and yet stand as a member of this council. I hereby resign my post." Murmuring's overtook the rest of Lucast's speech and Mordin's reply but suddenly Lucast's voice boomed like thunder and it condemned the Ilma, "If you will not stand with Earth, then I will."

The moon illuminated all before Tom as he skirted the edge of his estate to the lake where they would swim in the summer. The moon illuminated the silhouette of Sophie sat by the edge of the lake, but it was not that which took his attention. It was the crashing of water against the bank that concerned him. Great waves rose from what should have been the still pool and hurtled against the edge. Tom charged towards Sophie, she was crying, her head buried in her knees, her hands white from the power she unknowingly exhorted on the lake.
"Sophie what's wrong?" Tom asked as he skidded to a halt beside her crying form and sat cross legged to her left. She fell onto him then, her head in his lap, her arms clawing at his jeans, but the lake continued to act violently. His eyes scanned the distance and his heart dropped. Dog walkers were everywhere, and someone would be bound to hear it.
"Sophie. You need to control it." Tom said sternly, "Please Sophie people will hear."

Vengeance of the Gods

She sobbed louder but no change came over the lake. His hand stretched towards the lake and he felt her power, pulling and crashing against the water but he could not break her sway, she was too powerful.

Tom instead stroked at her hair and begged, "Sophie please I need you to help me."

He could hear the dogs barking at the crashing waves, but he could not worry about that. He focussed on Sophie, running his hand through her brown hair and slowly her breathing began to calm, "I'm here for you Sophie." Suddenly her hands relaxed and the lake calmed in an instant,

"Thank you."

Her eyes shot open like she had suddenly realised where she was. He could see they were blood shot from the tears but her crystal blue irises seemed to catch the light of the moon stunningly, "I saw him Tom." She said in a breathless whimper and she sat up swiftly, her head spinning to catch sight of something he could not see.

"Who?" He asked her as he used his hand to force her attention back onto himself.

Her eyes were wide with fear, "The Tempter."

"He's gone Sophie. He can't hurt us." He did not believe it, but it was what he was meant to say, though it seemed Sophie was not listening.

"I was walking, and I felt something behind me. All my hairs stood on edge and there was that smell, the mould and decay. He was staring at me with his golden eyes. When I stared at them it was like he was reading all my desires. I felt like I was naked. Then it all went black and I could feel him inside my head. He was laughing at me just like when I was trapped in Cirtroug's mind."

Tom's heart stopped. He had spent hours, they all had, trying to coax out of Sophie what had happened when she had collapsed in the mountain chamber but she had never divulged a single word and always her face paled at the thought.

"Was he there then?" Tom asked, his own fire burning inside of him.

"Cirtroug was in my head, learning all about me through the nothingness and he learnt about you. I tried to fight him. Then there was nothing, until I could hear your voice. You were talking about crossing a road and then another noise began." A tear rolled down Sophie's cheek and Tom stroked it away, "It was his walking stick. He was walking towards me and the blackness lifted slightly but I could not break free. He said, "Tom is in danger, only you can save him.""

His hand grasped hers, "And you did. We were trapped and you sat up and used water to charge at the warriors." Or that was what it looked like to him.

"It wasn't me." She sobbed, "I wasn't strong enough, so he worked through me. Everything I wanted filled my head then and I knew I could

never have any of it, but he corrupted the power and saved you. The effort I think nearly broke him for he screamed and seemed to turn to rot in front of me and then all I was left with was Cirtroug's laughter." Her eyes widened again, "I won't go back Tom, I won't."
He pulled her into a swift embrace, "It's memory now. It hurts but it's just memory." He hugged her tightly, feeling the coldness of her arms, "You are freezing." He smiled as he let go of her, "I don't feel it, but you will catch a cold out here like this. Please come back to mine?"
Sophie smiled, her full goofy smile but Tom caught again the want in her eyes. They flicked onto his lips, just the way Kat's did whenever she leant towards Price. Swiftly Tom stood up, he took her hand and lead her towards his house. She cried a bit more on the journey, silent tears that she seemed to be holding back but her hand gripped his tightly to give her strength.
Tom led her in, and Sophie climbed the stairs towards his room. He poked his head into the living room, "Sophie's having a bad moment Dad, is it okay if I make us some soup?"
His dad sat up slowly, his mum asleep beside him, "Is she okay?" He asked.
Tom knew he had a soft spot for Sophie, "She will be fine. We just need to have something warm."
"I will do it mate. You make sure she is okay,

and I will bring it up."

Tom and Sophie sipped at their warm soup, for a time becoming the young people that they were. The familiarity seemed to have calmed Sophie completely. She sat by him, gossiping. The full smile on her face melted away all his barriers. Without thinking he took a strand of hair from her face and tucked it delicately behind her ear. Sophie looked down, her face blushing. He sighed, a million questions circling through his head. His eyes closed; he could hear the television downstairs, but it was being drowned out by Sophie's nervous breaths. Tom did not open his eyes when she sat up and moved towards him, not even when he could feel her hot breath on his cheek. Only when her lips touched his cheek delicately did he open them.
His heart was racing, his palms sweating but before his mind could offer any argument he turned his head, looked into her eyes and placed his lips onto hers.
The world was spinning around him. He had never kissed a girl before and the contact was strange. He tried to follow the movements of her lips, but he could not match them, and his teeth clattered into hers. She broke away suddenly, a smile twitching onto her lips.
"Sorry." Tom said suddenly, feeling more awkward than he had any right to be.
"That's okay." Sophie looked at him again, her

smile beaming, her eyes glistening, "You just need some more practise."

She leant forward again, and Tom allowed himself to kiss her. They stayed that way for a couple of minutes, no parts of their bodies touching but their lips and the occasional bumped nose. Tom had never felt so close to someone but in the back of his mind voices screamed at him. He was not sure what this meant, were they now together? Tom wanted that more than anything, but he knew it to be a false dream of his link to humanity. To be with her was not his path, he would not watch her grow old and miserable beside him.

This time Tom broke away but her lips lingered there, her eyes closed like she was trying to hold onto the moment.

"I need a drink." He gasped, "would you like one?"

Sophie smiled at him in a dreamy way, "No I'm fine." She grabbed her phone and hurriedly began typing to someone, then she stopped and stood up, "Actually, I think I better get home. My dad will be worried about me."

He wanted to say something, but his mind would not function. Her hand came up to his cheek and she knelt on tiptoes to kiss it gingerly. Then with an embarrassed smile she crept from his room. Tom sighed and collapsed onto his bed. The warmth that her hand had left on his cheek disappeared in an instant. He lay there, thinking of the moment he would have to leave them. Dark words circled through his head, words he had heard back on the Island when he saw the vision of Kat, words embedded in the curse of all those of Ilmgral who come to earth, the curse of the King.

Chapter Five- Hidden dangers and terrible truths.

"You should not have angered them." The guard of Eternity said as he marched alongside Urgarak, condemning him with his sweet musical voice.
"I only sort to share with them my views." Urgarak replied coolly.
The Graul had to duck as he walked the hallways of his ship. It was designed for the small stature of the Murka's and not for one such as himself, the guard had the same problem and the constant crouching seemed to have put him on edge.
They reached the bridge and the relief of the vast open space was blissful. The re-enforced glass gave a great view of a storm over the continent of infinity as the ship sat in orbit over Abgdon. The Murka's stared at the guard nervously but not as nervously as when their eyes strayed onto Urgarak.
"Engage thrusters." He ordered, "Break us out of orbit."
The ship lunged violently but Urgarak's powers rooted his feet to the floor. Soon Abgdon disappeared and the dark vastness of space was before him, "Set our course to the Ingarly jump. Then set the Virdact engines for Earth."
"Earth." The guard yelled viciously, "Ignore that command, General Urgarak is suspended, I

command here, you will set the Virdact engine for Uralese."
None of the Murka's moved and Urgarak laughed viciously, "These Murka's do not represent Abgdon and they do not answer to your authority."
The Guard stared at Urgarak as black veins rose and fell on the Graul's skin, "You cannot do this, you will be killed if you touch me."
Urgarak licked his lips and black smoke poured from his mouth, "I serve a higher purpose and my life was forfeit when I gave over to it."
Flame kindled in the guards hands but Urgarak seemed undaunted and as the flames charged a figure of smoke burst out of Urgarak. It took the shape of a man before driving at the guard. His scream was enveloped by the shadow and his flames extinguished. Urgarak watched as the guard fell to the floor, writhing in torment until the last of the shadow passed into him. At which point he lay there sobbing, "Finish him." Urgarak whispered and the guard went rigid, a high-pitched scream shot from the guard and he slumped to the floor. Urgarak licked his lips and pain soared through him. He could hear the guards screams inside his head and could feel all the hurt that had gone into making this prison. His nightmares would be terrible that night.
Mirkan, Urgarak's Murka commander approached him slowly, "Is he dead?"
"No." Urgarak said bitterly, "Even this weapon

cannot kill the Ilma so easily. He is trapped inside his own mind and his body is a vessel that I can use for a while. Our mission will be long complete before he wakes from his torment." Urgarak turned back again to the stars, "Let us finish this."

*

The next morning the rain drove against Tom as he almost ran towards school. It was on days like this that he wished people knew of his powers. He would love to be dry, using his power over water to drive the rain back against the direction of the wind. He knew he could not though. His walk to school was surrounded by people all getting just as drenched as he was. Sophie was waiting outside the school gates for him, sheltering under an enclosed walkway. It seemed she did use her power. Tom stared down at his own uniform. The green wet and darkened, his shirt going see-through. Sophie's looked fresh on, without a drop of rain on it. She was smiling at him and Tom was sure she was wearing more lipstick than usual. Her hair was slightly more curled, and she stood on the balls of her feet, rocking on them as he walked towards her, "Did you sleep well?" She asked a little awkwardly as soon as he stopped next to her.
Tom tried to avoid looking into her blue eyes that seemed to sparkle even more that

morning, "Not really." He said and it was true. He had laid awake most of the night, trying to piece together his part in the tale and why the world made him feel so alone. He wanted to know things and more importantly he wanted to dream. They had never given him answers but in that world of dreams he had felt like he belonged.

He had also laid awake thinking about his feelings for Sophie and in the hours just before sleep did take him, he was sure he had found the words to say. Now though his mind was blank.

"That's a shame. I slept amazingly it must have been the soup." She said while staring at him. She continued to stare, with her goofy smile on her face, until Tom could not take it anymore. He looked back at her, the corners of his mouth twitching into an unwanted smile, "What?" He asked.

She rocked on the balls of her feet more vigorously, "Nothing, I am just happy is all."

"SOPHIE WOULD YOU DO SOMETHING ABOUT THIS." Kat yelled as she approached them, unafraid of who might hear.

Price trudged alongside her. Kat stopped by them, her usually frizzy hair hanging limply over her face, "I am soaked, and my handbag is ruined." She held up a bright pink bag that was clearly darkened by the rain.

Sophie's eyes twitched towards Tom before she lifted her hand. Every drop of excess moisture seemed to lift off Kat, hovering around her until Sophie let it fall to the floor. Kat shook her head and her blonde hair instantly became frizzy and sparks seemed to crackle around her. Tom's head whipped around but apart from two people that Tom knew to be Halves, no one had seen.

Tom pointed towards the handbag, his eyes turning to Price, "Hey did that come from your mum's collection?"

"Oh sod off." He replied, shaking his long hair that was still dripping wet.

"He thinks it looks good." Kat beamed, "Don't you?"

Price nodded while she was looking but the moment she turned away his eyes rolled dramatically, "Don't ever get a girlfriend." He said, stepping aside so that he was out of reach of Kat.

Tom went to laugh but before he could, Kat and Sophie began giggling, their eyes quickly straying towards him.

Price looked at them in confusion, "The only good part is the kissing." The girls laughed even harder now and Price finally realised he was missing something, he threw his hands wide, "Can someone please tell me what the hell is going on?"

Kat and Sophie went silent, attempting to hold back their giggles and smirks. Tom ignored them, storming off to his first lesson. Behind him Sophie's smile dropped, and she looked at

Vengeance of the Gods

Kat who gave her a gentle shrug of the shoulders before a push to follow him.
"I didn't mean to make you uncomfortable." She said as she finally caught up with him.
"You didn't." Tom said unconvincingly, "Just a lot going through my head."
Sophie squeezed his arm but didn't press further, "Hey, a new girl is starting today, I think she may be a Halve but I didn't get a chance to ask. Do you mind if she sits with us in English? she doesn't know anyone."
Tom actually smiled then, he was dreading English, a lesson on a table alone with her and Kat would be excruciating but they could hardly ask him difficult questions with a new girl there, "Sure."

Mr Laws was waiting for them when they stepped through the door, he stopped Tom suddenly, "I've just read your short story Tom." He picked up a piece of paper from his desk and took a deep laboured breath, "Then I felt the glass of the phial against my leg." Tom's face reddened and Sophie gawped at him, but Mr Laws seemed not to notice, "Hope seemed to fill me. I would not die this day. Death waited only for my enemy, there he may look out and see me, happy and in love, living a life he had forsaken." Mr Laws stopped and placed the paper down, "Quite powerful Tom. I wanted to ask what it meant?"
He racked his brain. He had written about his

battle with Cirtroug, with some changes to protect what had happened, "It's about our insecurities. I wrote it to deal with what happened on the Island, to help with the guilt. Cirtroug was everything I felt about what happened there."

Mr Laws nodded sadly, "I'm glad you found some way to come to terms with your grief." He handed Tom the sheet, "If it helps, I've graded that with full marks." He breathed deeply again, "If you ever need to chat, I'm here."

Tom smiled but it was impossible, he couldn't talk to Mr Laws any more than it seemed he could talk to Sophie about what he was going through. The pair walked towards their desk, where she grabbed the sheets, "I want to read this. I had no idea you could write."

"I just needed to get the words out of my head somehow." Tom didn't mean for it to seem so sullen but his frustration at himself for not finding the words to speak to his best friends came through in his voice.

Sophie nodded and sat down next to Kat, who seemed able to read the feeling on the table and did not start the barrage of questions that he was sure were stored in her head. A silence filled the room and Tom's hair stood on end; his eyes darted to the door. A girl was stood in the threshold. She seemed nervous, long flowing brown hair fell over one of her eyes that were green, sparkling with fear. Her chubby cheeks were dimpled with a nervous smile as she

waited on the edge of the classroom. Tom's senses seemed to heighten, a smell of decay came into his nostrils, his heart rate increased, and goosebumps covered him. He was afraid.
"Hello Hannah." Mr Laws said with a smile and turned to the class, "This is Hannah, she will be joining us." No one said a word so Mr Laws turned back to the girl, "It looks like everyone is here so please sit wherever you would like."
Her eyes caught Sophie's and her smile widened slightly. she glided towards the table, head down and face flushing. She looked at the seat by Tom for a second before sitting quickly into it and un-packing her bag.
Tom's breath caught in his mouth and his jaw locked. He could feel the energy burning in his fingertips and it took all his power not to let it out.
"This is Kat." Sophie said. Kat did not look up from the phone tucked under the table, but she nodded, "And that's Tom."
To seem normal he tried to breathe and he managed a muffled, "Hey."
He looked at her, cute and unthreatening but then why was his whole body on edge? His mind forcing him away. His eyes involuntarily fluttered between Hannah and Kat, but he could not understand why.
A strange thought grabbed at his mind. He had felt this sort of repulsion before, at the threshold of the mountain path when he had resigned himself to go and defeat Cirtroug. His

eyes scanned the rather pretty girl and
wondered how he could feel that way now?
"Hi." She replied with a smile, her eyes catching
his for the first time, "WOH!" She gasped,
"What colour are your eyes?"
Tom smiled nervously, "They look gold I know."
Mr Laws handed out some sheets for the lesson
and Tom set to work immediately. He felt
trapped between two dangers. A girl who loved
him, who would do anything for him and
another that he was sure would bring some
harm to him. Sophie's leg brushed his and he
felt all of the feelings he had for her that he
knew he could never act upon and then to his
right, he had this new threat, though he still did
not truly understand that. He was thankful that
English was first, Sophie were not in any of his
other lessons until drama at the end of the day
and even if Hannah was, there was no way she
could sit next to him in any of them.

*

Hannah wandered the unfamiliar school during
break time. Sophie had said that she could join
her, but she had lost her before then and she
had no idea where to look. The idea of starting
at a new school had not been that nerve
wracking for her, not when she knew the
people she would meet were like her. Her mum
was a Halve, an old friend of Tax and they had
both welcomed the chance of meeting others

like her and she had welcomed the chance to receive the training that her mum never did. What she had not expected was Tom.
Tax had mentioned the survivors, even made sure that is was Sophie who showed Hannah around, but she had not expected the power that Tom seemed to give off. His golden eyes locked onto hers seemed to take away all the insecurities she had. Hannah had always been plagued by a voice, a dark and dreadful voice that spoke to her out of the darkness, breaking her down. People had always told her that these voices were in her head, but Hannah did not think so, she thought they came from the devil. Always in the corner of her eyes could she see him, a figure in black, chain armour glowing faintly and broken sword at his belt. Always he was there, but she could never look directly at him and never did she have the strength to silence him. Not until in that classroom when she looked at Tom. Almost at once the voice became silent and she was filled with a strength she did not know was possible. As she wandered the halls she searched for Tom, the figure was there just out of sight and she wanted rid of him for good. To do that she had to get close to Tom, no matter what.

*

By the time they got to drama Tom's mind was whirling. Sophie had tried to question him at lunch, only getting angry when he could not answer her constant stream of questions, and always Hannah was there, doing whatever she could to get close to him. He was exhausted as he sat down with Sophie and Price, deciding on what they were going to do for their drama piece. He tuned in when Sophie turned to him, she was smiling viciously, "So in the end me and you should kiss."

"Why?" Tom felt like it was a trap.

"Because are characters are in love." She replied nonchalantly.

"I'm not kissing you in front of everyone Sophie." Tom was exhausted, mentally strained from all the fear and he did not mean it to sound as bad as it did. He knew it had hurt her by the look on her face.

"Didn't stop you last night." She blurted out, her face reddening.

Price looked between them, his mouth wide open, "You two did what?" He shook his head, "And I thought things were weird enough."

"Shut up Price." Sophie said her eyes never leaving Tom.

"It was one kiss in the heat of the moment." He whispered.

She stood up, hands on her hips, "How long were you going to lead me on?"

"I wasn't leading you on."

"What was it then?" Sophie was yelling but no one looked at them, clearly expecting it to only be part of their act, "You know you can't just."

"Sophie." Tom whispered but the sharpness cut her off in her tracks, "You just don't get it." He felt everything that had built up in him that day. All the fear for his coming solitude and the inevitable goodbyes, plus the threats that seemed to be always springing up around him. He needed some relief from that, he needed to find the right words, "I'm not human." He whispered, "I would love to be able to live a normal life, but I can't. In the back of my head I know I will always lose the people I love." Sophie's eyes were wide and wet with tears, "But you look human?"
"You know what I am." Tom growled, "Sophie you are everything I could ever ask for in a girlfriend but it can't ever happen." He ignored the fact that Price was staring at them. He knew that if he did not say the words now then he never would, "I am like a stone that will be constantly battered by time, broken down with every loss until I am nothing more than a spec of who I am now. Soon I will be devoid of shape or substance, buffeted between death and disaster, that is the fate that awaits me." He didn't know where those words came from, but they were about as close to what he imagined his future life to be. He would not be himself once his parents died, once Peter and his friends had died and he still had years of life left to live.
Sophie seemed stunned, all colour had faded from her face. She slowly sat down, her hand

coming up to wipe away the tears from her eyes.
Price looked between them, "Wow." Then he tried to laugh, "As much as I love an interspecies depth of the universe discussion, can we please turn this alien negativity into a drama piece?"
There was silence for a second before Tom laughed and Sophie giggled. It was hollow but it was better than silence. His hand cracked Price on the shoulder, "For you buddy, anything."
"Does that mean you will be at my funeral?" Price asked nonchalantly.
"You really think I would go?" He replied with a grin.
"Not even to dance on my grave?"
Tom laughed, "Now that's an idea."
Price stood up and took his hand, "Just promise me you will dress me up cool when they bury me. That way when I come back as a zombie, I will look good."
The pair walked off to work on a scene and Sophie gingerly followed them. She knew they were using humour to mask the pain and the terrible future Tom had accepted but she had no way to stop any of it.

*

"Tom." Sophie yelled as he was about to cross the road. He had avoided any more conversations until school had ended, instead

they had all focussed on being other people.
Where the problems were made up and could
be forgotten with the school bell ending.
Tom stopped and smiled at her, but she knew it
was forced.
"I'm sorry." He said sadly, taking her hand, "I
shouldn't have kissed you."
Sophie felt her heart break and a void filled her
stomach but she would not add that to his guilt,
"It was going to happen at some point." She
laughed but it faded as his golden eyes looked
away from hers, "We need to remember what
this must be like for you." She said, squeezing
his hands, "You mean the world to me and."
She paused to swallow away her tears, "I love
you Tom." His eyes showed his hurt, but she
pressed on, "I think I always will." She sniffed,
unable to look at the pain in his eyes, "But we
lost too many people on the Curamber. I don't
want to push you away."
He finally smiled then, "I don't think I could get
rid of you if I tried."
Her arms wrapped around him before she could
help herself. She wanted to show all he meant
to her but to do that she would have to kiss him
again and that would cause more problems
than it would solve. No, she would have to
forget that plan before it ripped them apart.
When they separated his eyes were like golden
stone, hard and un-readable but his shoulders
were slouched, like the weight of the world had
once again been placed upon them. She had

seen that look in him before and it always frightened her.

"I will see you tomorrow." He whispered and he turnt her back on her, closing himself off from her.

This had been probably the worst day for Tom since the Island. He was happy he had spoken to Sophie, but her admission of love hurt him, like he was guilty for what he was and the gap that put between him and his friends. It seemed to him that the further they got away from the events on the Island the more they seemed to slip into the way they were before. For Tom that was impossible. He felt like his old life was someone else's dream and yet he did not feel he belonged in his new life. Not unless he was training, readying himself for the next fight. Therefore, he once again found himself walking the familiar route to the Agency. There was something different about today though. He turnt his head, the feeling of unease growing. Hannah was there, following ten metres behind. Tom stopped suddenly to see what she would do and was stunned when she stopped also. He turned around to face her, "Anything I can help you with?"

Hannah licked her lips nervously and stepped onto one foot, "I was following you to the Halve place."

"Halve?" Tom asked, visibly shocked.

"Mr Warman wanted to see me."

Tom's eyes faltered, now there was one more thing to worry about, "Follow me." He said, forcing a smile onto his lips.

She almost skipped to come by his side and when she did, the same cold feeling swept over Tom, he shuddered trying to ignore it.

"What's your power?" She asked to break the silence.

"Fire." He said without thinking. An automatic defence, a way not too draw too much to the fact that he was different from the Halves.

She did not ask any more questions to Tom's great relief. Someone was ready to meet her at the front door. As soon as she was gone, a river of warmth seemed to flood back into him. He let out a long breath but cursed himself, "This is ridiculous, she should not make me feel this way." He whispered to himself, but he knew to trust the feelings of his subconscious, they had not failed him before.

Tom trained by himself for an hour, working through all of his gifts. A bird of flame he created, and he lifted small rocks before working with the metal ball. He created a whirlpool and mirrored it by turning the air into a tornado. He was busy trying to make a perfect flower, that never seemed to work, when Hannah found him again. The dread fell into his summer song and the flower withered and died before he could regain it.

She stared at the flower. She knew there was something different about Tom and wondered whether this was it, "Can you show me your gift?" She asked.

Tom hesitated but everyone found out in the end. He lifted his hand and flames danced between his fingers.

"Wow." She gasped, "So is it fire and plants? I didn't know people can control two things or is it more than two things?"

"It is complicated." Tom grumbled. His eyes fell onto David, he had his escape route, "It was nice meeting you." He lied, "And I'm sure you will do great here, but it is time for my lesson." Without waiting for her to speak Tom left her. His coldness only seemed to fall away from him as he approached David. They left together, never looking back at the young girl.

Chapter Six- Sam

"Oi Firestarter." Price yelled at Tom as he launched a small piece of quiche in Tom's direction, "Catch."
Tom looked at him in bewilderment as the pastry flew passed him and landed with a dull thud into the wall.
"Nick." Their form tutor yelled, "I saw that. Now behave yourself or I will have no choice but to kick you out."
Price gave her a half-hearted apology, knowing that the threat was not genuine. No one ever got kicked out of their Christmas party. He continued to fill his plate with food before coming over and sitting at the table with Kat, Sophie, and Tom.
"Have you got enough?" Sophie asked as she stared at the mound of food. A vast contrast to her own which included just a small sandwich and a slice of cake, of which she had touched none.
"If they offer it." Price took a piece of cake and didn't bother chewing it before speaking, "I will eat it."
Sophie scowled at him, "You know Kat, your boyfriend really is lovely.
"He might not be perfect." She grinned before finishing her drink, "But he's mine." The classroom became silent as she belched loudly. Sophie looked horrified but Tom barely looked

passed the magazine he was reading, "Good effort." He said nonchalantly.

"You guys disgust me." Sophie shook her head, but she concealed a smile that lasted when she caught Tom's eyes. Since he had spoken to her, she had been overly nice, almost trying to force the fact that everything was okay between them. It made him feel better that she understood but he was sure he was still on thin ice.

Price stood up, drawing all their attention onto him. His shorts, inappropriate for the time of year, lifted revealing a scar to his thigh from the battle, "What?" He said in response to their confused glances, "They've just brought out some Pizza."

Tom looked from Price's plate and then back up to him, "You my friend are a hoover." He shook his head as Price walked away but he looked around as a soft voice said his name.

The soft voice belonged to a boy called Josh, who Tom had seen at times at the Agency, but they did not yet know what his powers were. Josh beckoned Tom over and nervously the boy ran a hand through his brown hair and fiddled with his overly large nose, "Something's happened."

Tom leant closer to him, "What?"

Josh's hand extended outwards and nearby papers fluttered in a sudden but gentle wind.

"Your powers have come." Tom whispered with a large smile.

Vengeance of the Gods

Josh nodded nervously, his face white and clammy, eyes wide with fear. Tom thought he must have looked the same when his powers first showed.
"I haven't told the Agency yet. Should I?"
"Of course." Tom grinned as though it was obvious, forgetting that this was like going through puberty in a day, "They don't like surprises."
"I'm scared." Josh admitted.
"Don't be." Tom felt like jumping. It was always nice to be able to help someone through something, "This is the start of your life. You can use your powers and you can start training now. I've never met anyone our age who can control wind, we should train together when you get a bit stronger."
That forced a smile onto Josh's face. He would get the chance to train with one of the survivors, that was something rare for the young Halves who had heard so many rumours. He would not get close to them though. That was something that had never happened with the new Halves. For whatever reason, be it the Tempter or their own bond, no one had broken into their circle.

*

Sophie stepped from the basement swimming pool, dressed in a black shirt and a tight red jumper. She had not decided to dry her hair and it hung limply to her cheeks. A cold breeze blew through the Agency and she shivered, wishing she had a gift like Tom's that kept him warm throughout the year. As she turnt she nearly crashed right into Tax, who smiled down at her, "Ah Sophie. I was just coming to find you." Sophie's hands slipped inside her jumper, her thumbs nervously feeling the fabric but she tried to smile, "Okay."

"Can we talk in my office?"

Sophie gave a gentle nod and she followed Tax. He asked some questions about how she was feeling, all she answered politely but not exactly honestly.

All the heaters were going in Tax's office and Sophie sighed as she stepped into the stuffy warmth. Tax indicated to a chair and Sophie took it gingerly, her leg tapping against the floor nervously.

"There are a few things I wanted to say to you Sophie." He smiled, which helped to remove her nerves, "The first is about Tom."

She swallowed, her mouth tightening, "Is he okay?"

"Of course." Tax said but his smile had dropped causing a lump to form in Sophie's throat, "Well." He paused and the lump grew bigger, "I wanted to talk about supporting him. You need to understand that things will soon get very weird for him. We have never had a refugee grow up not knowing what he is. In a couple of years, it will seem like he does not age. I fear he

may try and push you all away."
Sophie shot up, "Well we won't let him." Then her eyes widened, "Wait, there are more?"
Tax nodded, "A few of the Ilma come here at times. They usually use their power to look human, but they always know what they are. Tom has spoken to us about his fears of losing you all. He feels he needs to push you away now." He gave a hearty laugh, "I'm sure you won't allow that." He grabbed a file, "And the second thing. You are probably the modest one of you four, wouldn't you say?"
Sophie shrugged her shoulders, "I don't know really."
Tax gave her a sympathetic look, "I need you to go on a recruitment." Tax handed her a photo of a boy, with brown curly hair and big wide eyes, "This is Sam Patten."
Sophie's mind immediately began to grow, to mature as Lucast's changes kicked in. She looked hard at the picture, memorising his face, "Where is he?"
"Here in Southbrook." Tax said, "It gave us quite a shock when he moved here. We were going to send someone to Oxford to go get him. Coincidences don't happen Sophie. A Halve doesn't just move here by chance, which means we want him here as soon as possible."
She nodded, not really understanding what Tax meant, "What are his powers?"
"We don't know yet, we are not even sure if they have shown. If they have, we want you to

bring him in at once. If not, then we can approach this more slowly."

"When do you want me to start?" Sophie smiled.

"Well if you were still at school I would ask that you started Monday but I can't wait till after Christmas so I rather hoped you would start now."

Sophie's mouth fell open but she shut it quickly, "Where do I find him?"

Tax checked his phone, "The internet is an amazing tool. He is trying out for the football team. That would be a good chance to run into him."

"Yes sir." Sophie stood up and gave Tax a nod but before she could leave, he grasped her hand gently, "It really is good to see you looking happier Sophie."

She smiled, feeling it as well. Her conversation with Tom had opened everything up for her, she felt lighter for it. She almost ran out of the Agency, ready to carry out her mission.

*

He was small, Sophie realised when she caught her first glimpse of him, and his picture had done him no favours. He was cuter than it showed, his big eyes screamed for her protection, a vast change from Tom's steely and commanding eyes. She told herself that she was not comparing him to Tom but for the last three months, he had been her everything and it was hard not to judge all others based on him. Sophie followed him out of the field, hanging far enough back to not be noticed while he walked with two people from the football team. It was raining which always made Sophie feel more confident. The water falling around her seemed to be a safety net and she could feel some of its power inside of her.

His two companions soon left, and Sophie walked faster to catch up with Sam, but he walked quickly for someone his size and Sophie did not want to just run up to him. He came to the high street and Sophie hung back while he looked at all the shops in his new town. When he cut into one, Sophie realised she would have to do the same. She brought some gum, her eyes never falling from the shop Sam had gone in, so she cut back out just behind him. He looked her way, eyebrow raised but then shook his head and continued to walk down the high street. She followed him again, but her eyes widened as he suddenly stopped to check his phone. She could do nothing but continue walking and as she passed, her eyes scanned his phone. There was a click and she saw a picture of herself.

"Pervert." She yelled, stopping in her tracks. Sam was running, sidestepping people nimbly while Sophie charged behind him. He cut down a side street and she grumbled as she gently followed him. The air suddenly became icy cold

and her heart rate increased. A gutter dribbled water into a nearby drain and she lifted her hand, bringing the water to her.
She stepped further into the alleyway and the floor glistened like frost in the morning and it was hard for her to keep her footing.
"Why are you following me?" A voice asked from the darkness.
Sophie stopped dead, "Just come out."
He burst from the shadow and charged at her. She threw her arm up in defence and water moved towards him like a rushing wave. His arm came up instinctively and the water turned instantly to ice. Sophie's eyes widened; the ice was no longer in her control. He barged passed her, but Sophie flicked her wrist and a funnel of water collided with his ankle and sent him sprawling to the floor. Sophie ran to hold him down, but Sam was stronger than she thought, and he got up ready to push her into the wall but the gutter beside her creaked before giving way and water from the rooftops charged at Sam. His hand came up and turned the first droplets to ice but her mature power broke through and water hit him in the chest, drenching him.
He cried out, "Please stop."
The water fell to the floor instantly, "I'm sorry." Sophie whispered; her chest was heaving but she tried her best to smile.
"What do you want?" Sam asked and he looked close to tears.

Sophie surprised herself by laughing, "Just to talk."
He looked at her curiously and then at the water at his feet, "I had heard rumours of others, even heard rumours of them coming from Southbrook but I never truly thought."
"There are loads of us." Sophie interjected, "We have a place where we can train. There are people who will look after us."
"A place where we train?" He asked incredulously, "That just sounds like a fairy tale."
Sophie stepped towards him, "You see that I have powers. Please, that has to give me at least one hour of your time."
He still seemed dubious, "One hour."
Sophie and Sam left the alleyway together but Sophie could tell that he didn't believe her by the way his shoulders slouched and the fact that his eyes never left floor. She never realised how confusing this must be for others. Being friends with Tom and then the Island, meant she slipped into this role quiet easily. She had never really been alone with her powers and the thought of it made her shudder. Her hand reached out and grasped his wrist, "You will be fine, trust me. There are many of us to help you."
He gave her a quick fluttering smile, but it broke away as he looked at the seemingly abandoned office building, with the burly guard stood outside.

"Passes." He said calmly in a voice that Sophie thought carried further than it should have. She reached into her pocket and pulled out a small ID that had a picture of her and different letter's to indicate her power.
The guard scanned it with his phone before smiling and handing it back, his eyes quickly turned on Sam, "Pass son?"
He looked close to bolting again so Sophie cut in front, "He doesn't have one yet. I was sent to recruit him. Tax... I mean Mr Warman knows he is coming."
The guard looked hard at Sophie and then back at Sam. He gave a sharp nod before going over to a phone that stood on the wall beside the door. Sam was white so Sophie turned towards him, "They don't want people knowing what we are. We all sign a non-disclosure thingy when we join so we don't tell anyone."
"What happens if you did?" Sam asked and Sophie thought that asking questions was the only thing keeping his mind from panicking.
"I don't know. Tax never did explain it." She shrugged.
Sophie went to the balls of her feet as the guard returned, he was smiling, "You can go in. The director isn't in his office, but he will be around." He turned on Sam, "It's good to see you here son, it's the best place for you."
Sam nodded meekly as Sophie led him into the main door. Once inside he breathed a sigh of relief, "I thought he was going to shoot me

then."

"He won't shoot you." Sophie grinned, "But he might steal all the air from your lungs."

"You mean he is one as well?" Sam's mouth was wide open.

"Most people who work here are." She said, "I think it is hard for us to live properly once our powers are matured and it is easier to work where people understand."

Sophie signed Sam and herself in with one of the desks and began walking up the stairs. She went to shout as Tax ran down the stairs towards them, but she did not need to. He stopped right in front of them with his eyes wide open, "Blimey Sophie, you work quick." Sophie blushed at the compliment but Tax continued as though he was in a rush, "Good afternoon Sam, my name is Michael Warman, head of the Institute for the detection and protection of Halves, though most refer to us as the Agency."

Sam took the Director's hand limply, "Nice to meet you?"

"I'm sure you have plenty of questions, sadly Sophie has caught me by surprise, why don't we go up to my office and have a conversation. Sophie can meet you in the training rooms."

Sam was going white again, but he nodded, "Okay."

Sophie gave Sam a warm smile as he followed the director up the stairs. He had to hop multiple stairs at a time to keep pace with the

Director who marched in long strides so by the time they reached Tax's office, Sam was out of breath and even more nervous. They walked in and Tax offered him a drink which he politely declined. The director took a gulp out of a glass of water before beckoning for Sam to sit. Tax followed him and pulled several forms from one of his draws.

"You must have a lot of questions. Ask away."

Sam thought of all the questions he had in his head from before his move but they were blanked out by one more pressing, "Why do they call you Tax?"

Tax's smile widened, his eyes glinting, "Now that wasn't what I was expecting but I should answer every question. When I first became director of an agency full of conspiracy theorists, it did not pay well so I drove a Taxi to pay my rent. They called me Taxi Warman and in the end just Tax."

Sam nodded, wondering why that question had seemed so pressing but he guessed it was to calm himself before asking the next one that came into his head, "What am I?"

"Now that is more like it." Tax's eyes became suddenly cold, like he was weighing Sam, "Basically you descend from experiments done by an alien race."

Sam's eyes widened and beads of sweat formed on his brow. *Aliens.* He did not think any of this made any sense until he realised that he could freeze whatever he wanted. He reminded himself to keep an open mind.

"I know it is a lot to take in but don't worry it is all explained in your introductory handbook." Tax looked down at his sheets as though he was now reading from them, "If you agree to register with the Agency, you will be given training to control your abilities and learn practical applications. You will meet people going through the same experiences as yourself and you will be supported throughout your life." He looked up from his script, "What do you reckon Sam?"

"Is Sophie involved?" He asked, trying to make the question seem normal but Tax was weighing him again.

"One of our best." He sat back, "I'm sure she will be happy to work with you."

"Okay I will do it." Sam said, laughing slightly, feeling suddenly relieved to have some of his questions answered for him.

"Are you sure?"

Sam nodded, his face reddening, "Everyone so far has said this is the best place for me. I've been alone the last few months and I am ready to understand what I am."

Tax was thoroughly pleased, "Okay, I just need to ask you some questions. Name?"

"Samuel Lucas Patten."

"Date of birth?"

"Twenty fifth of June, two thousand and three."

"Gift?" Now Tax looked up from his sheets.

Sam struggled for the words, "Ice I guess."

This seemed to peak Tax's attention and he placed his pen on the table, "A demonstration?" Sam indicated towards Tax's glass of water and reached his hand towards it. His finger touched the edge of the glass, it became suddenly misty and little veins of ice crystals grew like a spider's web from his finger.

Tax's eyes widened, "One for Professor Harper whenever he returns." He said mysteriously but he never explained who Professor Harper was or what was so interesting about his power to shock the Director, who must have seen it many times before.

"Is that all sir?" Sam asked nervously now.

"Yes Sam, I just need to speak to a parent or guardian. Is anyone home?"

"My mum should be. She doesn't know about it; does she need to?" Sam asked, worried what his mum would think of her only child being some alien experiment.

"Of course." Tax said like it was obvious, "She needs to agree for you to train here. We cannot have you hiding it from her. Some parents react badly, and we have homes to protect those who cannot return home but once most see what we do and understand how common this is, they often come round to our way of thinking." Tax adopted a friendly tone, "I know this is scary. If you let me have her number I can explain everything to her."

Sam grabbed his phone and read the number to Tax, "Thanks, why don't you go and see Sophie

and I will find you once I have spoken to her."
Sam stood up and said, "Thank you." meekly.
He was worried what his mum would think. It
was not the shock she would need after the
divorce, but it would be a massive relief to him.
He found Sophie on the threshold of the
training room. When he saw her, he could not
help but smile widely.
"Well?" She asked as she rocked again on the
balls of her feet.
"I'm in." Sam grinned but winced as Sophie
screamed in a high pitched voice, "So." He said
once she was done screeching, "This is where
you train?"
Sophie beckoned for him to step inside and
when he did, his eyes widened. She watched as
he scanned all the different stations and
laughed as he gawped at a fire Halve and a wind
Halve, who battled in what looked like a dance,
"This is incredible. I couldn't even cool a room
like this."
"We could have used you on the Island." Sophie
said without thinking.
"I read about that." Sam said going sheepish
again, "Were you there?"
Sophie gave him a smile and a nod but went no
further. Even between Halves the truth of what
happened on the Island was a secret. Tax did
not think it right for fear of alien invasion to fall
on its members. Tom was religious about it also,
not wanting others to think differently of them
or even blame them for what had happened.

"What is upstairs?" Sam asked, feeling Sophie's tension.
"Research and development." She replied, "We aren't allowed up there."
She walked Sam around the training room, showing him all the stations and introducing him to some of the Halves. Just as they completed the circuit, Tax found them again, "I've just spoken to your mother. I think she was ready to hang up on me, but I made her log into our secure site. Think she nearly dropped the phone bless her. I've invited her and yourself to come and visit later this evening so you can truly see what we do here."
"Alright then." Sam said sheepishly, fearing the conversation that would await him at home. He wondered if he should just come out and demonstrate his powers, but he did not want his mother to have a heart attack on him.
Tax turned on Sophie, "I think you should introduce Sam to Tom and the others, I'm sure they would love to welcome him."
"Good idea." Sophie said but her voice did not match the words. They had a close bond that had been formed in the worst of experiences. Sam might not fit into that too well.

Chapter Seven – Christmas Gifts.

Tom woke from a blurred dream that he tried to guess had something to do with snow and ice, feeling somewhat refreshed and ready for the new day. He had finally finished his plan for the Christmas decorations. He had not told the others about it, wanting to have his idea perfect before he did.

"Tom." His mother shouted from downstairs and he charged to meet her, tossing his breakfast bowl into the sink as he passed. His mum was walking in the door, carrying bags through the threshold, "Can you get Peter out the car please sweety.

He nodded and quickly un-strapped Peter before placing the toddler on the driveway. He looked and pointed to a ball that sat in the footwell of the car, "Toy." He demanded, hands on his hips.

Tom gave his little brother a raised eyebrow smile, "Say please Peter."

"Toy." Peter demanded again.

The use of the boy's name in a stern voice caused a wicked smile to grow on Peter's face, "Pooey bum head." He whispered and he turned around to make sure their mum was not behind him.

"That's it." Tom feigned anger, "Now I'm going to eat you up."

Peter turned to run but Tom caught him in

three long strides. The boy screamed with delight as Tom turned his world upside down, "What did you call me?"
Peter giggled, "Pooey."
"I'm a giant." His voice went deep as he began to sweep the pavement with the toddler's curly hair, all the while Peter laughed, drooling as he swang. With a heave, Tom righted Peter who stared at him with big eyes, "Again."
"Not now." He replied and when the toddler's lips dropped, he added quickly, "Go and see what mummy has for you."
Peter turned quickly and charged at full speed back into the house. Tom grabbed the ball from the car and shut the door without touching it before moving back into the house.
"Have you eaten?" His mum said while she filled the cupboards.
"Yeah, I'm just about to go and meet the others down in the field so we can plan Christmas Eve."
"Have fun." She said and before Tom could run away, she added, "I know you Thomas Lita, don't you go swimming in that lake it is far too cold."
"I wouldn't dream of it." He said wickedly.
He charged out of the door, grabbing his scarf, and wrapping it tightly around his burns. He was in a jumper, not that he really needed it. The grey sky kept the temperature relatively mild and his gift kept him warm. He ran from the estate, into the field where he had met

Vengeance of the Gods

Sophie the night they had kissed.
Sat by the lake, on an old log that Price had found for them, he could see Kat and Price were sat. They were laughing at something on her phone, her loudness breaking the calm of the morning. That was not what shocked Tom though, what shocked him was the fact that her hair was tied up and underneath her pink coat, she was wearing a dress.
"Oi Oi love birds." Tom smiled as he stopped by them.
Kat scowled at him, "Why do you always ruin a good moment?"
"Why are you dressed like that?" He asked in reply.
Kat swished her ponytail in disgust, "I've got a christening to go to later and my mum said." She adopted a high pitched whine, "since it's at the church, you need to wear a dress.""
"A church." Price said in a shocked voice. He knew the story already but now he had an audience he couldn't miss that chance to mock his girlfriend, "Just make sure you don't burst into flames when you walk in."
Tom laughed at his best friends bravery but he laughed harder when Kat pulled away from him and turned with a cheeky smile towards Tom, "Its fine because this older boy I know is going and I'm going to get his number."
She gave a sigh, pretending to text someone. Price looked between Tom and her before reaching over and grabbing her phone. She

scowled at him and stood; hands placed firmly on her hips. Price jumped on the log and part of it began to suddenly swell. He held the phone above his head, the swelling branch keeping himself and the phone out of her reach.

She lifted her arm and little shocks shot from her fingers into his ribs and he convulsed awkwardly.

"Will you two get married already." Tom laughed.

Kat turned towards him, "Get my phone back." She glared at her boyfriend, "I hope you die Nick Jones."

Price went all sweet and the log reduced in size while he bent down to her height, the phone slipped behind his back, "If I get a kiss you can have it back."

Kat leaned forward and kissed him but her right hand came up and shocked him. His arm went limp and the phone fell. Tom caught it with his power and Kat snatched it out of the air. After a quick tussle between the pair, Price turned to Tom, "What's with this secret meeting?"

"I better wait till Sophie gets here." He said as he glanced around, searching for her.

His eyes fell onto two people walking towards them. One was clearly Sophie but the other he did not know. It was a boy, but he was not much bigger than Sophie.

"Who is with her?" Tom asked, all this would be for naught if she brought someone new and un-powered.

"It is Sam." Kat deadpanned.
"Sam?" Price asked.
"Sophie recruited him yesterday."
Tom gave a small smile, at least now he could reveal what he had to say. Sophie approached and nervously began to introduce Sam. Tom smiled at him, while Kat and Price basically ignored the newcomer to look on her phone again.
"What is your power?" Tom asked as he took Sam's hand, who murmured nervously, "I create Ice I think."
Tom looked at him weirdly. He searched inside of himself, imagining causing the air to grow cold but he realised in shock that his body was not capable of it, "That's pretty sweet. I'm glad you are joining us."
Price yawned before speaking in a bored voice, "Come on then, what is the big plan?"
Tom took a deep breath and looked between them all, "My parents want us to use our powers to decorate my house on Christmas eve."
Their eyes widened in shock and there was a moments pause before they all began speaking at once, yelling at him about all that they could do. He lifted his hand to silence them, "I was thinking." He said once their jabbering had ceased, "that I will buy some mistletoe and Price can spread it around the room. Kat can control all the decorations, making the lights dance and Sophie can create a winter water

feature."

"I can create icicles." Sam said excitedly.

Tom looked at him weirdly, that wasn't in his plan mostly because he had no idea it could be done, the thought put him off a bit, "Yeah we could."

Price and Kat began again then, asking Tom about all the decorations, Sam seemed to withdraw into himself so Sophie turned to face him with a smile, "I think it is a great idea."

He seemed unsure, "When did you discover your powers?"

"About a year and a half ago. I always loved to swim and one day when I was getting out of the pool, I thought about getting dry and all the water just fell off me."

"That must have been a shock." He looked into her blue eyes and his face reddened, they were fixed on his and it made him nervous, "I found out when everything I touched from a cup of tea to a can of soda became suddenly cold. I didn't know what to do."

"It was easier for us." Sophie said, "I found out Kat and Tom had powers almost straight after." Sam watched as Sophie's eyes strayed towards Tom, they began to sparkle and jealousy filled his heart, "What are his powers?"

Sophie came back to look at him but she didn't meet his eyes, "Fire." She deadpanned.

"We are opposites then." Sam tried not to make it sound like a competition, but Sophie clearly had feelings for Tom, the hurt when she looked at him was plain, but Sam was growing very fond of her.

"In more ways than you know." Sophie was now looking down, "It's all complicated with Tom."

"How?" He asked.

He had the feeling that she was hiding something. He knew that the four of them here had escaped a volcanic eruption but whenever he tried to steer the conversation towards it over text, she would hurriedly change the subject.

"He can control more than one power." Sophie deadpanned but Sam knew that was not the whole story but did not have time to ask before she started speaking again, "It was only because of him that we made it off the Island."

Sam decided to press, "What actually happened?" His eyes went to Tom then, below his scarf, Sam could see scars. He looked back at Sophie, she was staring behind him, like she was lost in some memory. A mental scar compared to Tom's physical ones.

"We released something." Sam wasn't sure she even realised she was saying it, "An alien who wanted to restart a war or something, we never did find it all out."

Sam's head turned as the lake beside them began to rumble, the others had stopped speaking also and were looking at Sophie but she seemed not to notice, "He killed all of our friends and an alien made us stronger, made us into soldiers to fight the war for him. Tom managed to defeat that monster."

"What monster?" Sam asked, looking between them all nervously, wondering what he had gotten himself in for.

"Cirtroug." She whispered and a great wave charged into the air and came crashing down on the far side of the lake.

"SOPHIE!" Tom's voice was louder than it had any right to be. To Sam, it sounded like it came from the ground itself.

"What the hell?" Kat asked, more quietly but not without concern in her voice.

Sophie seemed to snap out of the dream suddenly, she looked around at them all, tears falling down her face, "I was only talking to Sam." She said nervously.

"We don't know him." Tom did not look at Sam as he spoke, "We can't tell anyone what happened, we just can't."

Sophie felt embarrassed, hurt and strangely angry. Her hands flew into the air defensively, "At least he wants to listen to me." She reached down and grabbed him, her cheeks burning, "Come on Sam, I thought my friends were ready to speak about it but clearly not."

With her head down she charged away from them. She had lost control; they could not see that she was ashamed of it. Sam followed behind her, worried what he had become a part of. As they became hidden by a thicket of trees on the edge of the lake, Sophie collapsed to the floor and began to quietly sob.

Sam sat cross legged beside her. He had no experience with crying girls or girls in general, so he just sat there quietly, waiting for her to speak.

"Why can't." She paused to sob, "Things just be normal?" She bit on the end of her thumb to stop the tears.

"What do you mean?"

"He was always different." Sophie said distantly again, "Even before the Island he always had such terrible dreams and it seemed like he had the world on his shoulders."

"He seems a bit full of himself." Sam replied, shocked that it sounded so sulky.

"You have no idea what he can do." She laughed wickedly but it was not meant to sound cruel, "When he was on the Island it seemed like he was complete, like he had found himself. It was there that we found out he was one of them."

Sam gawped at her, "He's what?"

Sophie ignored the question, "We never would have survived if it wasn't for him."

Sam couldn't help but grasp her arm, "I'm sure you all did your part."

Sophie finally looked at him, "He was the one who charged into the mountain, the one who finally trapped Cirtroug forever. He was my hero."

"Why don't you marry him then?" Sam asked. Sophie laughed again but it was a melancholy laugh, full of hurt, "That was on the Island. Now it is like he is waiting for something and until it happens, he will not be complete again. I see him training day and night, but he does not ever say what he is training for. I think he is waiting for the Tempter."

"The Tempter?" Sam asked but she once again ignored his question, though the lake did begin to rumble again at the mention of the ghostly figure.

"I don't think he will ever be right until he is fighting a war again."

A smile flickered onto Sam's face, "You know what." He said more sternly than he thought possible, "We are young and we don't need all this worrying."

Sophie smiled but Sam wasn't sure whether it was a kind smile or a pitying one for someone who did not know the cruelty of the world. Sam built up his courage, "I mean if you want, we could try and be normal kids. Like we could go to the cinema after Christmas."

Sam could barely breathe as Sophie's eyes examined him. She sat up and gave him a quick peck on the cheek, "It's nice to talk to someone not corrupted by the island." She whispered, "The cinema would be nice."

*

Vengeance of the Gods

That night, Tom had spoken to Sam and again over the following days, explaining to him about what they had done on the Island and all that Sophie had been through. Tom was impressed with how he had taken the news and he saw in him, the tools for Sophie to heal and to forget her dream of them being together.

When Christmas eve finally came, Tom was more than happy to have Sam's help and he had factored his new friends' powers into his scheme.

Tom was charging around his empty house, going over all of the decorations, all of which held for him some memory where he would sit up passed his bed time, trying to stay awake until he would hear a bell and footsteps on the roof. Then he would charge up to his room and fall asleep. He knew it was all a game now. Last year he had even helped his dad set up the act, but Peter had loved it and it helped bring back some of his love for the occasion. This was surely going to top all those memories though.

The knock on the door stopped him. He opened it quickly and gave both Price and Kat a warm hug before he laughed at their matching jumpers. Kat was beaming but Price gave Tom a look, daring him to say anything about them. A few minutes later, Sam and Sophie came in. Sophie looked around, "No Nicole?"

"She is with Daniel." He replied.

He turned towards the four of them, "Okay, my mum and dad will be back in a couple of hours,

so we have to have everything ready by then."
Tom picked up a pot full of soil with a small
stem growing from it, "Can you weave this
around the room?" He handed it to Price who
nodded, "Sophie I need you just to relax at the
moment and just help anyone who needs it."
He turned sharply on Sam who was cowering on
the sofa, "Can you begin working on your
icicles?"
"I will do my best." He beamed, "I'm not sure
how long they will last though."
Tom turned his attention onto Kat, "Can you
please help me put up the lights." He knew it
was always best to ask Kat to do something,
demanding anything of her would usually leave
you with a sour look and a bad attitude.
After a quick discussion of what they needed to
do, they set to work. Price picked up the pot
and placed it in the corner of the room and
began to speak soft words to the plant inside.
The stem began to grow, crawling its way up
the wall, flowering, and growing leaves as it
slowly climbed its way towards the ceiling. Price
was a genius with his movements, never
hindering those around him, and making the
berries grow in places where they reflected the
Christmas lights or the occasional icicle.
Once the mistletoe reached the ceiling, Price's
song, that had at first sounded like a spring
after a harsh winter became suddenly a song of
bountiful summer. The plant began to weave
itself around the lamp shade, hanging with

beautiful white berries, waiting for someone to stray beneath it. Satisfied, he grabbed a drink from the coffee table and crashed on the sofa, watching all the others while they continued to work.
Kat and Sophie held the lights up for Tom while he used his power over metal to force tacks into the plaster board and Sam worked to create his icicles.
Sam's hand was held outstretched above a bowl of water and Tom watched as slowly the top of the water began to freeze. As Sam's hand moved the ice turnt, becoming a cone that slowly reached up towards his palm. When Sam was satisfied, he lifted his icicles to the ceiling and with Sophie's help, secured them there.

After another hour of work, the room looked just as Tom wanted it. The tree was up, decorated by dancing lights. Mistletoe was nestled in every corner of the room and across the ceiling, icicles created beautiful patterns in the light. For Tom it was almost complete. As night settled outside, Kat cut the power and Tom came in with a bowl of water, a ball of fire hanging in front of him for them all to see by. He placed the bowl beside Sophie, who looked at it suspiciously, "What do you want me to do with that?"
He smiled, his golden eyes glowing in the firelight, "You and Sam are going to use it to create snow."

Sophie squealed so loudly that Price came from his watch behind the curtains, his hands clenched into fists. Once he saw they were all okay, he shook his head and returned to his hiding spot.

As soon as she was done screaming, Sophie hurriedly explained what she wanted Sam to do. Her hand went above the water and it lifted from the bowl. With a splash it separated into tiny droplets that filled the room, suspended at their eye height. The droplets flew into the air at her command and danced just under the ceiling, amidst the icicles and mistletoe.

Just then Price gave a yell, "They are here." He charged back into the room.

The flame in front of Tom blinked out and he whispered to Kat, "Wait until they are inside." None of them seemed to be breathing as the door slowly opened and three pairs of feet, two large and one small, walked into the house. They seemed nervous, clicking the light switch, and murmuring about the fact that they did not work.

"Tom." They heard his mum say, "We have bought your friends some chicken, why don't the lights work?"

The door crept open and at that moment, Kat released her hold. All the lights turned on and the living room danced with colour. His mum stopped on the threshold of the door, her husband behind her, staring at the transformed living room. Just then Sam lifted his hand and the water droplets became snow that was no longer in Sophie's control so it gently fell to the ground, where it thawed so Sophie could take control again and launch it back into the air. At the snow, Peter screamed, and he ran around the room chasing the snowflakes, trying to catch them on his tongue.

The snow was the icing on the cake for his mother, who suddenly burst into tears. She charged at him, pulling him into a tight hug that he struggled to return. Once she released him, she grabbed Price and then all the others in turn, including Sam who blushed vividly.

"This has to be the best Christmas present ever." She wiped tears from her eyes and pulled him into one more hug, "Just look at Peter."

Their eyes all went to the toddler, who charged around the room, trying his best to touch everything. For him Christmas was still a magical time and what their gifts had done must have truly looked magical. Tom felt the hairs on his neck stand up and an emptiness filled him. He had always thought of his powers as a weapon and now they were revealed to be something so much more than that. The four of them could create magic if they put their mind to it. The thought was beautiful, but it left him hollow and he realised as he watched Sophie smile at him, that it was because this was the life he could never have.

Tom wiped away a tear, but he bit his tongue and tried to live in the present and not the

battles that were surely going to come. He
nodded at Sam, who ceased the snow and
Sophie collected all the water into the bowl.
Then they all sat down to eat together, all
except Peter who still ran around the room. He
was chasing different toys, which turned on and
off just as Peter was about to catch them. He
was not sure who was having more fun, Peter
or Kat, who was making it happen, a rare full
smile on her face.

Once they had eaten, Sophie and Sam removed
the icicles while Tom and Price worked to
extract the mistletoe. Due to their gifts and a
considerable amount of luck, there was no
evidence of either. Then the others left to
spend the rest of Christmas eve with their
parents. Tom thought of staying up until
midnight but by ten he was exhausted. He
trudged up to bed and said a prayer for all those
that would not see Christmas day before falling
asleep. If he dreamt, Christmas day might have
come quickly but this night was set to be as long
and as black as the next.

Tom woke up to a high-pitched scream. A
scream of joy, a scream of a three-year-old boy
who fell asleep before midnight and woke to
find the carrot by his bed eaten and the milk
half drank. Tom dressed slowly and made his
way downstairs. His dad was in the living room,
trying desperately to keep Peter away from the
presents. His mum was in the kitchen and the

smell of bacon and fresh vegetables were wafting from it.

They ate their breakfast together and then opened presents. Tom got a scarf of his favourite football team and several games for his console but his favourite present was from the Sophie, Kat and Price, who had given him a book by a professor Alexander Harper, a paranormal investigator that worked secretly for Tax to look at mutations of gifts. He was looking forward to guessing what the truth behind his stories were.

Through the day the Lita's played games and then ate and as evening settled in his dad played Christmas songs on the vinyl player. Peter fell asleep early and Tom felt like dosing off while his mum stroked his hair. It was hard to think that three months earlier he was fighting for his life, the prospect of never seeing another Christmas not even entering his train of thought. For once that night, he did not pray for forgiveness. Instead he prayed for a peaceful life and happiness for his family. He fell asleep more content than he had for months but little did he know that across the stars, vengeance was swiftly hurtling towards him.

Chapter Eight- Shadows of the Darkness.

"We have returned to Earth General, establishing orbit now."
Urgarak's eyes flickered open. He had been having a nightmare, all his dreams were nightmares since he had found that weapon. He dreamt of the children of his home world, starving, ripping eachother apart for flesh while Thomas Lita laughed in the heavens above. Urgarak looked towards the possessed guard, whose eyes still burnt black, "Thank you. Maintain orbit."
Urgarak sat from his bed and rubbed at his eyes. He was wasting away. He had not eaten in months, another side of effect the power that now coursed through his veins, "I am just a vassal." He said to himself, "To bring doom upon the Gods and establish a new universal order, where all are free to live in their own designs." He looked at the guard whose head was tilted observing him, waiting for a command, "Why does it hurt?" Urgarak asked but the guard did not answer, he could not answer, his mind was filled only now with the darkest of thoughts that had circled through Urgarak's head at the time the sentinel had been released.
"Because it is the weight of destiny." A dark and terrible voice said behind Urgarak, but he did

not turn to face it. He knew that if he did, he would be shocked by the lack of any presence. He heard in his mind, the sound of chain mail rustling and a smell of decay reached his nose. Not the musty decay of the Tempter but the smell of death itself, for that was who spoke to him, "Return yourself to Agraldin devil."
Urgarak muttered to the air, "I will carry my weight and soon you and your kind will fall." Urgarak dressed in his parade uniform, metal armour under his control and a cape, in the colours of Uralese, bright green and hemmed with gold. He placed the badge of Uralese on his armour and left the disembodied voice of Agral behind. The climb through the ship was effortless for the Graul who had taken this walk more times than he could count. He climbed the steps to the bridge and stared at the Earth as the sun crept above the continent of Europe, "Earth date?" Urgarak asked.
"Third day of their first solar cycle month." Mirkan replied, "We are searching for Thomas Lita now sir."
"The internet." Urgarak licked his lips, "A good name for a global information hub, we shall soon know all that he knows."
"And when we do my lord?"
"Then we must make him act as a human." Urgarak smiled to himself, "We must make him so desperate that he challenges me. He will confess his crimes and then no one can stop me from my vengeance."

"Sir." The Guard said in a hoarse voice, his black eyes were staring into space, "There is a ship approaching with one of the Graul."

"The Ilmgralite's." Urgarak snarled, "How many ships?"

Mirkan ran to a scanner but confusion filled the grey face of the Murka, "Just one." He said harshly and his low hanging arms slammed at the controls, "It is the ambassador's ship."

That made Urgarak falter, to kill Lucast would be a step to far. War would not come from that, only a closer union between Ilmgral and Abgdon in their hatred of him.

"Let him dock." He commanded, "Assemble the second battalion for parade on the launch deck. We shall show him our might and see if he will see sense to aid in our cause." He turned to the guard, "Follow me."

He walked again the cramped halls of his ship, down the elevators until he reached the main launch platform. Dropships and fighter crafts, all shaped like birds, sat dormant in the hall. Murka's in their brown uniforms were lined up orderly, their one-handed rifles hanging at their side. These were weapons for the weak. He was already powerful for one of the Graul, but his new power made him a rival to the gods themselves.

Urgarak held his head high as a ship sped into the hold, slender and ornate, a jewel of their craft but not equipped for battle. It landed with a dull thud and from it stepped a Graul like

Urgarak, though his skin was covered in less red scales than the general's. Lucast's hooked from his jaw and levelled out either side of his face. His golden chest piece was ceremonial, but everything else was loose fitting as though he expected a battle.

"You will leave now Urgarak." Lucast ordered without any of the customary formalities, "Forget this venomous dream of you and your kin."

Urgarak's arms raised in feigned surrender, "And where is Ilmgral's fleet to stop me or do they stand by the judgement that Thomas Lita is a criminal, like these earthlings harbouring him."

The silence told him all that he needed to know, "I have an army Ambassador."

Lucast looked at the Murka's, "Of slaves."

"They were freed from bondage when they joined our cause, slavery is a product of your profession, not mine."

Lucast lifted his arms and the metal armour around the Murka's began to constrict, not enough to hurt them just to make them uncomfortable, "They still wear metal as our slaves did of old. Is that so they cannot argue against you Urgarak?"

"They do not fear me." Urgarak took a step forward, "They fear the power I possess." His arm shot outwards and from his fingers black smoke charged.

Lucast's eyes widened in fear and a shield of fire

burst out of his hands and met with the smoke which ignited, screaming as it did. When it subsided, Lucast breathed heavily, strained from that small encounter with the Darkness, "The use of that weapon is illegal."

"As you can see Ambassador." Urgarak's eyes began to leak the same dark smoke that had charged at Lucast, "My power has outgrown yours. The curse of Scaraden runs through my veins and soon Thomas Lita will succumb to the darkness that I weild."

Urgarak moved with frightening speed and darkness charged for Lucast whose only defence was to throw fire as a shield. With a duck he charged back onto his ships and fired up the engines. Urgarak felt the metal of the ship and tried to hold it but the thrusters ripped it from his control, "FOOL." Urgarak barked as the craft went for the exit, "Let him go, if I cannot strip his mind from his body then he must live."

Urgarak turned and looked at the guard who still stood patiently beside him. With a smile he lifted his hand and the smoke fell from the guard all at once. The guard collapsed and a smoke like figure stood in his place. It would have looked like Urgarak's shadow if it wasn't for the way its body seemed to flow and the piercing golden eyes that stared at him intently. The guard was writhing on the floor, Urgarak turned to Mirkan, "Kill him and when he tries to take shape, lock him in a phial, we will send him back to Abgdon in that with our regards." He then turned back to the black figure, "Get to Thomas Lita before Lucast can warn him."

Dawn crept in while Tom tossed and turned in his bed. His dreamless sleep was disturbed by something and the darkness that usually accompanied his sleep un-nerved him. His sleeping mind was working, searching inside itself for the coming threat but it found nothing but blurred images and faceless voices.
Tom's eyes shot open when his alarm sounded. His chest was heaving, and his pale skin glistened with sweat. He looked around the room, desperate for some form of comfort. He found it with the fabric of his scarf. He held it tightly, bringing his mind away from his dreamless night terror.
He dressed in his Southbrook uniform, the scarf wrapped tightly around his neck as though it was armour for his protection and he slipped his old reliable lighter into his blazer pocket.
The air was cold, the morning frosty as he began his walk. The blue sky above him made him feel very insecure and he checked behind himself constantly, even jumping at the movement of his shadow across the wall.
He moved off for school, his eyes now watching the shadow. It seemed to follow his movements, but he felt as though there was a delay. Some talking school kids took his

attention and when his eyes turned back to his shadow, his eyes widened, and his mouth fell open. It scaled the side of a large house and it seemed to be leaning towards him.

Tom's eyes shot around but he could see nothing to create such a vast mass of blackness. Something in his mind said one thing, run. He launched himself away and like a real shadow, the black mass began to follow. It appeared as though it was part of the walls, ducking down and around obstacles to keep pace with him. He glided round a corner and gave a shout of horror; the shadow flew in front of him and came darting along the road by his feet. He ran again but a trail of smoke lifted from the pavement and wrapped around his ankle. Tom's heart flew into his throat as the shadow turned him over. He was falling, the ground came up slightly to support him, the cold tarmac of the road ripped at his hands and he let out a gasp of pain as skin on his knees was torn by pavement. He clenched his fists as he lay on the cold ground and he reached for the scarf that had flew from his neck in the fall but he faltered. The world was turning dark, a real shadow spread across him, cutting off the winter sun from the burns on his neck. Tom nervously turned his head and his eyes widened again. The shadow was receding but stood now in front of him was a black shape. It was growing from the reducing shadow in streams of black smoke as though the tarmac was on fire. Soon it stood to its full height in the image of a man, but Tom could see a gleam in its face, the gleam of the golden eyes of Ilmgral.

Without another thought Tom stood and a stone flicked from the floor into the figure. It gave a muffled moan and the stone was devoured but it seemed like nothing more than an annoyance for the ghostly shape. The next stone he flicked burst into flame before passing through the black smoke. This time the figure roared in a high-pitched wail and the golden eyes seemed to burn with rage.

As the figure stepped closer, patterns in the smoke seemed to become clear. The faint outline of a nose, and different shade of scales could be seen. His mind thought of the Ilmgralite's but none, not even Cirtroug, had repulsed his body so.

The shadow charged suddenly and Tom took steps backwards, flinging stones from the floor into the smoke but it seemed not to feel it as it continued to move forward. Just as Tom could feel its dreadful presence next to his skin it, stopped, distracted by something. A door opened to his left and a mother stepped out, a child beside her. She stared at the ghostly figure, eyes wide with fear and she pushed her child back into the house. The figure seemed to smile, and it moved towards the door, a long arm spreading smoke towards the mother who screamed. Tom's fear gave way, a ball of fire collided with the arm and a high-pitched wail filled the air.

"Oi." Tom said, "I'm the one you are after." He turned to the mother, "Shut the door."

He heard the door click as the smoke once again turned towards him, its wispy arms seemed to blacken and harden and it swung for him in a vicious movement. He ducked the first blow but did not see the second arm before it grasped at his wrist. His lungs gasped as though he had suddenly been plunged into cold water and ice seemed to creep into his veins. Despair filled all his mind. In defence his body acted on instinct, he felt the small static charge swell in his left hand and with a crash of thunder a blue light flashed against the ghostly figure. His hand broke free as the smoky arm was burnt away by the power. With a cry the figure withdrew slightly but as it went back to its full height, many arms of smoke burst suddenly from it like a great black octopus. All Tom could do against this barrage was ignite his hand and block every blow with the flame.

Every time fire met smoke, a scream would reach into the heavens but more of the black smoke would charge at him and it took all of his will to keep his hands alite.

A great gust of wind came from behind him and charged at the ghost who was blown backwards by the fury of it but it managed a swing at his legs and the distraction enabled it to strike again. Tom caught the arm in his flaming hands and the smoke cried. With the smoke held between his palms its darkness began to seep into him again. Ice cold seemed to pierce him and dark images of his beheading of Cirtroug filled his mind. He tried to blank them out, tried to think of all that Lucast had revealed to him. With a cry his flames roared, and the arm was devoured by flame that turned a sickly green colour before faltering. The burst of the smoke launched Tom into the air, and he crumpled onto the floor but not for long.

He felt tendrils of smoke grasping at him and he was soon being lifted off the ground by the arms of smoke and he looked now into the golden eyes and saw only pure hatred for him reflected in them. Another arm grew from the figures shoulder and slowly it entered his nose. The sensation of water being forced down his throat made him cough and convulse but the shadow kept penetrating him, moving into his lungs, and clouding his mind. The world was darkening, voices of his dead friends screamed inside his mind. His fingers were going numb but slowly he reached for his one chance of salvation. He could just about feel it, the plastic of the lighter but his hands were failing him, his whole body was failing him. Slowly his hand slipped from the lighter and no matter how much he willed them to move, they were locked in place.

In the blackness of his mind, he saw a figure. The Tempter was staring at him, weighing him. How strong was he? How strong was he too become? He was of Ilmgral, he did not need hands to use his power. With no sight to distract him, he sort for the metal of his lighter and connecting to it he lifted it from his pocket. The darkness seemed to sense the use of his power and it plunged more of its darkness into him so images of Kat, surrounded by the same dark smoke, a young girl laughing as Kat was overcome, filled his mind. He gave a yell of despair, but he pushed out the image, sort for the striker and put all his remaining energy into striking it.

The scream was the loudest yet and Tom felt suddenly the warmth of the flame as it drove at the smoky arms binding him. He collapsed to the floor, his mind clearing but the un-relenting cold was still on his limbs. Then the fire surrounded him, protecting him, and warming his body until he could move his fingers and then his arms. He stood and the figure regarded him curiously but with a smile it withdrew suddenly, became shadow at Tom's feet and moved behind him but Tom was ready for this. The fire balled in his hand and just as the smoky figure regained shape, he plunged the swirling mass of fire into its midriff. There was no scream, at least none that Tom could hear this time, but dogs howled in the town and the windows around him seemed to vibrate. The flames devoured the smoky figure, pulling it apart and igniting every strand until it lost all shape and was consumed.

Vengeance of the Gods

Tom fell to one knee, desperately clawing for breath. He felt like pulling at the flames to regain some strength, but they had turned the lurid shade of green and they seemed to give off a putrid reek. He could hear in the distance the bell for the beginning of school, but he had no thought, no strength to go there. He just collapsed on the pavement, waiting for the next strike that he would surely be unable to fight. He knew he needed to reach the Agency, only there would he be safe, but the coldness had seemed to strip his limbs of all their strength. He did not even move at the sound of the door opening and barely lifted his head as footsteps charged towards him, "Are you okay sweetie." Came a soft female voice. He finally lifted his head; it was the mother who had stood in the doorway.
"I'm fine." Tom sighed with a pained expression as he clumsily rose to his feet. His legs felt like jelly and his hand reached out to force against the earth, the only thing that could keep him standing.
Her hand grasped his but shot back swiftly, "You are frozen." She then bent down, picking Tom's scarf from the floor before handing it to him. She smiled but her eyes lingered on his scars. He thought he caught then a measure of understanding in her expression, "You really need to go and see Director Warman at once." Nothing she could have said, would have surprised him more, "Excuse me?"

"I know who you are Tom, if they are chasing you again then you need to go and see Tax."
Tom wasn't sure whether he was imagining this, "How do you?" He asked in a stutter.
Her daughter rushed to her side and with a smile and a flick of her wrist, her front door slammed shut, "Let me see your hands?"
Tom held them out and she examined the grazes, "They are nothing major, but they are frozen." Her eyes then looked around, searching for the figure, "Was it one of them?"
"No." He suddenly recognised the woman, she worked on one of the desks in the ground floor of the Agency office. Tom never thought that she may have been a Halve, "this was something different."
"I will take this one to school and then I will be heading to the Agency. Get in and I will drive you." She ordered.
Tom smiled, he didn't think his legs would carry him and he could feel the power keeping him up wavering, "Thank you very much."

It was a commotion outside his office that startled Tax from his work. He knew there would be trouble. It had been nearly half an hour since his sensors had picked up on an anomaly. He suspected a Halve had been using their power irresponsibly and had ordered the person to be found and brought to his office. What he did not expect was his secretary bursting in, her eyes wide with fear and her lips quivering.

"What is the problem Ashley?" He asked, standing up.

"There is someone here to see you Director." She replied in a haggard voice.

"Do they have an appointment?" Tax asked and when she shook her head he continued, "Well then ask them to make one."

Her eyes widened again and Tax wondered what could make her lose her composure so, "But sir it is one of them."

Tax stood up straighter and nervously began to adjust the suit he wore, "Tell them to wait five minutes."

Ashley disappeared but there was another commotion and suddenly an Ilmgralite burst through the door, "I'm sorry but I do not have five minutes." He shut the door with a slam before turning with a smile aimed at Tax, "Director Warman."

"Ambassador." He replied with a courteous nod, but he regarded the Graul with squinting eyes. He had seen him in his normal form only once before. Lucast had a way with minds and could often trick the eyes into making himself look human but not today. He was also in his full ceremonial armour and not the suit that Tax was accustom to.

"It is just Lucast now I'm afraid." The Ilmgralite said sadly.

"Shouldn't you be using your mind games." Tax said as he beckoned for Lucast to sit but the

Ilmgralite refused, "You have scared half of my staff to death."

"My mind is elsewhere Michael." He replied dramatically.

Tax sat on the edge of his desk, examining the alien, "What can I help you with?"

"You must bring the kids here." Lucast demanded as he began to pace.

"Kids?"

Lucast stopped pacing and his golden eyes bored into Tax, "The survivors of the Island." His face seemed to tighten with pain, "They are being hunted."

Suddenly Tax's smile faltered, his demeanour crumbled and he became a concerned human, facing a wider universe that he knew nothing about, "By who?"

"I will explain once they are here." There was a stutter to Lucast's voice, showing the fear in his mind and it made Tax panic. He was usually so calm, so assured and his voice held a musical rhythm but all of that was gone now.

"I need to know what sort of threat we are facing?"

Before Lucast could answer another commotion started outside. Tom burst through the door. He looked set to blurt something out, but he stopped when he spotted Lucast. Tax though was equally as silent, looking at the wounds on Tom's hands and the paleness of his cheeks, "Yes Tom?" He said finally.

"Lucast." Tom murmured in astonishment.

"Hello Thomas Lita." He replied, "It has been a long time since we have seen eachother,"
Words seemed to fail Tom again, so Tax stepped forward, "Mr Lita." He said sternly, "Since you are clearly not here to see the Ambassador, may I ask what has brought you here and in such a state?"
Tom's eyes seemed to harden and to Tax, the twelve year old seemed to grow taller.
"I was attacked." He deadpanned.
Lucast moved with frightening speed and grabbed Tom's shoulders, leaning in closely to him. His eyes seemed to be searching inside him, looking for something. Tom could barely hold that glance but slowly Lucast seemed to relax, "By what? tell me everything."
He recounted his story of the shadow, the visions it created and the way it had seemed to freeze his limbs. While he spoke Lucast seemed to become more frightened, his eyes widened, and his red scales seemed to lose some of their colour. His worst fear had not come true, that Urgarak had got into Tom's mind but it still meant one thing. He would not stop until he had completed his vengeance. Urgarak turned back to the Director, "Get those children here now."

Chapter Nine- News of the wider universe.

It started as a typical art lesson for Sophie. She worked while rubbers and pieces of paper were launched across the room. Their teacher minded little, soon many of these students would stop taking art and she would be left with those of talent, of which Sophie was one. She had always been drawing and now the pencil flowed gently across the page as she sketched a woodland scene, her headphones helping her to concentrate over the noise. The seat beside her was empty, Tom had not arrived at school that day and she had no text to explain why. Kat and Price were at opposite ends of the classroom, having long been separated but Sophie expected they were the ones doing the throwing.

Suddenly though the noise seemed to stop. Her eyes shot up; everyone was looking behind her to the door. Sophie gently removed her headphones and turned her head. Men were there, two of them and they were both wearing expensive suits, but she could see Agency lanyards around their necks.

"Can I help you?" The teacher asked nervously. One of the men nodded and stood forward, "We need to speak with Miss Carter, Master Jones and Miss Dalton please."

Without thinking Sophie stood and she saw

Price and Kat do the same. She like they, trusted the Agency more than their own teachers and they would follow them without thinking.

"Sit down you three." The Teacher ordered and they moved to sit but never actually made it back to their seats before they halted. The teacher stared at the men, "Why may I ask?"

"That's an issue of national security." The second man replied in a level voice.

Murmurings began around the room and the teacher looked between the children and the calm men stood in the doorway. She may have been about to argue but she was silenced as the headmaster burst into the room. His balding head was glistening with sweat and he was pale, a look of shock in his eyes. At his shoulder Nicole was stood. She seemed nervous as well, her deep brown eyes looked at Sophie and gave her a quivering smile.

"Nicholas, Kathryn, Sophie." The headmaster said with a shake of his head, "Please go with these men at once." He looked at the teacher, "I have informed your three parents about where you are going."

The class now spoke together in hushed voices. Sophie dropped her head, feeling all their eyes on her as she hurriedly packed up her things. She could not catch their words, but she knew they would be making the connection that all those summoned had survived the Island. She wondered what story they would think of and knew it would not come close to the truth about the knights of earth.

They were rushed from the school and driven the short distance to the office's that served as the Agency Hq. None of their questions were answered and they had given up asking before they had even left the school. Sophie could feel her heart beating in her chest. She thought about Tom, about his absence, that could not have been a coincidence. As they walked through the offices she turned to Price, "I think something has happened to Tom."

He nodded but did not speak, his hand just reached out and took Kat's. Sophie wished that Sam were there. Not that he was strong enough to protect her, she just wanted his presence. He would not know the danger and would not be panicking like she was. Instead it was Nicole who grasped her hand and squeezed it gently, "Don't worry Sophie. It would take an army to hurt Tom and we would have known if one of them had come."

Sophie nodded but she wasn't convinced. She was looking for the Tempter, wondering if that ghostly figure may have played some part in this.

They were ushered into Tax's office and Sophie's eyes widened as she spotted not the Tempter but Lucast, who looked down on them with a wide smile on his face, "Hello children." Her eyes looked passed him to Tom who looked shaken but alive. Before she knew what she was doing, she was crossing the threshold and was in his arms. He hugged her gently and when she broke away, he tried to give her a smile.

"Umm." Price muttered, still unable to take his eyes off Lucast, "What is happening?"

Tax, who was perched on his desk, hand rubbing at his forehead, answered, "Tom was attacked."

"What? How?" Nicole charged across the room and grabbed Tom, examining him.

He squirmed, "I'm fine. Really."

"Can everyone please take a seat." Tax ordered, his voice was strained but he tried to smile, "Lucast is going to explain everything to you all.

The five of them slowly took a seat on the floor, facing Lucast who was pacing the room. Little specks of dust seemed to be swirling around him whenever he was caught in the light. He seemed troubled as he spoke, "I have learnt a lot since that day on Curamber. I learnt that what may have at first seemed like a simple plan of Cirtroug's, is in fact a vast conspiracy spreading through both the empires of Abgdon and Ilmgral. The seers are declaring that war is imminent. The governments of the two empires are doing their all to stop it while the Gods work through the warrist movements to bring forth the destruction of the Ilma. Urgarak, the Graul who planned the attack is now their latest pawn in that endeavour." He stopped pacing, his golden eyes looking at each of them, judging how well his maturing had taken hold, sensing whether they could fight this next threat. Behind Lucast, Tax's hand slipped into his pocket, he casually removed his phone and pressed record. "Tom was attacked by something not from this world." Lucast continued before turning his gaze onto Tom, "Tell them what attacked you."

"It was like a shadow." He began and the hairs on his arm stood on end at the thought of that figure, "but wispy like smoke and it had features like a face and gold eyes. When I used my powers, it seemed to scream. It could be hurt by my powers, but it was strong, it probably would have killed me if I didn't have my lighter."

"Or do something worse than death." Lucast deadpanned.

Nicole looked confused, "What could be worse than death?"

"This power could kill you. Freeze your limbs until your heart gives out but it can also trap your mind in a prison. A torment of your own creation with your own doubts and failures screaming at you, screaming until you eventually consume yourself. The worse thing this power can do though is lock who you are away in the dark prison and then use what is left for its own means. I fear that was the mission." Lucast took a deep breath, "What attacked Tom goes back to the second great war between Ilmgral and Abgdon." He began to pace the room again, "It is a thing of pure

energy."
Sophie butted in, "Is it alive? You speak of it like it can think."
"To a sort it can." Lucast continued, "After Abgdon's enlightenment they sort to challenge Ilmgral once more and so they liberated the planet of Murk from our protection. With the Murka's on their side, they launched fresh waves of attack against our people and so King Guram Grinoma became the second king eternal." He stopped his pacing and looked at their confused glances, "It is a title bestowed to the kings of Abgdon during a time of war. Their king now is a peaceful man as were most who have held the title of Abgdon's rulers. Only three have become King Eternal's and the second of these was the vilest." The room seemed to darken at his words and Tom felt the others shift closer towards him.

"When Abgdon was losing the war, he performed an act so evil that it created a power that was just that, evil." Visions came back to the children, the same visions that had seen once on the Island, only now they seemed to make more sense.

Tom felt Kat stir. That image seemed clearer now and two of the powers of the darkness seemed revealed in that image. Tom was not dead on the floor on that battlefield, he was asleep, trapped in a dungeon created by the darkness and Kat, was she being killed by the darkness or overcome by it? Was that the obstacle that she was destined to become? Tom felt his heart stop at the thought, and he breathed deeply to bring his mind back to the present.

Lucast had charged across the room and grabbed a piece of paper from Tax's desk, on which he crudely drew a semi-circle which he then cut with lines that joined in a central spot on the edge of the paper, "This is the spectrum of powers. Each of the powers possessed can be traced upon this line. From earth and metal on one side, to water in the middle and fire, power, and wind on the other side. Halves have only the ability to channel one part of this spectrum. Now what was created is the central spot, the opposite of all our powers. That is why when Tom used his powers upon it, the darkness was consumed."

Tom nodded, "My fire turned green and sickly when it touched the darkness though."

"Did you absorb it back in?" Lucast asked, a gleam in his eye.

"No, I didn't want to connect with it, I just let it disperse."

"Good." He sighed, "That fire was now tainted, and part of the darkness would remain within the flames. It would probably do nothing more than make you sick, but the darkness is a terrible weapon. It is more adaptive than our powers and somewhat alive. It can manipulate our gifts, mutate them into other forms as it did with Cirtroug, giving him the power to control the molten rock and fire within without being hurt. It makes the Ilma more powerful and the second king eternal took it into war with him. Only betrayal of one of his own stopped him in the end but the darkness could not be controlled and in the third great war its terrible power was unleashed. Only Infeon the gift holder was able to withstand them and he found the source of the darkness and split it into many pieces, scattering it across the universe."

Price raised his hand, "Why didn't he destroy it?"

"A fair question." Lucast replied, "I do not know for sure. Maybe to do so would have killed the Ilma or he had some plan to use it in the future. Still he thought that the small amounts he split it into could not be used but he did not understand the power of the darkness. Once inside a host it becomes no longer dormant, it feeds off them and their power, to grow in strength and then it takes many forms. The strongest of which attacked Tom, a sentinel of eternity." Now the room visibly darkened and clouds rolled in the sky. Tom looked to his side, Kat was staring down, the hairs on her arm stood on end and she was trembling. Lucast seemed not to notice the change, "They hold some of the mind of the host, designed to be generals on the battlefield, thinking with their master's thoughts but separate from him."

Tom looked hard at Lucast. He now knew the

tools being used to kill him but he didn't yet no the wielder, "Who is Urgarak?"
"He is a pawn but why he is hunting you is a better story and it may show how he was easily swayed to this path. He was a soldier, A Graul in the armies of Ilmgral but born on a planet called Uralese. It is a mining planet, poor and vastly populated. He loves that planet and so when it was traded to Abgdon he forsook his people and went to join their forces. He watched the people of his home planet starve and its manifested hatred inside of him. He wanted Uralese to be important and the only time it is important is at times of war. So, he became a member of the warrist party and moved for the high council of Abgdon to expand its empire, but all his attempts were fruitless. Until one day, while scouting Uralese, guess what he finds?"
"The darkness." Tom muttered.
"Exactly." Lucast smiled, "He then discovers where Cirtroug is captive and learns that an army had been positioned for the general and his eyes turn to Earth. Cirtroug will be the key to starting his war. Through the criminal he will find the strength and will to turn Earth into the base of his new empire."
"Why didn't he just release him." Nicole asked, "What did he need us for?"
"Because the darkness he wielded would have prevented him accessing the terminal. It was believed by those of Ilmgral that only those who

wielded the darkness would want to release
Cirtroug." Nicole nodded so Lucast continued,
"So he uses the darkness to try and connect
with a servant of Agral's, but the Tempter has
already sent you. Now Urgarak wants to use
you as a way of forcing Ilmgral to intervene and
in doing so create war in the universe."
Tom wondered something, "Where is Cirtroug?
Didn't you take him back to Ilmgral?"
Lucast's eyes faltered again and Tax shuffled uncomfortably. They looked between eachother
before Lucast finally answered, "I could not." He
deadpanned, "To do so would surely have
meant handing him back to Abgdon. He was
imprisoned on earth and here he remains. I do
not know whether Urgarak knows this but I
deem it is safer here, protected by humanity
than it would be with the Ilma who have failed
many times as custodians."
"How do you know all this?" Nicole asked
quickly.
"Some I have learnt through study." He cast his
eyes downward in shame, "Most I know
because he told me."
Price stood up before anyone else had realised
what had been said. His hands were balled into
fists and he stared at Lucast with the strength of
a forest in his eyes, "Why did he tell you?"
Lucast didn't seem daunted by Price's stare, his
eyes went away from the twelve year old boy
and focused on Tom, "I did as I am obliged to.
They had a right to know why one of their

people were held captive on Earth. Once I found out his intent, I begged the parliament of Ilmgral to intervene."

Price suddenly seemed to relax, his shoulders slouched, and he sat back down beside Kat who took his hand before looking back up at Lucast, "Are they coming to help?" She asked, a rare stutter to her voice.

"Sadly not. They deemed that peace was more important than your lives. I do not agree and so I resigned my position so that I could aid you." There was sadness in Lucast's voice, a sense of loss but mingled within it, Tom caught a sense of pride and the strength of that filled him.

"Will he send more of those things after me?" He asked.

"That was a mistake on Urgarak's part, something that I may have forced upon him. The darkness is finite within a host. It can use some of your own power, but the body cannot re-produce it, nothing is evil enough. Eventually it will either consume the host or simply become too small within the host to take any shape. Until Urgarak can find more, it is a weapon he must use sparingly and that may prove our opportunity."

Once again Kat asked a question about the darkness in her unusually nervous voice, "What happens to somebody when they have used all of it?"

"No one is ever truly free of it." Lucast gave her a sad smile, "To weild something so dark and

terrible will always leave scars. It becomes like an unquenchable craving while awake and sleep brings only nightmares."
Tom felt Lucast's maturing, the invisible barriers placed within his mind to zone out all his child like thoughts and become only the cool calculated soldier that he had forced them into. His heart seemed to cool and his mind focused, "What must I do?" He asked in a steady voice.
"You must stay strong and you must stay vigilant." Lucast warned, "He will seek to force you into action Tom. He has many soldiers on his ship, Murka and Grignar and more of his darkness. He will strike again but it will come as targeted assaults until he leaves you no choice but to face him."
It was at this time that Tax turned off his phone and stood up, drawing the children's attention on to himself, "I have ordered uniforms for you all. The same ones that the strike teams wear. If we can have some indication of Urgarak's attack, then we may be able to better arm you for what is too come. For now though, would any of you like to go back to school?"
"No." Price replied slowly, standing up again, followed by Kat and then Sophie, "I want to train while I'm scared enough."
Lucast gave a loud booming laugh, "The Knights of Earth stand again. May Livella light your path."
Price and Kat charged from the room and Nicole slowly followed, shaking her head, and

muttering about getting caught in this once again. Sophie remained behind, watching Tom, seemingly being able to read him better than anyone else.

Slowly He stood, "Is there nothing else we can do?"

Lucast shook his head, "To challenge him now would only make his attack legal. We will force him to act in the hope that Abgdon finally intervene."

"We will get you all some panic buttons." Tax said, "Just in case you should find yourself under attack."

Tom nodded, his eyes then caught Sophie's, the blueness was exaggerated by the sparkle of tears and her lips were nervously quivering but he didn't think it was nerves for herself that caused it. Her thumb stroked something, a bracelet on her wrist, a gift from Sam, "Sir." Tom said finally understanding her nerves and the role that he must play, "I know it costs a lot of money but."

"What would you like Tom?"

"Well sir." He paused to lick his lips, "Sam is a part of this now. He might not know it, but he likes Sophie and the rest of us. He will not hold back if something were to happen to us. I think he should get a uniform."

Lucast looked between Tom and Sophie, "He is not one of the Knights of Earth." He murmured, "Your coming was prophesised to us by the Tempter but he was not mentioned."

Tom had guessed the Tempter had long held sway over his life, manipulating his dreams and surrounding him with his friends. Knowing that it was not in his control did not make him feel any better.

"Prophecy doesn't take into account what people will do when they care about others."

Tax said with a wide smile, "I will see what can be arranged Mr Lita."

Sophie took hold of Tom's hand as they walked out of Tax's office and as soon as they were clear she threw herself around him, hugging him tightly, "Thank you so much. He is not one of us, protect him please."

Tom hugged her back but only gently, "I will Sophie. I promise but he may need to learn to protect himself."

With that, they charged down the stairs to train like their lives depended on it.

*

Urgarak sat amongst his most faithful general's, staring down at the planet below them. His mind was dark, his thoughts wicked. He could still see the face of Thomas Lita as his sentinel was destroyed and yet he was so close to achieving his goal. He had to work differently, no more would he waste his darkness to force a confession. He would find other means for that, "This boy, what do we know from Cirtroug's attack?"

Mirkan, his Murka commander answered, "He was able to defeat Cirtroug and trapped him in a phial."

"But he was not alone?" Urgarak asked.

"He had help from the abomination's my lord." The general licked his lips, seeing now the means to fill his end. The Ilmgralites had sort for the death of Halves before, they would not mind some now, "He is friends with them isn't he? Close to the freaks of nature?"

"We believe so." Another Murka said with a nod.

"They are powerful and with them he may wish to do to me what was done to Cirtroug, but this connection can be exploited, it can make him irrational." He turned to Mirkan, "Where is your assassin."

Mirkan clicked his long grey fingers and a figure stepped forward. Even in the low light of the bridge, Urgarak could see that his grey skin was scarred from years of combat, his low hanging arms were full of sinewy muscle and his eyes seemed dull like he was awaiting the next kill. He was still bent backed as all Murka were, a degeneration from when their race had first been conquered. Years of labour had turned them into what they were now, but their looks did not tell the whole tale. This Murka was educated, learnt in the arts of war.

The Murka's intelligence had been what the Abgdonese had used to wage war against the

Vengeance of the Gods

Ilmgralites. Even if not all of Urgarak's foot soldiers shared that trait of their race, they were still a worthy army.
Urgarak stood to address the Murka assassin, "You will be taken in one of our ships. We will find a target close to Thomas Lita. I want you to exterminate his friends quickly but I must warn you that this is a one way trip and when you fall after killing his friends, he will know that he must face me."
The Mirkan assassin snarled, "Yes my Lord."

*

The Saturday morning was cold again, frost hung on the ground, but Tom seemed not to notice. Little had happened since Lucast's warning and some of the nerves from what he revealed had slipped from his mind. His hand reached into his pocket and found there the lump of plastic attached to his keys. His finger ran gently over the rubber of the panic button. He had been given it the day after the attack with a stern warning from Tax not to press it unless absolutely necessary. He quickly withdrew his hand. He did not think he would need it that day, not since he was walking to the Agency. He stopped at the end of the street and smiled when Nicole ran towards him. She was wearing a bright red jumper over tight jeans, but she still seemed cold as she gave him a quick hug.

"Ready for this?" Tom asked.

Nicole's brown eyes seemed full of frustration, "I thought I was done with all this. Now they are giving us a silly uniform."

Tom laughed, "We may need it." His laugh faltered when he realised how true that was. No matter what they might want, war was coming and they would need the advantage the uniforms gave them.

They walked to the Agency, talking a little about what Lucast had revealed and what the next threat they would face may be. Once signed in, they cut to the training room where a wide smile suddenly seemed to spread over Nicole's face.

Tom looked over. Daniel was there, learning basic martial arts. While they watched he was flipped over, and he landed with a dull thud onto a soft padded mat. Tom winced but Daniel caught sight of Nicole and shot up as though it was nothing. He whispered something to his instructor before walking over. He was in a vest that was soaked in sweat but Nicole didn't seem to notice as she kissed him quickly but she soon broke away, "God you stink."

Daniel gave Tom a wink before sticking his hairy armpit into her face. He laughed as she recoiled in horror, "You are an animal." She said but anger lasted only until he kissed her again.

"What are you doing here?" He asked as soon as she had stopped eating his face.

"Tax wants to see us." Tom said in reply.

Daniel gave him a wide smile, "What you done this time?"

"We've done nothing." Nicole replied, "I'm an angel."

"I don't quite believe that." Tax said from behind them, making all three of them jump into the air and he laughed as he turned to Daniel, "How is the training going?"

"Well thank you sir. When I am not on the floor at least."

"Good to hear it. Do you mind if I take your girlfriend for a while?"

Daniel winked at Nicole, "Have her."

She gave him daggers but allowed herself to be escorted away from Tax. Tom followed them out. On the stairs, Sophie, Kat, Price, and Sam were waiting. They all followed him up the stairs, passed the floor with his office, all the way to the research and development room, which caused excited murmurings from the kids. He punched in a nine-digit code before the door opened. They stepped through into a maze of offices, all messy, strewn with different documents. They were led into the largest of these, where a bald man with big round glasses, that magnified his eyes, stared at them. Behind him was a box with their names on. Tax stood by the man, "This is Dr Pentka, he has been working on your uniforms." He rummaged into the box and pulled for each of them a bundle with their names on it, "There are rooms to change next door. Once you are changed, we will discuss each aspect of your uniforms."

The boys found an office for them to change in. They stood at separate corners and changed swiftly. Inside each bag was a pair of durable trousers and a long-sleeved shirt that seemed heavier than it should have. It had a zip instead of buttons at the neck and the collar covered his burns perfectly. A belt he slipped through his trousers and looked at the clips on that as well. Also, inside were socks and shoes. his shoes were made of rubber, but round metal studs were forced into the soul and when he thought about it, he used them to lift his feet slightly off the ground. Left in the packet was a wrist strap. The back of which had a clip to hold something and cables went to a small pressure pad that strapped into Tom's palm. He pressed it, expecting to feel something. He did feel something, but he did not think it was from the pressure pad. He seemed suddenly to be full of adrenalin, like he had drunk a full can of one of the energy drinks that Price always did to wake up with in the morning.

The feeling was strange but Tom enjoyed it. Soon Price and Sam came over and joined him. Sam's uniform was identical to Tom's, but Price's uniform looked like his only in the fact that it was the same trousers and shirt. Other than that, it was vastly different. Price's uniform seemed to be pitted and the zip on his shirt did not go all the way up his neck. His belt also had none of the clips that Tom's did and was bare at

the front apart from two hooks. He also had no wrist strap.
"How does it feel?" Tom asked.
Price suddenly seemed to be shaking, "I don't know but I'm buzzed." He then looked harder at Tom's, "They covered your burns. They really did think of everything."
Tom gave his best friend a malicious smile, "Yeah, they made yours extra-large."
Before Price could work out that it was an insult, he had charged from the room. The girls were already changed and stood waiting by Dr Pentka. Tom didn't have chance to look to closely at their uniforms before Price jabbed him in the ribs and Dr Pentka began talking in an eastern European accent, "Director Warman has had to go but I will explain your uniforms and how they complement your powers." He went to a box beside himself and grabbed a small cylinder with H20 stamped upon the side. It was only six inches long and Tom realised it would fit perfectly in the clips on his wrist strap. He beckoned for Sophie to come closer and she did nervously, her hands hidden in the sleeves of her shirt, "Let me see your wrist strap."
She gently lifted her arm and Dr Pentka clipped the tube in place before joining the cable from the pressure pad, "This contains pressurised water vapour." Dr Pentka began, "When Sophie presses the pad, the moisture will be released and will be there for her to use. This allows her to use more of her power while using less of her

own personal energy. Once the cartridge is spent, simply press the button on the back of the strap and the cartridge will release." He gave Sophie a warm smile, "Please show us your power."

Sophie looked back at Tom, who gave her a confident nod, "Okay." She giggled before taking a step back from Dr Pentka. She pressed the pad and there was a spurt of spray that suddenly became a ball of water in her hand, "Wow." She murmured, "I would need to strip the ground to get that much."

Sophie breathed in and the water absorbed back into her hand. She shuffled uncomfortably, the water gave her a boost, but she suddenly needed to pee.

"Your suit." Dr Pentka explained, "Is waterproof and designed for swimming. Tax thought you would like that."

Sophie's cheeks reddened, there was nothing she liked more than swimming, "I do, thank you."

Dr Pentka asked her to remove the cartridge's which she did willingly before stepping back into line. She got with her uniform a pointed bar, filled with water that she could throw and brake open when she needed a more direct approach, but he didn't let Sophie demonstrate that, or the water balanced throwing knives that he mentioned other water Halves used. He turned instead towards Kat, "Now, the pretty blonde."

Price stepped forward and received scowls and moans from them all. He gracefully stepped back into line allowing Kat to step forward.

Dr Pentka shook his head in Price's direction but when he looked at Kat he was smiling wickedly, "I like your gift. For you I have these." He pulled out another tube, but it seemed heavier and a lightning bolt adorned it.

"And these are?" Kat asked, in a blunt and unappreciative way.

Dr Pentka seemed not to notice, "These are batteries. They connect to your pressure pad and give you an extra power source to work with."

Kat's eyes went wide from the sudden surge of power she had not expected, and sparks arced between her fingers.

"You like?" Dr Pentka asked.

"You bet sunshine." She grinned, "Now I can super zap people."

"No!" Dr Pentka said sharply, "For that you need these."

He pulled from a box two metal rods which he hastily connected to the battery. Flows of electricity seemed to move across the rods and at times a bolt would shoot from them connecting with Kat's body.

"These will make it easier for you to channel your power onto a specific target." He then turned on Sam, but he did not have much for him, who had sat cowed at the back wondering what he was doing there. He received a cooling agent that attached to his wrist and nothing more. Tom wondered whether Dr Pentka did not believe Sam would be hunted or that he would not have the strength to fight if he did, but Sam seemed relieved to not be holding any pieces of sharp metal.

The doctor then pulled Price and Nicole forward while Kat reluctantly disconnected the rods and the batteries, "Your gifts come from the ground. You cannot create that which you control, only use what is around you. That is why neither of you have any wrist straps. However, your gifts respond well to radiation. Within the pitting of your suit is a small radioactive source. You can use the energy boost received when absorbing the radiation to aid you in the use of your powers."

Nicole was given nothing extra, the earth was her weapon and she would find no small amount of it to use. Price though was given two plastic rods with a metal spike, the inside of which held soil and a seed. Also, with his gift were many small boxes of offensive and defensive plants for him to call upon when they were needed.

Once Dr Pentka had taken back the weapons from Price, he turned on Tom, "Now you were a challenge." He gave him a warm smile, "I think we have accommodated for all your powers. Your wrist strap is universal. It can carry propane cylinders, batteries or whatever else we need. Also included in the wrist strap is a slightly more powerful radioactive source to aid you in battle." Tom received nothing extra, but he wasn't worried about that, a knife would do nothing more to aid him. Everything around him was a weapon, he was the weapon.

Dr Pentka ordered them to change and they did this much more reluctantly than before. When they returned the uniforms to him he was smiling, "These will be stored here."

Tom raised his hand, "What use is having a uniform but then not being able to keep them."

Dr Pentka looked sheepish, "We cannot allow the members of the public to see them or for you to go around with these weapons without proper training." He gave them a stern look, "You will learn to train with these, and we will find a way to incorporate them into your day to day life. The best chance you have now is to be vigilant and your panic buttons are your greatest weapons." A smile flicked onto his face but to Tom it made him look more like an insect, "You can go now."

They left the research room together and gathered in the training hall, "That was amazing." Kat exclaimed, "I can think of a few people I would like to use my rods on."

Nicole laughed, "I'm sure you would. I just know I will be happy if I never have to see them again." She shook her head and walked over to where Daniel was still training.

"What are you guys doing now?" Tom asked, he was eyeing up the fire room, wanting to release some of the energy he had absorbed from the radiation.

"Me and Sophie are going shopping." Kat exclaimed, Price looked horrified, but she gave him a quick smile, "Don't worry sweet you won't want to come to this type of shopping."

Price looked at Tom, "Gaming?"

He looked at one of Fox team, wearing uniform similar to the one Tom had just given up, a cold look in his eyes, "I'm going to stay here for a bit."

Price gave his best friend an exasperated look but turned to Sam, "Fancy coming round mine for a game?"

He nodded his head, blushing slightly at being asked, "Will be nice to do something to take my mind off the fact we might soon be attacked."

Kat snogged Price so hard Tom thought he was going to collapse while Sophie gave Sam a hug. To make it not seem weird she gently threw her arms around Tom before they all went their separate ways.

Chapter Ten- Hunted

Together, Price and Sam walked out of the Agency and cut through the town, to get back to Price's house from there. They cut passed the empty school, through a lane crowded by tall and thick evergreen's, "Things seem to be going well with Sophie." Price grinned, the sun reflecting off his braces.
"We aren't together yet." Sam said and Price watched as his face reddened, remembering when he would have done the same.
"Had your hand up her shirt yet." He asked and laughed when Sam's eyes widened, "Best feeling ever." He exclaimed, un-sure whether Sam could get any redder.
It became cold as they walked into the shadow of the trees and Price immediately stiffened. He stopped dead, the hairs on his arms rising. The wind brought words from the trees to him, words of a nearby threat.
"What's up?" Sam asked looking back at him.
"I don't know." Price muttered, searching the trees for something, "I just don't feel right."
Sam looked around, "Stop messing okay."
Some birds flew up from a tree and Price relaxed, wondering if that was what he had sensed, "I'm probably just being paranoid."
He was about to take a step again when his eyes widened. He pushed Sam into the

undergrowth as a shot echoed in the alley way and sparks shot across the pavement. Price shoved Sam to the floor and he connected to the trees. They seemed to rustle and there was a moan as a branch broke and a figure fell to the floor, landing with a dull thud. With a turn it stood nimbly and even though they were concealed in the undergrowth, it was looking right at them. A gun clattered to the floor between them and Price looked from the grey skinned, long armed creature to the weapon that was like none he had ever seen.

Price charged for the gun and his finger slipped to the panic button. Sam was behind him, but the creature was quicker. It dived on Price and swept him away with a powerful swing of his arm. Sam was braver than he had expected, and he grasped the creature's arm just as it wrapped around the gun. The creature gave a primeval yell before jumping back. It stared down at the silhouette of Sam's hand; his arm burnt by the freeze. Sam kicked the large gun away but squealed as the creature pulled from its belt a long-curved blade.

Price was on his feet again and he charged, pulling for a root but before one could break the surface, a boot caught him painfully in the stomach and the Murka slashed with its good arm to keep Sam away.

It turned again on Price, and Sam tried to kick out but the figure turned, caught his boot and span him to the floor. The knife was coming down for him before Sam could stop it, but a root snatched at the creature's wrist. Price was pulling with all his might but the muscular arm of the Murka was slowly getting closer to Sam's chest. Its numb, frozen arm grabbed at Sam's neck and he tried desperately to breathe. In a last desperate measure, his hand went to the Murka's face. Ice glistened on his fingers and the Murka screamed. The knife fell, grazing Sam's cheek and the distraction allowed Price to pull the Murka away from him. Regaining itself it span, grabbed the gun and smiled at them but more roots were bursting from the ground and Sam's hands were sparkling with the ice that covered them.

With startling speed, two knives flew at Price and Sam and they ducked to avoid them. When they looked up, the Murka was charging away with a frightening turn of pace. They chased it as far as they could until it disappeared into a spinney at the end of a long field.

"What." Sam paused for a breath, "The hell?" Price felt his mind darkening, the strength of a forest filling him, the same coldness that had formed whenever he had seen molten warriors in his path back on the Island, "I don't know." He sat on the grass of the field, staring into the spinney. He could still feel it, the alien tearing through the plant life, maybe looking for somewhere to hide.

"What do we do now?" Sam asked nervously. Price lifted his hand and summer seemed to come to some of the spiney and brambles, thick with large thorns, formed around the side that faced them, "It could attack us again at any time. I think if it were only just one of us it would have killed us. We need to call the others; we can't let this thing escape."

*

Tax had expected an un-eventful day and it had proved to be. The kids had their uniforms and he was leaving the office for home before one o'clock on a Saturday for the first time in months. The motorway was also blissfully clear of cars. The in-built phone on his car blared into life and Tax answered calmly, "Warman."
"Sir. We have a problem." A voice said on the other end of the line, "Nick Jones's panic button was activated twenty minutes ago."
Tax shook his head, "He often plays tricks."
"I know sir but just seconds later so was Sam Patten's. We were able to contact him and he claims they have both been attacked."
A month ago Tax would have put it down to kids being kids, but he knew Price was a target. His eyes swept to the passing junction and his foot slammed to the floor, "Mobilise Fox." He said through gritted teeth, "Make sure they take whatever it is alive. We need to know everything we can. I will be twenty minutes to co-ordinate. See if you can get hold of the children and make sure they don't do anything

stupid."

*

"What's going on?" Tom asked as he rounded on Price who was still standing watch in the field.
"Something attacked us." He said swiftly but before Tom could reply, Kat and Sophie arrived. Kat flung her arms around Price but when she let go, she was smiling with feverish delight, sparks arcing between her fingers.
"You are lucky." She said, "We were almost on the bus."
Price scowled at his girlfriend, "Oh yes I'm that lucky I was nearly killed."
Tom stepped in front of them, "By what?"
Price seemed to tune back into the fight, "Not by what you described. It was an alien, it had like grey skin and long arms. It nearly got hold of Sam."
"Sam." Sophie exclaimed, "Where is he?"
"He is the other side of the wood to make sure it doesn't go that way." Price deadpanned.
"WHAT?" Sophie screamed causing Tom to wince, "Why didn't you just go to the agency?" Her cheeks were reddening, "He isn't ready for this, he..." Sophie paused for a breath, her eyes looking between them in a panic, "He..." Then before they could stop her, she charged across the field.
"Sophie." Tom yelled after her but before he

could charge away as well, Price grabbed his arm.

"I sent Sam away to keep him safe." Price explained, "I can sense things in the wood. I think I know where he might be."

Tom looked at Price and Kat, it reminded him of when they had first had their mind matured, when they were first setting out to look for survivors. Price held the same hunger in his eyes and Tom knew his fear was true. They would never be who they were before, no matter how much they pretended to be, "Did you warn the Agency?"

Price pulled from his pocket the panic button, "First thing I did and Sam has spoken to them as well."

"They treat us like children." Kat said suddenly, "They don't even trust us with our uniforms after we helped defeat an army of molten warriors. We should capture this thing and bring it back to show them how good we are."

"I think they know how good we are." Tom replied but the idea of being the hero once again filled his mind, "On the other hand if it escapes before they get here, then who knows what it will do."

Kat was smiling wickedly and even Price had a determined look in his eye, probably planning a Price is a hero month instead of a day in his mind.

Tom sighed, "Let's see what we can do."

Price gave a wide grin and set off for the

spinney with Tom and Kat following him. He lifted his hand and part of the bramble died, giving them a clear path to walk through. With winter still in full strength, the wood was littered with debris but with nothing much to conceal them or the Murka but Price pointed to a thicket of evergreens further into the spinney, "That is where I sense it."

Tom turned back to Kat, "Phone Sophie. I don't want us separated for too long."

"On it." Kat smiled as she grabbed her phone and held it to her ear.

"Did it have powers?" Tom asked.

Price shook his head, "If it did, it didn't use them."

"Well that would be cheating." Kat laughed, "If something else had powers."

Tom laughed as well. This seemed so natural, them walking into unknown danger. This was what they had been made for and Tom knew it was the design of both the Tempter and Lucast, that they acted so.

"No answer." Kat replied solemnly.

"Keep trying, I don't like us being separated like this." Tom ordered, "I will press my panic button again as well. See if we can get some help."

*

Sophie had not run like she did now since the Island and all though swimming kept her fit this sprint around the spinney caused a stitch to form painfully in her side. She could not give in though, she had to reach Sam before something happened to him. Her phone was ringing but she did not want to waste time answering it. Just as her legs began to cramp, she saw him standing in a clump of tree's looking at the woods nervously. Sophie came to a walk and breathed heavily as she edged towards him, "SAM!" She yelled and he jumped, staring at her with wide eyes, "WHAT?" She had to gasp to pull in more air before she could speak again, "ARE YOU DOING?"

Before Sam could answer, she threw her arms around him and hugged him tightly. When she let go, Sam kicked at the dirt.

"I was attacked." He said. His bottom lip quivered, and a tear formed in his eye.

"You should have run home." Sophie said as she took his hand and rubbed away the tear, not with her power but with a delicate finger.

"You wouldn't have." He replied tartly, "I've heard the stories. You would have fought to make sure it did not hurt anyone else."

"No." Sophie whispered, "Not you. I don't have a choice, my mind was changed so that I do those things, but you do have a choice."

"Where are the others?"

"They are moving into the woods I would have thought. They are the warriors." She replied.

Sam looked around with a small smile, "Well I haven't seen or heard a thing. If we cut in here,

we might be able to trap it in the middle." Sophie pulled at his hand, bringing his attention back onto her, "I'm taking you home, I'm not having my boyfriend killed trying to be a hero."
"Boyfriend?" He stuttered while staring at her.
"Oh, shut up." She let out a nervous laugh that faded as Sam repeated, "Boyfriend." In a shocked voice.
"You are adorable." She smiled as she gently kissed him on the lips, not that he seemed to realise, "Let's get out of here and wait for the Agency to arrive."
Sam looked from the woods and then back to her. She seemed so sweet, so innocent but he knew there was a power inside of her. A strength that had saved the world, "No." Sam said, "You say that you are changed and that your life is fated to go a certain way. This may be part of that, you might need to be with Tom and the others right now."
Sophie looked towards the woods and her mind darkened. She could feel it. A voice was shouting in her head, forcing her to enter the woods and regroup with the others. It was the connection the Tempter created between them. She almost laughed, *The knights of Earth*, it did not seem true to her but there it was, the voice in the back of her mind, "He has Kat and Price." She said out loud, unsure if it was in reply to that voice or to Sam.
"I'm going in." Sam said defiantly, then he stopped, "Is that your phone ringing?"

"Yeah. It is Kat, she has been trying for a while." Sophie replied.

"Answer it." Sam ordered and just as her hands released his and went for her phone, he span around and before she could reach out, he darted into the spinney.

Sophie sighed, grabbed her phone and charged in after him.

*

"Finally." Kat yelled, earning a stern glance off Tom and Price, "She answered." Kat mouthed to them before starting a hurried but hushed conversation with Sophie.

"This takes me back." Price smiled. He had his arm outstretched, feeling for the trees and what might be disturbing them. Tom gave him a quizzical glance and he shrugged, "Us fighting together I mean."

Tom raised his eyebrow and gave his best friend a small smile, "It would be better if it was a molten warrior right now. We would see them straight away."

Kat turned to them, "Sophie and Sam are coming in the other way.

"Shh." Price said swiftly, his hand was quivering, "Something over there."

Tom looked over and reached out his own power. Even though it was less in tune than Price's, the little thicket did seem different. They edged towards it until Tom could make out a small shack. It had been put together by things that had been dumped in the woods in years previous, most of which seemed to be bits of rusty metal. Tom looked at his feet and he could see large boot prints, wider than any human feet.

They crouched down in a group of bushes that suddenly seemed to grow leaves as they hid behind it. Price sat down and breathed heavily beside them.

"I don't like this." Tom said, tapping his friend on the arm, "Why come here and set this up?"

Price lifted his head exhaustedly, "It is an alien, it probably lives in something like this."

"I do love you Price." Kat said in an exasperated tone, "But sometimes you are an idiot. If an alien were capable of space flight, I don't think it would live in a metal shack."

"Or build them when they know they are being hunted." Tom scanned the tree lines, but he could not see or feel a thing.

"Well then it is a trap." Price gave a tight laugh.

"Oh great." Tom pushed him to the floor, "That is one more thing to worry about." He became serious, "Kat go left, Price right. I am going to pull the shack down, as soon as anything moves get onto it quickly."

Kat and Price moved away, not as quietly as Tom would have done and in the silent winter wood it seemed to echo. Tom lifted his hand and felt the metal under his control. His cell's producing the same charge given off by the metal, linked them. Tom pulled and the shack toppled inwards. Kat and Price moved towards it, but they stopped dead, it was empty. Tom's eyes widened as a high-pitched scream spread across the spinney.

*

Sophie's hands reached towards the ground and from it, moisture came up to her, leaving the ground cracked and dry.
"What do you want me to do?" Sam asked from behind.
"Just stay alert." Sophie ordered. She was amazed at how calm she was. Usually the barriers that Lucast made crumbled easily after the doubt that Cirtroug had put inside her mind but they seemed like a wall, keeping out her twelve-year-old nerves.
The crack was the first thing she heard. She acted instinctively, and water flew in front of her. She did not see the bullet that passed through the water, but she saw its momentum lessen and its course shift so that it missed her by a couple of inches. Suddenly her barriers were completely intact, and her eyes darted to where the shot had come from. Her arm came up and the water charged like a cannon towards a tall evergreen. There was a yell and a body fell from it, grasping at the branches, catching one enough to slow its descent so it landed with a thud and a groan on its two thick legs.

Vengeance of the Gods

"WHAT DO YOU WANT?" Sophie yelled.
She took a step forward, but the creature charged and launched a small knife in her direction. She screamed, desperately pulling for more water. Time seemed to slow; the knife reflected the winter sun as it soared through the sky towards her. She saw Sam reach out, the tips of his fingers turning to ice and then the ice seemed to spread across the blade. With a whine, the knife shattered from the intense cold.
Sophie watched as Sam fell to one knee. He was breathing hard and his arms looked like they were bruising from the strain. Sophie pulled water just as the creature charged. She threw herself in front of Sam and blocked its first few swings with jets of water. Then as it came for another barrage a great swirl of flame grasped at the warrior and pulled him away. The flame swirled, surrounding Tom, who stood there with his eyes burning. Kat and Price were at his side, both ready for the fight, "Surrender." Tom yelled.
The beast did not even seem afraid and it searched for more blades. Tom smiled and reached towards them but whatever metal, if they even were metal, was out of his control. The three of them had to dive out of the way to avoid the blades as they were thrown. Price ducked and with anger from the earlier attack fuelling him, he charged headlong into the creature, who smiled and turned, delivering a

powerful punch that crumpled Price to the floor.

"Keep your distance." Tom said, "That is how we beat it."

Kat and Sophie nodded. The creature was moving towards Price, but a vine reached out under Tom's control and pulled him away. With a snarl the creature launched more of his knives causing Tom and Kat to separate, then his attention turned towards Sophie. She launched water at the creature, but it dived out of the way and with tremendous speed it grasped her in its thick arm and in a swirl placed a knife to her throat. She screamed, staring at Kat and Tom, who held up their palms but moved to protect those that were down. Kat protecting Price and Tom protecting Sam. Tom tried to give Sophie a reassuring smile but she was quivering, not daring to move with the knife pressed to her throat.

Hairs stood on Tom's neck as he heard movement behind him, then a voice whispered, "Keep calm." He relaxed; it was the voice of his metal instructor. Members of Fox team began to emerge from the undergrowth and the creature stared at them wide eyed. Tom wondered what it was thinking. It could kill Sophie in a heartbeat before they could even react but was Sophie its mission or all of them. While four members of Fox stood watching, the fifth, Luke Wood, crept from behind on feet that did not ever seem to touch the ground and

silently he reached for the Murka. There was a flash of blue light and Sophie screamed but the arm holding the knife fell limp and the blade fell to the ground. Sophie collapsed to the floor, holding her neck while Callum Hart, the youngest member of Fox team, used his power over metal to pull at the zip of her hoody, the buttons on her jeans and the watch on her wrist, to drag her to safety. The creature's useless arm swang round, catching Luke in the face and knocking him over but Peter Ward charged passed Kat and pressed the pad on his palm. A great swirl of fire swept around the Murka, surrounding him in a cell of flame.
"What were you thinking?" David yelled as he charged at Sophie. She removed her hands from her neck, and he smiled. The cut was small and had already stopped bleeding. His eyes turned back to Tom, "Why didn't you wait for us?"
He looked down, "We didn't want it to escape before you got here."
Before David could reply, a roar came from the fire. The Murka charged through the flames, its eyes had gone as black as the night and black smoke leaked from its mouth. It charged towards Tom, but David lifted his arm and a dart launched at the Murka. It met flesh in an instant and the Murka fell dead at David's feet. It was motionless for a second before it writhed and black smoke charged at David. Flame erupted from Tom's hand and he yelled as the fire consumed the black smoke and turned his

orange flames to sickly green.
David looked down at the body, "I'm guessing that was the darkness?"
"In all its weird glory." Tom replied, "That was only a little bit though."
David put a hand on his shoulder while Fox tended Price and Sam, "We have got you some transport. Come on, let us get you all home."

*

David stepped from the jeep, parked outside the Agency headquarters. He had never seen it so busy. People were charging around everywhere. The huddle included other strike teams, scientist, and politicians. The latter wondering about the impact of harbouring an alien body in their constituency. Two men came and lifted the body of the creature.
He turned sharply towards them, "Maximum quarantine." He ordered, "It was possessed by some of the darkness, we don't know what that will do. See if Lucast will look into it."
David stepped away from the bustle at the door, aiming for the back entrance when Tax called him back, "Where are the children?" The Director asked.
"I thought it was best they went home." He replied coolly, "They needed rest after what happened."
Tax spoke through teeth that seemed to be grinding together, "I need them for a d-brief."

"Then you can call their parents and explain to them why you are dragging them out here after they had been attacked."

Tax nodded to concede the point but David didn't think that was what really was bothering him. The Director's eyes flickered to the body that was now being paraded to the front entrance, "What happened out there?"

He stared at his boss, "We did as instructed."

"I WANTED HIM ALIVE." Tax yelled in a sudden outburst but it stopped as David grabbed him by his suit and forced the Director against the wooden rail, the only thing stopping him from the fast flowing river beside the office block. "And the death of one of my men, or the children. Did that mean nothing to you?" David asked but his eyes widened, and he swiftly let go of Tax. He didn't know why he had reacted like that, the vision of the Murka charging through the flames filled his mind.

Tax just smiled at David as he straightened his clothes, "They are not your men David."

He gave the metal Halve a stern nod before departing. David looked down, knowing how true that was. His life and the life of every other Halve relied on Tax, no matter how much they did not like it.

Chapter Eleven- Howls in the night.

"How are you feeling?" Tom asked Price as he met him outside the school gates.
Price moved himself around, wincing from pain, "Better than I was last night, I could barely sleep."
Tom dodged a charging older kid just as the bell for the beginning of school began. He looked at his friend, "It would be nice if we got some peace."
"We would." Price smiled, "If you didn't want to go up that stupid volcano."
"Shut up." Tom gave his best friend a slight nudge causing him to grit his teeth in pain. He looked at him with concerned eyes, "Sure you are okay?"
Price tried to stand up straighter and Tom knew it was only his ego keeping him from letting out a sigh. After a second Price grinned, "See, all good."
They walked towards their art classroom.
Sophie was already there texting on her phone while Kat waited patiently for them. She threw her arms around Price's neck at once while Sophie gave Tom a small smile, "How is Sam doing?" he asked casually.
She shrugged, "He is not coming in today."
"Guys." Said another voice. Tom turned as Nicole charged towards them "I just heard." She said quickly, "Is everyone okay?"

"I think so." He muttered, "Shaken more than anything.
"What does this mean?" Her hands went to her hips and she looked down at him in a very mothering way.
"I think he wanted to stop me from being with you lot." Tom tried to give them all a reassuring smile, "I think he is scared of us being together."
Nicole nodded, grasped all their hands and whispered comforts to Sophie before walking away with Daniel who had stood waiting for her. Slowly they were allowed into their art room.

Sophie sat down next to Tom and immediately placed her headphones in her ears and clicked play on her phone to drown out the noise of the classroom. Her pristine artbook she opened onto an old sketch of the church in town. Methodically she began shading, preparing the work for marking. Tom worked beside her, but he was doodling more than drawing. She recognised the doodle, it was of two birds, a crow, and a dove battling eachother. She knew it was one of the symbols carved into the floor of the volcano. Thinking of the volcano suddenly made Sophie stop. The hairs on her arms stood on end and a slight smell of old clothes filled her nostrils. Her hand reached to her phone and paused her music. There was silence.

The room was silent, but it should not have been. She could see people talking, see her teacher berating Kat for throwing something at Price, yet she could not hear it. It was like she had stepped into a bubble.

Then she did hear a noise, a click. Nervously she froze, another click. Her head turned and before she could stop herself, she let out an almighty scream.

The noise returned in an instant, but it was not the noise of classroom chatter. Instead all Sophie could hear were mumbles and whispers. Everyone was staring at her; she could feel their gazes, but she was staring at the door of the classroom where seconds earlier the Tempter had been stood. His golden eyes had been staring at her from the shadow of his hood, his cracked blue lips twitching into a smile.

"Everything okay Sophie?" Her teacher asked, more confused than angry.

Sophie felt her face reddening and heat building in her ears. She tried to laugh but it failed her, "There was a spider on my leg. Sorry." She murmured and before anyone could say anything further, she buried herself in her work. The Teacher gave her a concerned look and some others laughed to their friends but slowly the normal chatter returned. Sophie kept her head down, but her hand could no longer hold the pencil steady. She felt Tom lean towards her, "You aren't afraid of spiders." He said swiftly.

Sophie carried on looking down, she didn't want to show Tom that she was upset, "It was nothing. I just." She closed her eyes to compose herself, "I just scared myself."
Sophie did not wait for his reply before placing in her headphones. She stared at her page for the remainder of the lesson, waiting for any sign of the Tempter's return but the lesson continued as though everything was normal. As they packed their belongings, Sophie hesitated, so much so that she was the last one out of the classroom.
As Tom and the others cut out of sight she stopped. Click.
She turned without thinking this time and a scream nearly slipped from her lips again. The Tempter was stood before her. His ragged cloak blew in a non-existent wind, revealing the black clothes underneath. He held onto his walking stick with two hands and looked hard at Sophie. A rotten hand was risen and it beckoned Sophie closer. Reluctantly Sophie took a step forward and as she did the Tempter seemed to glide backwards through an adjacent door. Sophie did not want to follow but she could not stop herself. Her hand reached for the door and opened it. Her gasp was swallowed by the deep darkness that surrounded her. Only the Tempter could be seen in what should have been just another classroom.
"You are not real." Sophie said to the ghostly figure but that earnt nothing more than a smile.

Vengeance of the Gods

"Listen child." The Tempter's words seemed to echo in the darkness, "War brews in the outer universe. Agral the Vassal of death will use Urgarak to force a war that will destroy the Ilma, the Graul and Humanity, leaving the Gods as the forsaken custodians." Sophie listened, understanding nothing, "The death of Thomas Lita will lead to this. Lucast will rise in vengeance and when he kills Urgarak, Uralese will seek retribution and the dominos will continue to tumble until the Ilma are destroyed. Thomas Lita will fight Urgarak and he will aim to do it alone. You must not allow this; you must be by his side when he fights the forces of Uralese, or the universe will soon fall."
Sophie looked hard at the Tempter, "How do you know this?"
"I am cursed to follow the temptations of others but in my heart, I feel mostly the temptation of those who created me. The Gods desire the ultimate power and the Ilma stand in their way. You must believe my words Sophie Carter. The knights of Earth must stand together, or events will rip you all apart."
"We will do what we must." Sophie whispered, trying to find some strength but she was certain the words spoken came from the Tempter and not from her own thoughts. She blinked and light streamed into the classroom, the Tempter was there no more.
Sophie looked at her watch and gasped, nearly half an hour had passed while she had speaking

for just seconds with the Tempter. She could not sneak into English now. Seeing no other option, she sat down at the desk and wrote down everything the Tempter had said and everything Lucast had said, tying them together so that she might hope to find some sense in the universe.

Tom sat in English, his head ever rising to look opposite himself, but Sophie had not arrived. He thought about her screaming. *What had she seen?* He asked himself. He thought back to the moment before she screamed. He felt or thought he did, the presence of something behind him and he was almost certain he heard faintly the click of a walking stick.
As they were dismissed from English, Tom held himself back and found himself walking the corridors of their English block alone. He was searching for something and yet his mind could not remember what. Then he heard something, the sound of footsteps and with them, the sound of a walking stick tapping against the floor. Tom turned a sharp corner and stopped dead, "So that is what she saw." He said out loud.
The Tempter nodded, "I needed to speak to your friends."
Tom thought that the sight of the Tempter might have scared him but his mental barriers had fallen into place swiftly and he felt again as

he did while sitting alone in the farmhouse, with the Tempter beside him.

"What is your desire Thomas Lita?" The Tempter asked, his white lips forming into a smile.

"To live a peaceful life." He replied, matching the Tempter's gaze.

Laughter seemed to come from the walls around him and the ghostly eyes brightened, "Yes and what will you give to earn it. Will you fight Urgarak, kill him as you killed Cirtroug."

"I did what I had to." He said but his words faltered.

"I see your deepest desire." The Tempter said and he pointed to a door beside him.

Tom took a step towards it, shaking his head, "That's just a maintenance cupboard, what could I possibly desire in there?"

"Look." The Tempter ordered.

Tom opened the door, his heart in his chest. A box sat on the floor beside him and faint words seemed to come to him from within.

He felt the Tempter beside him, "Your desire will only bring death to you Thomas Lita. Trust to your friends, they will guide you."

He knelt down and opened the box. All the air fell out his lungs in one loud sigh. His hand reached towards the only object within and wrapped around the glass tube with silver tipped ends. A fiery essence still swirled within, Cirtroug's essence. Was this his desire, to have Cirtroug freed, what for? To apologise or to defeat him again and again, a thousand times to pay for all those that he had killed. Tom could not deny he had thought about it.

"Tom." He jumped at the new voice, the phial slipped from his hand, "NOO!" He yelled as the phial fell to the ground, with a deep and plastic sounding thud. His eyes widened. The phial was gone and all that lay on the ground was an old brush.

"What are you doing?" Tom realised it was Price speaking.

"Going insane." He said as he collapsed against the door, head in his hands. The encounter seemed like a blurred dream, with only the slightest memory of the Tempter's words remaining, "It's all this waiting for something to happen, I think it is getting to me."

Price sat beside him, "It must be if you are screaming about an old brush."

Tom rubbed at his eyes, "I think we need another chase."

"What?" Price asked, "The Agency won't like that."

"They also don't like us training properly. They have us practicing on targets, at nothing that fights back. It won't be like that when Urgarak comes knocking."

"It will make it easier for him, if we are all running around town looking for eachother." Price reasoned.

"We will keep it small." Tom said in reply, "Meet up on the green so we all find

eachother."
Price smiled, "It would be good to beat you into the ground without one of the teachers stepping in." He then laughed, "Good luck convincing the others though."
"I will tell them it's training." Tom grinned, "They won't be able to say no to that."

"I was thinking we use it as training." Tom said to Sophie over the phone as he laid on his bed, "Just that little bit extra so that we can actually fight eachother."
He heard her sigh on the other end of the phone, "But we have been told not to go out after dark."
His hand reached for the ceiling where flames were dancing for his amusement, "I think we need to be more prepared, we can't do that at the Agency."
Tom could almost hear the doubts that must have been circulating around her head but eventually she conceded, "okay." She whispered but her voice became stern, "I'm leaving Sam out of it though. I don't want it turning into what happened Saturday."
Tom grunted, he wanted Sam there. He knew Sam would be there when something really happened, but it was not worth reminding Sophie of that or she would not join them that night either, "Okay." He said finally, "Five Am on the green."
Sophie paused again, clearly debating it, but she

replied, "See ya then." Solemnly.
Tom hung up and absorbed the flames. He set an alarm on his phone and began texting Price all about what they were going to do. Little did Tom know that somewhere in the atmosphere, Urgarak received the news with hunger in his eyes. He turned to Mirkan and gave the order for his next attack.

*

The wind whistled in through Tom's window as the night wore on and all through it, he tossed and turned. He was hearing the Tempters words, hearing Cirtroug's words about the path he had to take. Blurred visions passed through his mind during that sleep but all that seemed to do was un-nerve him. He was almost thankful for his alarm sounding. He was heavy eyed as he looked out the window, the clouds were rolling quickly past a moon almost at its full. He wished he could go back to sleep but as his feet hit the floor and he grabbed the dark clothes he had prepared, the anticipation soared through him. Opening his window, Tom took a deep breath and slid through it. The air rushed past him, but his outstretched hands created a buffer against the approaching earth. He landed with only the slightest of thuds and charged across his back garden. Using his power over the earth, he leapt high and crashed down on the street beyond. No one seemed to have seen him and in his dark clothes he made his way like a shadow through the sleeping town.

He arrived at the field that was now illuminated by the moon. He could see Price, his thick frame making him stand out on the opposite side and he knew that somewhere Kat and Sophie would be lurking. As it hit five am their phones blared into life and Tom charged. He was running for Price but he turned at the sudden flash of blue light but he could do nothing as one of Kat's bolts caught him in the leg, numbing it and forcing him to the ground, where he rubbed it painfully.
Tom stood, his legs shaking as she walked towards him, sparks shooting everywhere as she rubbed her hands together. There was the sound of a crashing wave and Kat screamed as Sophie drenched her, the sparks on her hand now shooting back at herself. She tried to run for the cover of the tree's but was knocked suddenly back into the moonlight by a gnarled root. Tom span to face Price but ducked a quickly thrown ball of water. A fire ball he launched behind him and he used the earth to shift Price off balance, who rolled to the floor but not before a root snagged at Tom's ankle making him join Price and Kat. Only Sophie was stood, her pale skin reflected in the moonlight and a ball of water spinning in her hand. With a laugh she launched it at Tom's crotch, and he

gasped in pain as the water drenched him.
"Look." Sophie giggled, "Tom has…"

She stopped abruptly at the sudden howls that echoed across the field. Tom and the others stood as more broke out in the opposite corner, answered by the first that they had heard. Instinctively the four of them moved together, covering each other's backs.

Tom's keen eyes scanned the field and he saw shapes moving slowly towards them, shapes with four legs that moved like normal dogs, but he knew they were not. Even from a distance he could see their golden eyes and from each, some part of their bodies seemed to reflect the moonlight like metal.

"What are they?" Kat asked nervously as she clutched Price's wrist.

"I don't know but I don't think they want their bellies rubbed." Price replied in his cocky tone but his attempt at humour fell flat after another round of howls broke out. Tom's hand reached into his pocket, but they found nothing, "A panic button?"

"On it." Sophie yelled, lifting it from her key chain and pressing it.

Tom was happy that some form of help may be coming but it was early morning and the Agency would be empty. Some of the wolves, as he called them in his mind, were now close enough to see and he gasped. They may have been dogs or some close relation, but they were taller than most breeds and well proportioned, with strong back legs and long necks. Their claws were sharp and almost all were moulded with metal. What worried Tom most was the understanding in their golden eyes, and he was almost certain that there were words within their howls. His hands went out to feel for the metal parts, but his heart sunk. Just like the knives of the Murka assassin, this metal was beyond his control. They were soon becoming surrounded, at least ten had moved around them and Tom could see more moving on the edges of the field, blocking exits or waiting for their chance to pounce. A howl went up from one standing alone in the empty field, watching them cautiously. Like the howl was a call, the ten began their attack by charging straight at the four of them, causing them to scatter.

Price jumped as one attempted to knock him down, but it went immediately for Kat. It stood on its two hind legs, its muscles rippling before it leapt into the air. A spark arced from her hand, colliding with the wolf like creature that yelped and lay twitching at her feet but the distraction allowed another to knock her to the floor, that only stopped by a blast of water from Sophie. Tom dived in the way of one that had attempted to blind side her, but it swept him aside with a swift shoulder charge before knocking Sophie to the floor. Her heart leapt into her throat as teeth dug into her shoes. Her fingernails grasped at the wet mud as she desperately clawed to get free of its iron like grasp and she screamed as she was being pulled away.

Tom stood up and his hands became flame. He dived over one wolf, forced another away with a stone before launching his fire at the gripping wolf. Its fur caught in an instant and its jaws released her.

Screaming and howling, it charged around the field like a torch, forever being chased by Tom's flames. He almost felt sorry for it but that slipped from his mind when he saw Price narrowly avoid the jaws of another, its metal teeth aimed for his neck. Lucast's barriers formed at once. These things were there to kill, and he would need to do the same to survive. Pulling some of the fire towards him, he wielded it like brand, attacking any wolf that came near him.

While they fought, Tom realised they were once again being herded. The wolves went for precise attacks where brute strength had failed, and they buffeted each of the children towards the others. They took out two more, one with a spear of wood and another covered in Sophie's water and shocked by a passing Kat but four more seemed to take their place.

Two charged at Price but he turned and from the nearby river a bramble charged, wrapping around one of the beasts and pinning it while a swirl of flame and water attempted to keep the others at bay.

Then a new noise caught Tom's attention, there were joggers approaching. Tom saw them coming closer through one of the lamplit walkways. Wolves snarled but the pack guarding it slinked into the darkness, allowing the joggers to walk blindly by. The flames surrounding the children absorbed into Tom just as the first set of wolves turned and charged at the newcomers. Tom felt for the connection to two distant trees and felt the pressure of the earth ready to force him upwards. Then just as the wolves charged for another attack on the children, he launched himself into the air.

It had seemed like such a good idea when Tom had thought of it but now that he was flying his heart was racing. He had overtaken the wolves, but the joggers and the ground was fast approaching. Wind came up to buffet him while his arms reached out to the earth. He landed with a heave and turned on a dead leg to face the advancing wolves. The joggers gasped, looking between both Tom and the wolves, unsure what frightened them more but the first growl and leap from a leading wolf answered that one for them.

The shock of Tom flying wore off for the others quickly at the first wave of attack. Sophie pulled moisture from the ground, launching it at the charging wolves like a cannon and all they could do was retreat and try to find a way round her.

Vengeance of the Gods

This led them towards Kat, and she sent bolt after bolt at the wolves, wishing more than anything that she had her rods to channel her power. As one pounced, knocking Kat to the floor, Price reached out. The night was split by a tremendous crash and a huge branch launched from a nearby tree, it bounced over Kat, carrying the crying wolf with it. A howl went out around the field and the others on the attack snarled but backed away towards the edge of the field.

Tom watched as the wolves surrounding the joggers slowly backed away but they didn't go far, they gathered around the one that Tom guessed was leading and all around him he could see pairs of golden eyes watching him intently. Price and others charged towards him as growls and howls broke out in a chorus again. Tom looked around, lights were coming on in the houses, soon people would be coming out to investigate, too many for them to protect. It would be a blood bath.
"What are they waiting for?" Price asked despondently.
Tom stared at his friends with wide eyes, showing his panic that seemed to crumble their resolve, "They want more people. They want us to chase them while they attack those around us." He tried to harden himself, "The button Sophie."
He looked around, they were the target. He

needed to get out of the open, to force the wolves to come to them, to channel them somewhere where their speed and numbers would count for nothing. Suddenly his eyes fell onto the church that stood at the edge of the field. It was a new build, replacing one that had burnt down in a fire. Tom had been there before to look at a memorial in its grounds for those killed on Curamber. It was perfect for what he wanted.

"The church." He said commandingly as he grabbed the joggers and forced them to start moving, "Get there now."

They all began to run towards the church. In half an attempt to provoke and another to protect them, Tom launched fire at the wolves and Price pulled down the trees they passed. A howl echoed and the wolves advanced.

Chapter twelve- In God we Trust

The joggers ran as fast as they could with the others hugging their flanks doing their best to keep up and to hold back the encroaching wolves. The joggers reached the church first and nervously they hammered on the locked door. Tom burst passed them. He closed his eyes and imagined the pins inside the lock before sliding them into position. The door opened with a heave and the group charged into the cold, black church. Tom turned and re-locked the door while Price and Sam moved stuff to block it.
A ball of fire he launched into the air and he seemed to shimmer as he aimed to keep it alight. The ball of flame illuminated some of the church. It may have been new, but the builders had tried to give it an aged feel. The stone walls were nearly bare and old wooden pews were screwed to the floor. The artifacts saved from the old church were proudly displayed and Tom felt bad that they had lured the wolves here. The church was cold and Tom watched his breath curl towards the ceiling and also the breaths of all those that were panting hard after their run.
The joggers babbled to eachother, but Tom did not think any actual words were produced. They all looked lifeless, with wide eyes and shaking hands. They would be no good for him

right now. They leapt at the sound of a wolf crashing against the door and then they all became silent while they listened to the sound of scratching feet and sniffing noses.

Tom ran to the shaking adults and the ball of flame followed him. The adults were scared, their advance of years helping them little, "I can't explain what's happening." He said, "Help should be on the way, but you can't stay out here. You aren't safe."

"And you are?" A woman with blonde hair and bright sad eyes said, her hand reaching to ruffle his hair.

Tom tried a reassuring smile, "Safer than you are right now." He looked around to a back room that might have been a bathroom or waiting chamber for the vicar, "I need you to go in there. We will stop these things."

That seemed too much for one of the men, a tall burly man with a thick chest and large arms, he stamped his foot on the floor, "No. It is you who need to hide, what are you like thirteen?"

"Twelve." Price yelled from the far corner while himself and the others continued to move what they could to give them room to fight, "And trust me we are experienced with this."

The adults looked at eachother and shook their heads, "This isn't a game." The man yelled before clapping his hands together, "Right kids. I am going to phone the police; you just hang tight and everything will be fine."

"You can't." Sophie yelled innocently, running

towards them, and putting on her best good girl smile, "We can handle this I assure you. Please do as Tom says and hide."

The man shook his head at her and Tom noticed the sad look in his eyes. Maybe he had daughters and couldn't believe what he was hearing. He moved away from Sophie and quickly grabbed his phone.

"Kat." Tom yelled.

Kat turned and her hand shot outwards. A bright flash leapt from her fingers and connected with the man's phone. It beeped and whined before going black, the man stared curiously at it but a vein bulged inside his head, "WHAT DID YOU DO?"

Kat looked guilty, "Just charge it when you get home. It will work fine."

"Tom?" Price yelled as he pointed at a large metal cabinet.

Tom nodded and held his arms towards it. A screech echoed in the church as the filing cabinet began to move towards the door. His face was red from the force of moving the cabinet and the fire winked out putting them all back into darkness. Once it was in position, he turned to the now stunned adults, "The police will only be in more danger if you call them." He said sternly, his golden eyes the only points of reference in the darkness, "We have called people trained for this and they are coming to help but we can't defeat these things and defend you if you are out here so please." His voice boomed from the stone walls, "Go inside that room."

One by one the adults left for the safety of the room at the back of the church. Once the big man, who still seemed reluctant was inside, Tom locked the door and he set himself as its protector. He turned to his friends, all standing ready to die to protect the others. All of them just as resolute as they had been when they had decided to march up the mountains peak. They were not complete though. He wished more than anything for Nicole, with her they may have been able to go on the offensive but with just the four of them they had to make their stand there.

"This is Urgarak's next step. Prepare yourselves."

They all nodded, the barriers Lucast had put inside of them were in full strength. They could still hear the wolves gathering and what sounded like a conversation between them. A body thudded against one of the large windows, cracking it and they knew that it would not survive one more of those attacks. Price broke a rail from one of the pews and wielded it like a club until Tom fashioned for him a makeshift spear from a piece of the filing cabinet. He had no plants to work with so this would have to do. Sophie and Kat produced their own powers and stood ready for whatever came.

"Kat we could use some light." Tom said while he once again stood by the door where the adults rested.

Kat went to lift her arms but stopped as all the lights suddenly came on, all eyes turned to Price, "What?" He asked, "There was a light switch."

Tom went to laugh but the light coming on seemed to be the signal. A wolf crashed against the window again and this time it gave way. The wolf crumpled to the floor in the middle of the room, whimpering, a piece of glass protruding from its stomach. Following it a pack of wolves burst through the breach. All large, black, or brown furred, most with paws, legs or pieces of flesh replaced with metal parts. Only the odd exception remained how it would have been when born. Fresh hounds for the fight, Tom thought.

Two rounded immediately for Tom who created a brand of flame to defend himself. The first pounced and Tom ducked, his arm gently pushing it away but the other charged instantly and he swang his brand of fire to defend himself. The wolf dived out of the way, missing it by inches but both landed like cats and moved again. Tom swung his brand like he was possessed, moving through different stances he was being taught to keep the two wolves at bay but with each swing they were getting closer. After another pounce and another duck, the two wolves landed side by side. Tom panted, feeling his strength starting to ebb. He pulled strength from the stone and spread his legs,

one behind the other, ready to move into whatever strike he wanted.
The wolves charged at the same time. Tom pivoted, a strike struck his back, but he held his connection to the flame and brought it through the other like a blade, tearing the skin of its ribs like paper. Tom stumbled, wincing from the pain in his back but he regained his feet quickly, but another strike knocked at his hand. The flames dispersed and he looked at the blood. A howl caught his attention and he rolled away from another strike, launching a stone statue into the wolf's snout to knock it backwards. The wounded wolf then pounced again, and Tom watched it with steely eyes. The brand of flame reformed in his hand, the flames burning almost white from the power he poured into it. The beast howled as its stretch split the wound further and as it crumpled from the pain, Tom launched his burning brand into the wolf's neck. The sound of the flames piercing and searing the flesh was sickening but it was nothing compared to the dog like whimpers that followed as the wolf collapsed and lasted until it had gone still.
Tom faced the other, guilt and doubt were forming in his mind, "It is just another kill." He whispered to himself, shaking out the demons from his mind. The wolf lunged while Tom was still distracted. He turned but gave a sharp yell of pain as metal claws dug into his back, tearing his shirt and his skin. The weight forced Tom to

crash into the door and he heard the yells of those beyond. The wolf was readying for its strike, but Tom felt the power of the stone, felt it resisting against him. The rock cracked as Tom launched himself backwards and the wolf went with him. He landed on top of the beast and as he rolled over, the floor collapsed into the cellar, taking the wolf with it. In that cellar Tom sent fire but the beast lunged desperately, its fir burning and in its panic, it began to run around the church, attacking everything it saw in its madness. Tom collapsed against the wall, earning himself some respite while the others battled on.

On the far side of the church, Price charged at the wolves that poured through, while over his head Kat and Sophie launched their powers into those still jumping. His club he brought down on one who had nearly regained its footing, sending it to the floor dazed. The club came upwards by instinct, crashing into another with the force of a large oak branch crashing to the floor. That wolf limped away with several broken ribs. He charged at others, but these were smaller, less enhanced and scarred and they scurried to the back of the church, runts waiting for their chance to feed. The injured wolf went to strike again, and all Price could do was swing his spear to keep it a distance. Most of the other wolves ignored him to move for either Tom or the girls and all Price could focus

on was the one wolf attacking him.
He got lucky, after sidestepping one attack, Sophie launched water at the attacking wolf that fell from the blast, allowing Price to drive his spear through it. He ducked out of the way of a maddened burning wolf before staring at the one he had just killed. It looked almost pathetic and he wiped away a tear as he pulled the spear from it, but the guilt did not last. A new wolf had dived through the window and its golden, knowing eyes were focussed on Price. It was the biggest one they had seen yet and the most enhanced. Metal covered most of its body, including its spine. Its claws were inches of shining metal and as it barked out orders, Price caught intelligence behind its eyes. Price readied his spear and waited for the leader of these pack of wolves to charge.

Tom had returned to the door. He was panting, desperately pulling to him what strength he could. His hands were bloodied from several wounds and these stung as he ignited his hands at the approach of more wolves. His brand swept upwards in a sudden flurry, cleaving the face of one of the beasts and killing it instantly. He dived out of the way of a bearded hound before a third clawed at his knee. He dropped to the ground and in a panic, a swirl of flame swept around him forcing the two wolves a side. Kat screaming distracted him, but the wolves could not attack before he launched himself into the air and balanced himself nimbly onto one of the pews. Metal objects flew from the walls, colliding with the wolves, knocking one into the cellar and the chandelier from the ceiling crashed at another. The runts on the outside barked and nipped at his ankles, forcing him back towards the main pack and only Tom's many powers kept them at bay.

Sophie was feeling exhausted, she was creating water from her own body while she desperately searched for a source and the effort was draining her. Kat was at her side, her arms shooting bolts of electricity at any wolf that neared them.

Sophie was knocked away by a wolf that twitched as Kat zapped it but one more had flanked their position. Price saw it coming, he swang at the leader of the pack before charging, jumping over a pew to come to his girlfriend's aid but the leading wolf dived, hitting him in his midriff and sending them both rolling across the floor.

Kat screamed as she was chucked to the ground. Sharp teeth gripped at her ankle, puncturing the skin, and threatening to rip her leg a part. Sophie ran over, kicking at the beast who held on for all its might. She breathed, her hand became water and she grabbed the wolf's snout. It howled and rolled away enough for Kat to shock it. Just then Tom knocked a wolf into a nearby wall. It gave way and a pipe broke from

the force. Sophie felt the water and she surrounded herself and Kat with it, shooting it like a fire hose at any wolf close enough.
"Throw some in the air." Kat said, "I will charge it, then crash it back down."
Sophie nodded, the water lifted into the air like a wave and Kat sent her power into it. Sophie yelped, the power working back to her so with a yell she crashed the charged water down. Metal parts on the wolves worked wildly, while the flesh went limp. Many of the wolves crumpled to the floor, spasming, their bodies steaming. The water Sophie drew back to her as the runts, seeing their warriors be defeated, began to charge.

Price coughed from the weight of the leader as its paws pinned his shoulders to the floor, it's hot breath falling onto his face. Price's spear was the only thing holding it back. He tried to press it upwards, calling on the strength of trees to aid him but the wolf jumped, grabbed the spear and shattered it in its strong jaws.
The beast went for a strike but stood up, screaming as water splashed against its foreleg, causing its mechanical parts to spasm. It looked at its leg in confusion while Price grabbed the shattered pieces of the spear. His eyes widened as the wolf grabbed its metal arm and with a growl ripped it from its body. Three-legged, blood gushing from the wound, it pounced again. Price turned, waiting for the end and the

beast howled. They fell to the floor together and Price felt the warm gush of blood between his fingers. His eyes opened, the spear in his hand protruded from the neck of the leader, its broken shaft piercing deep.

It stared at Price with golden eyes that quickly faded.

The runts began to panic, clawing at the door for a way out or climbing the walls to escape through the window but the remaining warriors would not be so easily defeated.

Two rounded on Tom, the first he used fire to launch towards Sophie who knocked it out cold with the force of her water but the other managed to knock Tom to the floor. He stared at it, saliva falling from its mouth onto Tom's shirt. Tom's eyes widened; he was waiting for the end. The wolf hesitated and then it flew across the room crashing against the wall. A flurry of wind burst through the open window and the wolves howled at it.

Just after, the door crashed open. Some wolves managed to escape the flurry of fire and water that burst through the door then as Dog team entered the church, but most were imprisoned or killed in that swift barrage. David charged in not long after and came swiftly to Tom's side. His hand reached out and he helped him up with only a wince from Tom.

"Panic button worked then?" Tom asked.

"Thank god it did." David said without a hint of a smile.

Tom looked around; the wolves littered the church, but he was grateful to see that his friends were all in one piece. Kat was being held up by a big member of Dog team while Price and Sophie walked behind her. Price was moving awkwardly and when Tom looked, he saw that his shirt had been torn across his back and it was soaked in blood.

"Looks painful."

Price gave him a stern look, "No it tickles."

They walked out of the church together where a crowd was gathered but Agency staff were hurriedly trying to remove them. Tom noticed that there were no bodies of the wolves.

David's hand forced Tom's head down and he ordered the others to do the same, "Make it look like I'm arresting you." He said, "A report will say that kids broke into the church." He explained, "There will be no pictures of you though."

A jeep suddenly stopped in front of them and with some help they all got seated, "I just need to ask." David said sternly, "What the hell were you doing out there?"

Tom looked around at the others. Kat looked sick, holding onto her ankle that was still bleeding. Sophie was close to tears and Price winced with every movement. His little bit of freedom did not seem worth it now, "I will explain it to Tax." He said guiltily.

David shook his head and shut the door.

Kat winced as the junior doctor scrubbed at the bite with a disinfectant wipe that stung with every touch, "We are currently studying what germs these things might carry but we will give you some anti biotics just in case."

Kat nodded, hiding a sniff as she tried to retain her image, "Thank you."

Next to her Price was laid on his stomach while a nurse scrubbed vigorously on the wounds, earning yelps that made Tom snigger from across the room, "You sound worse than Peter when he has to have a bath."

Price shot him a vicious look, "If I could move I swear to God."

Tom went to laugh but it stopped dead as Tax came into the room. His hair was messy, and his suit looked like it had just been thrown on. He stopped in the middle of the room and faced them with his hands on his hips, "Morning all, perhaps you would like to tell me what happened?" His voice was calm, but Tom could see the vein bulging in his head.

He stood up, drawing the attention onto himself. He would not let his friends take the fall, "We were stupid sir."

"I will say." Tax frowned.

Tom kicked at the floor and could not meet the Director's eyes, "It was just meant to be a bit of fun." He said shamefully, "We just wanted some freedom, I never thought he would come after us like that."

"LUCAST WARNED YOU!" Tax yelled and Tom

felt heat rising in his cheeks and his eyes widened in fear. Tax looked to the floor and ran a hand through his messy hair, "So what happened?"

Tom began explaining about the chase, about the feeling of unease and restlessness creeping over them all. He left out the Tempter and what he had showed him. Kat and Price described what had happened when the wolves had attacked and when they had gone into the church. Tax listened intently and did not interrupt but he didn't seem to be any less angry. When the story had finished, he sighed, "No harm done then I guess." The four of them looked hard at eachother, each trying to work out what that meant, "No harm done?" Tom asked, the shock clearly coming through in his voice, "People saw our powers."

"Lucast is handling that." Tax deadpanned and when he saw their wide eyes, he realised he would need to explain further, "As you know, Lucast's power have mutated slightly. He has a way of working with people's minds. He will not be able to convince them that this morning did not happen, but he will be able to put some form of understanding into their minds. Enough so that they do not run around shouting it to the world, we here at the Agency will do the rest."

Sophie looked down, "So that is it then?"

"It is the way we like it." He smiled, "Life might be easier for you four if the world new about

Halves, but it wouldn't work well for everyone. Imagine how scared people will be knowing that their kids go to school with others that could bring the school down on top of them."

"None would do that." Price said sternly.

"You have more faith than I." Tax laughed, "Paranoia does not usually contain much logic Nick."

The room became silent again until Lucast came in, "That seems to be sorted."

Price's hand shot up, "Were they alien?" He asked, earning a stern look off Tax but Lucast just smiled, his golden eyes shining.

"They are from Ilmgral, or were originally. These breeds are more like those of Uralese, shorter and slender. They are a regiment of Grignar from the third Murka fleet."

"Grignar?" Tax said with a wink and smile at the children, "We need it in English."

Lucast looked confused, "Grignar are a form of Grignin, like canines of your world. They roam in packs in the wild lands of Ilmgral. At some time in our history one of the Ilma became a Grignin and from him a more intelligent breed were born, the Grignar. These things are highly intelligent and extremely dangerous strike units that often operate with the Murka's."

"And the Murka's, what are they?" Tom asked.

"The Murka's were once our slaves and they did not look how you saw them; they were tall and extremely nimble and very populous. Years of labour on our colonies saw them become the bent backed creature that attacked you the other day. They have deep resentment to those of Ilmgral and when Abgdon offered them freedom, they joined the Abgdonese empire and have become their foot soldiers ever since." Lucast explained, "Urgarak has a ship full of the Murka's and these he will unleash soon. These attacks have been nothing more than his attempt to make that attack legal."

"What is he hoping for?" Tom looked hard at Lucast, trying to work out what his next move would be. He needed to end this swiftly, if Urgarak was getting more desperate then his friends may not survive the next attack.

"They cannot attack Earth openly without angering both the Abgdonese and Ilmgralite councils. That will unite the two empires, which would not be sufficient for him." He began to pace the room, "They want Tom to challenge him, they want him to admit his crimes so that they can use the attack as an arrest and I suspect in the process, release Cirtroug who will bring with him some loyal members of the council."

Tom felt his heart racing. He had been chosen to defeat Cirtroug, not that he knew then about the giant chess board that he had become a piece of. The Tempter would probably suggest that he was a knight or a rook, an actual piece in the puzzle but he felt like nothing more than pawn, moving one step and waiting to die, "Why did he attack us tonight then?" He asked

to keep the dark thoughts out of his head.
"He wanted to kill your friends." Lucast
deadpanned, ignoring the sharp intakes of
breath from Price, Sophie and Kat, "He wanted
to make you lose everything until in your
madness you go to him willingly. The councils
would not care, would not know if an assassin
kills your friends and parades the bodies in
front of you or Grignar devour them before
your eyes leaving no trace, no evidence."
Tom's heart seemed to stop and every breath
that fell from his lips was painful. His fingers
were gripping the chair so tightly that his
knuckles seemed to whiten, "I have to go." He
muttered to himself before standing up on legs
that threatened to collapse from underneath
him, "I need to go. I need to hide, he can come
and find me when the others are safe."
Lucast charged across the room to where Tom
was about to leave, his voice boomed like
thunder, "AND WHAT GOOD DO YOU THINK
THAT WILL DO?" The sudden eruption of anger
made everyone but Tom jump, he simply stared
at Lucast with the same intensity.
"THEY WILL BE SAFE, THEY WILL BE ALIVE." He
replied sharply.
Lucast's shoulders dropped, "And you dead?"
"An end to it." Tom deadpanned, his voice
showing his maturity.
He felt the others looking at him, but he could
see Sophie most intently. She was looking hard
into his eyes and not that he knew it, but the

Tempter's words were circling through her head and she saw the truth in them.

"You are naive then." Lucast said in a condescending tone, "This is more important than you. If he kills you and gets his revenge, then he will only turn his darkness onto someone else. He will find more and use someone weaker to get hold of Cirtroug and whatever else may be held here. He will not just retire from his campaign; your death will only reassure him that what he seeks is just. As noble as your gesture is Mr Lita, it is a child's mistake."

Tom's jaw locked and the others clearly tensed, expecting him to lash out again so Price stood with only a slight wince, "It is stupid." He said, "We won't let you get away from us."

Tom looked at his friends, "You might die."

Sophie shrugged, "We certainly will if you let him kill you first. Then we won't have anyone to lead us when the Murka's attack."

Price walked to his best friend, "We had a choice on that Island to get on the boat but we weren't going to leave you and we won't now."

Lucast smiled at them, "There have been times in war when people who think they know better sacrifice themselves to save others, only to find that their enemy has then slaughtered millions after. Then people like me look back on those events and realise that the sacrificed may have been the only one who could have saved them. Do not be that first Thomas Lita. You have more to offer the universe. Stand up, you have friends and a world behind you."

Tom looked down. He was feeling no pull now either way, not from the Tempter or any other doom. He felt for the first time in a while that this was his choice alone and yet he had no argument against Lucast's logic other than the fact that his friends might suffer. He asked whether the risk was worth it, to stop Urgarak and to try to live his life, even with the risk to his friends. Was that his choice to make though? He looked at his friends, his stubborn friends. They would not let him escape and maybe the Tempter would make sure of that also. A goodbye would come between him and his friends but that was a long way away and his friends were worth that pain

"I hope you know what you are doing." Tom said to Lucast.

Sophie smiled at him and Price grabbed his arm, maybe to hold him there if he had a change of heart.

"I do Tom." Lucast smiled.

Tax finally stepped back into the centre of the room, "We will start preparing for Urgarak's next attack. I will have strike teams positioned in key areas. Now, I can understand if you don't want to go to school today."

Price, Sophie and Kat all nodded their heads and Tom could see their exhaustion. He was exhausted to but he wouldn't be able to rest at home and he needed to see some people, "I will

be going back to school."
Tax seemed concerned, "Are you sure?"
He stood straighter, his eyes burning. He had the beginning of a plan forming in his mind, "Positive boss."

Chapter Thirteen- The Edge of Something.

Tom could feel his body stiffening and the exhaustion of barely sleeping crept up on him as he was dropped off outside the school gates. The exterior of the school was eerily empty apart from the headmaster who watched Tom's arrival with nervous eyes.
"Morning Tom." He said with a forced smile. Tom could sense his nerves and wondered whether every time his name was mentioned, the headmasters hairline receded a little further, "I have a note and a reason for your absence, just hand it to Mr Wood and everything will be okay."
"Thank you sir." Tom took the note, but he knew it would not be. He was not in his Southbrook uniform, that was abandoned somewhere on the green. His mum would not appreciate having to buy another. Tom was wearing instead a tight black shirt, like the one with his uniform and the jeans he had worn during the fight with the blood stains quickly rinsed out. The walk through the silent halls made Tom even more nervous and he had to compose himself before knocking on the door of his classroom. He was beckoned in swiftly and all the class stopped their setting up of equipment to stare at him. He could hear the mumbled questions about what he was

wearing, and the bandages wrapped around his arms. Mr Wood frowned at him until Tom handed his teacher the note. He read it without his frown wavering all that much, "We are doing an experiment today, but you can't do it without first doing the written work. I will set you up with that, then you and Nick can do the experiment tomorrow."

That was the first piece of good news Tom had received that morning. His muscles were cramping, and he didn't honestly believe he would have the strength to do an experiment. As he settled in to do his work, Stephen, a survivor of Curamber, came and sat next to him, "Are you okay?" He asked in a whisper. Stephen was one of the only humans in Southbrook to know about Halves and he was sworn to secrecy like all the rest.

Tom tried a small smile, "You don't want to know."

Stephen's face paled, "Like the Island?"

"Those things aren't back." Tom said to re-assure him but that seemed to make Stephen more nervous.

"But something is." He leaned closer, "What's happening?"

Tom looked hard at Stephen. He could never have imagined what it must have been like for the human survivors. They had almost none of the support of the others and they had received no answers for what had occurred, "Don't come into school tomorrow." Tom ordered, "Just stay away. Something will be coming for me. You got off the Island, you don't want any part of this." Stephen's eyes widened, he nodded, unable to speak and shuffled awkwardly back to his equipment, which he set up with a visible shake in his hand.

Not long after returning back to work, another shadow loomed over his sheet of paper. Tom's heart dropped. He could smell her perfume and the shampoo she used in her long sweeping hair. He could also feel the absolute sense of dread that accompanied him whenever Hannah was near, "What happened?" She asked sweetly.

He tried not to look at her, "What do you mean?"

"The cuts on your hand. Are you okay?"

His knuckles whitened as he gripped his pen and spoke through gritted teeth, "Nothing happened."

She slinked away but her eyes kept falling onto him and stayed on him all through the lesson. Even as he walked between lessons, he could feel her presence and as they passed the library, she hurriedly came to his side, "You can talk to me you know. I'm here for you."

Tom stopped, "We barely know eachother."

Hannah gripped his arm in what Tom thought was meant to be a show of affection, but coldness seeped from the point of her touch and numbed his arm, "But we are going through the same thing."

The same thing, the words ran through Tom's head and he soon realised how false they were. She did not have an alien psychopath trying to kill her, she did not have to soon see her friends grow old without him, she did not have people expecting the world of him. His frustration for everything that had happened since the Island came out in his whispered words, "We are not going through the same thing."

Hannah nodded like she did not believe him and stormed off in the other direction. His heart began to race, and his body crashed. He slumped against the library walls as the exhaustion finally consumed his last piece of strength.

"What are you doing down there?" Said a voice that Tom recognised and it immediately made his heart rise.

He smiled at Nicole, who seemed suddenly to see the bandages on his arms, "Are you okay?"

Tom sighed, "Can we talk?"

She gave him a firm hand to help him up and then with a smile pushed him into the library, "I have a study period, come and sit with me." She dragged him to the back of the library where he was able to collapse into a large sofa, concealed from the librarian's desk.

"We were attacked." Tom said as soon as they were both settled, "Not by the Murka's but by some wolf like things."

"Are the others okay?" She asked quickly.

Tom nodded, "They are resting, I really need to

go and see Sam soon, he will be worried sick."
His eyes darkened, "I need to end this Nicole."
She looked at him with a smile, "I know."
That caught him by surprise, "I can't allow Urgarak to keep sending these things after the others. I need to face him and face him now."
"What will you do?" She didn't seem nervous like Tom expected, just resolute.
"I'm going to confess. That will make him act and then we are going to defeat him."
She almost went to laugh but stopped dead, "We?"
"I need you Nicole." Tom deadpanned, "We can't win this fight without you. The Tempter put us together for a reason and we need to stay together no matter what."
"I thought I was done with this." She shook her head sadly but Tom felt he caught the change in her demeanour, the sudden regression back to that state of mind on the Island, "But we all started this mess and we can't let others fight it for us. I will be there Tom. Not for Lucast or for the Agency but for you."
Tom took her hand and she gave him a warm, sisterly smile, "Get some rest here. I will go see the headmaster and see if we can get you off lessons for the day."
He declined politely but sat with her till after break.
The next few lessons passed and Tom had explained to Sam what had happened and given him much of the same speech he had given

Nicole. Sam might not have been a knight of earth and he may have been able to escape the doom that awaited them, but Tom would rather he be with them when the battle started. It would be better than him charging in halfway through to be a hero. During the lessons, a sense of calm foreboding had fallen onto him and it seemed that it was spreading throughout the school. At lunchtime, the feeling of depressive waiting loomed over the entire school. Conversations were hushed, laughter muted but none seemed to understand why. Even outside, under the dark canopy of clouds, the usual teenage chatter was subdued. Tom felt like he was caught in a bubble that was soon to burst. He knew he was on the edge of something and one step would see everything come crashing down upon him. He realised he would have to make his move this night, or Urgarak would make it for him.

The fear of the coming doom did not leave Tom for the rest of the day and the feeling followed him to the Agency offices. He was expecting there to be people, but he had not expected the volume of young halves that were gathered in the training room. They were not using their powers, but they sat in little groups, nervously talking amongst themselves. As soon as they spotted Tom, he found himself surrounded as they all began asking him questions about what was happening.

Vengeance of the Gods

He lifted his hand and brought them all to silence, "I don't fully know what is going on." He said, showing his maturity. He looked at them all, they were staring at him with determination kindled in their eyes. He realised they would follow where he led but he would not have any more dead on his conscience, "But something bad is coming. None of you should come into school tomorrow. I'm going to try and get it closed but even if it is open just don't show up and please tell your friends to do the same." Tom had not expected the sudden barrage of argument but there was so much that he could not focus on just one point, "LISTEN!" He yelled and the hall became silent in an instant, "It is time you all learnt the truth." His eyes caught Hannah's and the feeling of dread fell on him more sharply, but he used it now. The grimness coming through his voice, kept the arguments at bay, "I need to tell you about the Island." At the mention of the Island everyone became deathly silent, "On Curamber I released someone, an alien criminal called Cirtroug." The eyes of everyone fluttered to eachother but no words were spoken, "It was a planned event and Cirtroug had an army ready who tried to slaughter everyone. The person who planned his escape wants revenge for me foiling that plan. I believe he is going to send an army to kill me and the other survivors." There was some shuffling and nervous glances at eachother but that was it. Tom had expected them to laugh,

expected them to mock him but they had heard rumours and believed the sternness of his voice, "This will happen tomorrow and I don't want any of you in the firing line."
"We want to help." A tall girl with brown hair yelled from the back.
Tom smiled at her but shook his head, "I have enough bodies on my conscience as it is." His eyes scanned the crowd and they caught Hannah's. He was shocked to see that she was crying. Something stirred in him, these people needed him to be strong. He smiled and with it he seemed to grow, "I will always be here to protect you but you cannot come into school tomorrow."
Murmuring began but Tom did not let them leave until every single one of them had promised, even Hannah who he managed to give a reassuring hug to. He then left them to their whisperings and charged up the stairs and walked towards Tax's office. Ashley, his secretary, was sat by his door and she smiled at the young man, "Mr Lita, what can I do for you?"
"I need to see Tax." He blurted out and went to step through the door, but Ashley stopped him with a sharp cough.
"I'm sorry but he isn't here." She said with a sad smile.
"Can you ring him?" Tom asked quickly, knowing he was clearly pushing his luck.
She gave him a raised eyebrow smile that made

Vengeance of the Gods

Tom blush, "Is it urgent?"
"It is about the attack this morning."
Ashley looked at him with a frown and Tom did his best to smile. Eventually she nodded and began to call Tax, "Hi sir. Thomas Lita is here, are you able to speak to him?"
Tom felt his breath catch in his throat as he waited for the reply but eventually Ashley smiled and handed Tom the phone, "Hi sir."
Tax's voice seemed strained, "What can I do for you Tom?"
"Close Southbrook school tomorrow." He said sharply.
Ashley looked weirdly at him and Tax laughed, "What?" He said once he had composed himself, "Have you gone mad?"
Tom wondered how best to convince the director and decided to go for the truth, "Sir, Urgarak's attack is going to come tomorrow. I think he will use the school; we need to make sure no one is there."
The pause seemed like the longest of his life but when Tax spoke again, he sounded much more resigned than Tom had expected, "How do you know?"
"I have a feeling sir and I have to trust that." He deadpanned.
There was another pause that felt to him like it lasted a lifetime again, "Okay." Tax replied, a long sigh escaping his lips at the same time, "if you are wrong, then we will have to start having a conversation about your future here."

Tom didn't like the sound of that but he knew Urgarak would attack tomorrow, he would make sure of it, "Yes sir."
He hung up, wondering how he had convinced Tax so easily. He could still sense the foreboding doom looming over the town, and he wondered if Tax had felt it to. He charged out of the office again and sent messages to all his friends. The weather was strangely mild for the time of year and the dark clouds were not stirred by any breeze. Tom jumped a few fences and came to the lake where he sat by its edge and waited. Nicole arrived first, her black hair was in a pony tail and she wore a thick jumper and tight jeans but they seemed old, like she expected trouble. No matter how much she asked, Tom remained silent on the subject and continued to do so while Kat, Sophie and Sam arrived. It was not until Price arrived, fifteen minutes after the others, that he decided to tell them what his plans were. He gathered them around and they sat on the floor beside him.
"I've told Tax to close the school." He deadpanned and watched their faces all change to show their confusion.
"Why?" Kat asked.
"Urgarak is going to attack the school tomorrow." Tom said, expecting an argument, expecting some form of negative reaction from his friends but they looked back at him confidently, only Nicole seemed to be working through things.

"How do you know?" She said, only a slight nervous twitch to her voice.

He smiled despite himself, "Because I'm going to make him." He told her and joined in as the others laughed in resigned acceptance of the fate that had begun on Curamber, "I'm ready to fight him now." He continued, "and if no one else is in the firing line, I can be happy."

"Good." Price said, "We are more familiar with the school, that will give us an advantage."

Tom's heart sank. He looked at his friends, the most important people in his life. Kat and Price were cuddling, their eyes resolute. Sam and Sophie held hands and looked nervously at eachother, while Nicole gave him a warm smile. He still hoped he may have been able to convince them to go home and forget the wars to come so that no harm could come to them, but he should have known better. Sophie turned her gaze on him. She was the one who was always able to read his mind. He wished nothing more than to escape from those shining blue eyes, that considered him so carefully, "Yes, all of us together, the knights of Earth as Lucast said." She ordered.

Nicole was next to speak, "You don't think we would let you fight him on your own do you?"

Tom stood up slowly, thinking through it and Sophie followed him, "You heard what Lucast said, we will be stronger together." She took his hand, causing Sam to straighten, "Together forever remember?"

Price was next to jump up and he pulled Sophie and Tom into tight hugs, "Oh go on then, I didn't want to be a teenager anyway."
Before Tom knew what was happening, Nicole and Kat had joined the huddle, followed by a reluctant Sam.
When they broke apart, they were no longer kids. Tom could see it in the way they held themselves, the way they stared at him. He could also feel the strength coursing through them, he hoped Urgarak was scared, "It is not going to be like on the Island." Tom told the group, "We will be fighting things that think, that talk. These aren't like the molten warriors."
Sophie's voice was a whisper, "We don't have a choice."
Tom nodded and became their leader, "Right then, if we are going to do this, we need our uniforms."
"Tax won't let us have them." Price said a little bit sulkily.
Tom took a couple of paces away from them and looked at the Agency offices, it was starting to darken with people heading home, "He won't you are right. He doesn't believe me enough to let us run around with those." He turned back to them, a vicious look in his eyes, "We are going to have to steal them."
Sophie's mouth fell open, "Steal them?"
"How?" Kat asked and a cold gleam came into her eyes.
"Our abilities will give us access." Tom replied,

"From here we can see when they shut down for the night. Then we sneak in and get our uniforms before camping out at the school."
"What about our parents?" Sam spoke for the first time. He was not matured like the others, did not have the same block in his mind. He was just trying to keep up and not get killed in the process.
"My mum thinks I'm staying with Tom tonight." Price said, "Tom's mum thinks he's at mine. We can all try and do that."
Sam had clearly never done anything like that, and he seemed more nervous about lying to his mum than he did breaking into the Agency. Tom saw this and came swiftly to his side, "If you need to go home, go. Sneak out and meet us at the school later."
Sam shook his head, "I will convince her. She is more lenient since the divorce."
"Nicole?" Tom turned to the older girl, "Where can you be?"
"I've had a couple of study nights at Annabelle's, I will just say I'm there." She replied confidently.
"Just think though Nicole." Price laughed, "If an alien invasion destroys the school, I don't think you will have to sit your exams."
"Good job." She laughed in return.
Sophie sat down on the grass again and crossed her legs, her feet twitching, "Everything will change won't it." She said with dreamy eyes, "Even if we survive, it will all be different.

Everyone will know what we are, what we can do. The Agency won't be able to cover this one up."
Tom sat down beside her and smiled just as Sam gave her a kiss on the cheek, "Then let us hope." He began with a cruel smile, "That they either thank us or mourn us."

They watched from a group of tree's until the last few people ebbed from the Agency building, "There will be guards on duty." Tom said before he looked at Kat, "They are yours. Give them a quick zap, only if we need to but nothing that can harm them to greatly."
"Roger." Kat said with a smile that did not fill Tom with much confidence.
"Go Kat." He ordered.
She walked with a limp, her leg still stiff and sore after the dog bite, but she tried her best to seem confident. Her walk took her straight to the entrance where a guard was waiting. She looked around, there was no way in without going passed him. She quickly moved towards the guard, feeling the tingle of the power within her fingers.
The guard spotted her quickly, "You can't come down here sweetie." He said with a smile, but Kat could see his eyes watching her suspiciously, especially with the way she limped. She did not reply as she watched her target, not wanting to give away who she was too quickly.

"Didn't you hear me?" He asked and then his eyes widened, "Its Kat isn't it? The Agency is closed."

Kat was right next to him now and she gave him a wicked glance, "Sorry."

"What F." the guard didn't finish before her hand reached out wards and a blue flash caused the guard to collapse in a fit of spasms that seemed to knock him out. She placed her hand on his chest, his heartbeat was fast, but it was there, "Clear!" she yelled behind her and the others slowly emerged from the undergrowth.

Tom was the first there and he gave Kat a pat on the arm, "How long till he wakes up?"

Kat flicked her hair with her hand like she wasn't bothered, "I don't know, I'm not a doctor."

Tom shook his head but turned to Price, "Find something to bind him, we need as much time as possible."

The six of them spent as much time as they could moving the guard and making him comfortable, well as comfortable as he could be with a slender branch binding his wrists.

Tom felt sorry for the guard as he looked at him and he pulled out his panic button. He pressed it before slipping it into the guard's pocket, "We need someone to find him." He said to the confused glances of the others, "Come on, that's cut our time down."

Together they used the guard's keys to enter the Agency. They were met by the sudden sound of an alarm panel beeping but Kat's hand upon it soon silenced it. Tom gave them all a reassuring look, "If the inside is alarmed then we are probably alone. Any idea where our uniforms are?"

They all looked at him in astonishment, clearly shocked that he did not have that information. Sam answered the question though, "I saw some be placed in that locked room at the back of the training hall." He said quickly, "I think they are in there."

Price clapped him on the shoulder, "I always wondered what use you would be."

Sam laughed but Sophie threw daggers at Price with her eyes. Tom quickly set them back to the task, "Let us get them quickly. Fox will be here soon."

They climbed the stairs with their hearts in their throats. The empty building echoed all their footsteps and breaths, making them stop repeatedly, checking for anything that might indicate they were being followed but they found no one else as they reached the training room. If the rest of the building felt empty, the dark training room made Tom feel small and forced him to question what he was doing. Nicole's hands on his shoulder steeled him to the task. They found the locked door and Tom set to work. He took a deep breath and shut out all the demons that had suddenly seemed to shout inside his mind. He did as David would have told him and held his hand in front of the lock, feeling every metal component. He found the pins easily now and gently slid them into place so that the lock turned with a satisfying click.

They stepped into the room and took a deep breath. Racks lined the room, all filled with uniforms in tagged protectors. They scanned through them, searching through all the strike teams until they found theirs in a group in the back corner. The girls changed in the room while the boys stepped out of the training room to get into theirs. The old clothes they left behind, they would either be able to collect them the next day or would never need them again. The thought was not weird for Tom. He felt like he had back on the Island, where the next day was irrelevant compared to what needed to be done on the here and now. His mind was focussed on the task. He did not care about the sun setting tomorrow or rising the day after that. If he did not succeed, there would not be a world to wake up to anyway.

Price quickly walked over in his uniform, "Well this is great. We can look the part but we don't have any of our equipment."

Tom span round at the sound of approaching footsteps but he could quickly see that it was Sophie, "Are you guys dressed?"

"Yeah." Tom yelled and the three girls soon joined them followed by a nervous looking Sam, "These are useless without the stuff that goes with them." He continued.

Kat folded her arms defiantly, "But they are upstairs?"

"Exactly." He said, "That is why we are going to have to get them."

Sam's already white face became paler as his mouth fell open, "Aren't we going to be in enough trouble?"

Kat gave a laugh that seemed to echo throughout the hall, "Exactly, what harm could a little bit more do?"

Before Sam could offer any more arguments, Tom led them from the training room and climbed two more flights of stairs, until they came to the heavy security door leading to the research and development department.

Tom looked at Kat, "Any chance of cracking that code."

She shrugged her shoulders but placed her hand on the number pad. Tom watched her face contort and he could feel the energy she passed into the pad but in the end her hand flew backwards and she shook her head vigorously, "That is one complicated code."

Tom's heart sunk, he had never even tried using his power to work with equipment, without Kat, he was lost. To his surprise though, Sophie stepped forward, "It should be an electronic lock, right?" She asked.

Kat nodded, "Its insulated so I couldn't reach it."

Sophie looked hard at Tom, "Do you think it would be insulated against water?"

Vengeance of the Gods

Tom and Kat both shrugged and Sophie sighed loudly, "Never thought I would be breaking into a secure door today." She lifted her hand and in the small light of the fire escape sign, Tom saw it become suddenly slick with water. This she injected through a gap in the door, "I need you to guide me Tom." She said swiftly.

Tom placed his hand against the door, but he could feel little of the metal components, or in truth he could feel too much and even with his training he could barely tell one thing apart. Still he guided Sophie as best he could as she worked the water through the mechanisms. Suddenly to everyone's surprise, the door clicked and opened slightly but the automatic rollers failed to move.

"It might go if we all push." Tom ordered.

With all of them pushing, the door rolled far enough for them to squeeze through. They charged to Dr Pentka's desk and found amongst his things, the locked cabinet that they were after. A sudden sound stirred them all, the sound of car's roaring to a stop and doors being opened. Tom swore before whispering, "I don't have time for this."

His hand reached for the lock and he pulled with all his might. The metal door bent and with a crack the lock broke into pieces and the door swang loosely on its hinges.

"That is one way to do it." Nicole laughed and the older girl burst past him to begin handing out the weapons that were stored inside. Kat took a belt full of batteries and both of her rods and Sophie grabbed enough water cartridges to last her forever, with three water balanced knives that she still had only a little practise using. Price picked from a collection different seed boxes and his two seed filled spikes. When he felt them, his eyes widened and he turned to Tom, "This is a blackthorn, but I've never felt the potential like this. The thorns will be a foot long."

Tom stared at the spike nervously, "Then please throw it away from me."

He himself grabbed two batteries, two propane tubes for his belt and another two he connected to his wrist strap. He also took two water cylinders off of Sophie but when Sam handed him one of the cooling agents, he shook his head, "I'm sorry Sam, I don't think I share that power."

The others looked at him strangely, "You mean you can't do what Sam does?" Sophie asked.

He shook his head and instead grabbed two more propane cylinders.

Price clapped him on the shoulder, "Finally something you can't do."

Sophie was looking between the pair but if she had any more questions, she was unable to ask them as searching feet and voices could be heard on the floor's downstairs, "Damn." Price yelled, "What do we do?"

Tom looked at the others but it was Kat who had the answer, "The fire escape that runs

down towards the river, we can use that."
Tom nodded at her and led the way. They closed the door to the research room and moved downstairs to the offices silently. They could hear the training room being searched and knew that soon the missing uniforms would be found. A fire ball, just small enough to illuminate them, moved in front of them so that Tom found the fire escape instantly.

Kat silenced the alarm and Tom ushered the others in. There was no one on the metal staircase and no one watching the bottom either. The door to the outside opened silently and from there he sent the others around the edge of the river, where they could pass into the graveyard and skirt back round to the lake. He hesitated on the threshold of the door as he heard David speak only metres away from himself, "The uniforms are gone sir." He said. Tom walked to the edge of the building and peered cautiously around, his heart in his throat. David stood in front of Tax, who was pacing in the glow of the streetlight.

"Do you want us to continue the search?" His metal instructor asked.

Tax shook his head in a frown, "No. They will be punished for attacking one of my guards, but they are doing what they think is right. I want to see how this plays out but call all of our soldiers in, human and Halve, we may need them in the morning."

David nodded and turned. Tom jumped back

but he was almost certain that David's eyes had widened as they examined the corner where Tom was stood. He was breathlessly waiting to hear footsteps but when none came, he moved off to follow the others. By the time he reached the lake, every light in the Agency offices were switched on and Tom could hear vehicles constantly pulling into its car park. The others were knelt by the lake, talking joyfully about what they had just achieved but Sophie still seemed nervous and she shot up as soon as Tom approached, "Are they coming after us?"
"Tax wants to see what I do next." He explained, "I think we will be in trouble for the guard but if Urgarak does attack tomorrow, then a few things will be forgotten."
"What is the next plan then?" Price asked.
Tom gave them all a wicked smile, "We break into the school."

The walk to Southbrook secondary school was slow and steady, with them avoiding anywhere with too many people and they managed to reach the gates without seeing anyone. Using a low point in the fence, near the spinney where the Murka had escaped, they went onto the school ground and felt exposed on the many football pitches. The school, all in darkness now, seemed no longer to be a place of safety and Tom imagined a million eyes looking down at them from the windows above.
They found an unlocked door in the math

department and from there walked to a common room for those taking their senior exams. The large sofas would do for them to rest for the night and it was close enough to the exit should they need it. They all worked, removing the burdensome parts of their uniforms before waiting for Tom's next command.

"Let's try and get some rest." He ordered, "It will be a long day tomorrow."

Nicole found herself a sofa alone next to the one Tom had just sat down on, "I hope Tax has found a way to close the school."

Sophie and Sam also found two sofa's next to eachother while Kat and Price found some large cushions and pushed them together on the floor.

Price looked hard at Tom, "How are you going to do it then?"

"I am going to send a text to your phone." He shrugged, "I think that is how he learnt about the chase. We described everything to eachother."

Price nodded and rested his head down next to Kat's. She already looked on the verge of sleep, a smile on her lips.

Tom looked at his friends. Sophie and Sam were talking to eachother giggling, Nicole was texting Daniel on her phone while Price and Kat just looked at eachother smiling. He loved all five of them, not just for what they had been through together but for the people they were. He was sad he had dragged them into this, but he was also thankful that they were there with him. He grabbed his phone, just as his mind darkened and he typed out a message that was sure to bring his doom. He pressed send and rested his head against the armrest and fell almost instantly to sleep.

Price felt the vibration and gently removed his phone. He let out a loud sigh that made Kat look at him sleepily, "What does it say?" She asked with a yawn.

"I have Cirtroug." He deadpanned, "Come and get me."

*

"Another message General." Mirkan said swiftly.

Urgarak stirred from a vicious, darkness induced nightmare and looked towards his commander. A screen flashed in front of his eyes and he read the message with a cruel smile across his face, "He has challenged me at last. Now let those fools on the council deny my right."

He stood slowly, stiffly and his commander followed, "Should I arm the missiles, we could blow the school apart now and most of the town?"

"NO." Urgarak yelled, "This is still too early in the game. The empires will be watching, we will need his confession to keep them off our backs. With Cirtroug in my possession, he will dispose of that fool Crio and bring with him all our generals of old. War will come and Uralese will rise to prominence one again in our new empire, with me as its governor." Visions of his triumph filled his mind, "Ready the first and second Murka battalions. Arm what Grignar remain to us. Our soldiers must be ready for the fight. I want bombers fitted with the Virdact and armed with Uralese weaponry. We will show the worth of my planet." He then stared at the world below him, darkness lay now where Thomas Lita would be waiting, "War comes at dawn for this pathetic little planet."

Chapter Fourteen- The Battle Begins

Tom woke just after day was breaking but the world was dark, and no sun pierced through the clouds that hung low and menacingly over the town. Almost at once it became clear that Tax had kept to his word. The school was empty of people and a quick check of his phone showed the excitement of pupils for their unexpected day off.

Tom stood and stretched. He was not refreshed from his fitful sleep, but he knew adrenalin would eventually take over. Gently he woke the others and with yawns and stretches they readied their uniforms, re-attaching their belts and wrist straps, loading them ready for the fight that was sure to come. All of Tom's weariness seemed to be driven from him when the radioactive source began to be absorbed into his skin. It helped drive away some of his tiredness, but the increase of his heart rate sent his stomach fluttering. All of them seemed refreshed, apart from Kat who still limped from the tightening wound to her calf.

Tom clutched at his ears as the walls suddenly began to shake and a roar like jets grew in the skies above them. Price looked towards him and yelled over the noise, "Bloody hell that's low." He nodded, "And not flying over us. I think its them." He charged out of the common room with the others hot on his heels.

Vengeance of the Gods

The air was strangely muggy for the time of year but the sweat on their bodies was chilled by a wind that blew downwards from the skies above them. Tom's mouth fell open as he stared at large, metal, bird like shapes that were slowly descending towards the football pitches, dropping great metal barricades from their talons. The first of these ships landed and from their wide mid section's, units of Murka's emerged in rank and file. They did not rush towards Tom and the others but instead stood in their ranks behind the metal barricades.
At once they began snarling and yelling in their own language. A One-handed firearm were held in their strong low hanging arms and many of the Murka's wore goggles for long range shooting.
Tom looked to the heavens, five ships had already landed, with at least thirty Murka's crammed into each one and thirty more seemed to be coming down to land. It seemed hopeless but he would not go without a fight, "The grass Price." He said, "Let's form a barricade."
Price stepped forward and he sang a song that Tom quickly mimicked. Directly between the Knights of Earth and the Murka's, the grass began to grow rapidly, thickening into a grass hedgerow that rose almost four feet into the air, "Sophie." Tom ordered and she stepped up, her hands outstretched. The grass looked like it had been goldened by the sun and moisture

cracked at the grasses base but around Sophie, the ground was now a quagmire.

The guns of the Murka's began to clatter against their legs and they matched the rhythm of it with a chant that sent Tom's heart racing. One Murka stepped from the latest ship to land. He was slightly taller than the others. His uniform seemed to carry decorations and he took a position at the head of one of the formed columns. Tom wondered if he spoke English, but his first words were in a harsh language that carried to Tom, a noise like the crushing of rocks. Then a shadow fell from the heavens, too small to be a sentinel but it flew into the commander who went rigid and his eyes turned black, "I am Mirkan, commander of the Uralese third infantry division. You are under arrest for crimes against Uralese and will answer in the hall of flame for your crimes against her and her mother planet, Abgdon."

For a second, a thought other than battle filled Tom's mind. An insane urge filled him to abandon the fight, to go with these people and see Uralese and Abgdon. Price's arm gripped his and he returned to the present and the thought vanished. He knew he would not see another day, let alone another planet, if he was to abandon his friends.

"I think they are waiting for an answer." Price said, his cocky voice in full swing now.

Tom gave his friends an encouraging smile, "Then I will give them one." His hands whipped through the air and a shimmer followed them. As the shimmer touched the grass, it became immediately engulfed in flames that made the Murka's fall back slightly.

Mirkan gave a cry and the darkness left him, charging towards the friends. The fire took it and where it touched, the flames turned to sickly green and they parted obediently for the Murka's who began their march.

Tom ducked as something flew over his head. A dropship burst into flames as the ball of earth crashed into its engine and brought it spinning towards the ground. He turned just as men began to pour towards them from vans, that seemed to be streaming into the school grounds.

The men were all in Agency uniform. Some were Halves but the majority carried military grade rifles. These joined in a chorus of gunfire that was at once returned from the Murka's, as everyone seemed to suddenly take cover. Tom spotted David emerging from one of the vehicles with the other members of Fox team, "Dog and Hawk take the left flank." His eyes quickly turned towards Lucast who wore what he had on the Island and he seemed ready for battle, "Find me those kids."

"We are here." Sophie yelled beside Tom and the five of them charged to take cover behind one of the vehicles.

There the six of them joined the battle. Tom launched fire balls into the Murka's line while

Agency soldiers stood over him, the sound of their guns were deafening but the children could not think about that in the heat of the battle. Shots also whizzed over their heads or hit the metal work of the jeep and on the odd occasion some hit flesh and Tom winced as people screamed around him. His friends were fighting. Nicole hurled bits of rubble or anything she could find of stone and earth at the Murka soldiers. Price was directing Agency soldiers to targets, Kat and Sophie were working together to launch charged water into the Murka's line while Sam froze the water near their feet and launched it wildly. Tom was impressed with him, even if his ice never hit a target and his face was extremely pale.

Tom burst from cover for a second, his finger pressing the pad in his palm, launching a fire ball that caught a Murka's uniform, allowing one of the Agency soldiers to shoot him swiftly. He ducked down behind the jeep and Sophie edged past him for a look around, "There are more approaching." She said, her eyes fell to one of the dead Murka's and any colour that was in her face, faded for a second.

"Can you do something?" Tom asked to rally her.

She nodded; her jaw tight. She burst around the edge of the vehicle, her hand gently pressing the pressure pad. The torrent of water sounded like a jet and it flung the Murka backwards. Kat moved passed Sophie, her hand reached for the

heavens, sparks flickering between her fingers. The battlefield became suddenly illuminated by a bolt of lightning that struck the sodden Murka's, killing them instantly. The thought that she had just killed seemed not to touch Kat's subconscious. Of all of them, Tom thought she had become the coldest in her maturing, a probable side effect of seeing her own death. She moved back to the van, a smile spread across her face, showing an eagerness to enter more of the battle.
Seeing her like that turned Tom's head away from the battle. He started to hear everything, the screams of a wounded man being carried into the maths block, the sound of jets and the constant pop of gun fire. He closed his eyes to focus himself and when he opened them again, his golden irises seemed to burn with his own inner fire. His fingers found the pressure pad and fire launched into the sky before crashing down into one of the Murka barricades, causing those inside to scatter.

"Sam." Sophie yelled as she moved from beside Tom to go towards her boyfriend, "I need your Ice."
She saw his hands shaking and she gently took them, "You can stay here." She said, "No one will say anything."
He shook his head, "What do you want me to do?" He had to shout as the gunfire intensified but it sounded quiet to Sophie.

Vengeance of the Gods

"Freeze my water and launch it at the Murka's. I can't get enough of an impact right now."
Sam nodded just as Sophie began launching balls of water into the air. He used his power and launched the now frozen balls into the Murka's. An Agency soldier shouted triumphantly at them from the vehicle to their side, "More."
Sophie smiled, "Move with me."
Before Sam could answer, she ran towards the next car along. Every few steps she launched a ball of water into the air. Sam took deep breaths before following, turning each one to ice before sending them into the Murka's. One hit a Murka in its face, crushing its rodent like nose and sending it to the floor, where it lay there until the soldier ended its life.
Sophie squealed with delight as she crouched behind the next car and screamed as Sam came to a halt next to her. He looked panicked, almost close to tears, "Next time I invite you out." He said through gritted teeth, "Please say no."
Just as she was about to laugh, the soldier crumpled to the ground in front of them, blood oozing from a wound to his head. They stared at his lifeless form and all smiles vanished from their faces.

Price had felt useless during the battle so far. He crouched behind Kat while she screamed like a woman possessed, using her rods to direct bolts of lightning at any Murka's she could see. He looked over the car and stared at the bodies on the ground. He may have thought they were winning if it was not for the stream of drop ships still falling towards the school field.

"Are you okay?" He asked in a grumpy voice that did not suit the fact that they were on a battlefield.

"Just fine sweet." She replied with a cruel grin, "These batteries are perfect." Suddenly her eyes became cool, "They are pinning us down from a bunker." Price looked up and saw a barricade where a machine gun was firing into a vehicle that was already ripped to shreds, "Can you get a bush that far?"

He gave her a cruel smile, "Of course." He reached behind him and grabbed one of the soil filled boxes. He launched it into the air and yelled before it even hit the ground. His words drifted on the wind and a great twisting blackthorn grew in an instant, surrounding the barricade and trapping those inside. Callum Hart appeared across the battlefield and fire leapt from his hands, engulfing the barricade. The screams from those inside became just another part of the noise of the battle.

Tom found himself staring at the barricade, he was now next to Nicole who worked logically, ducking behind cover and finding something under her control before standing and launching it at the enemy. Then she ducked back down beside him. Tom though had a million thoughts running through his head. He had caused this, caused more death and danger for his friends. The noise of battle was like nothing he could have imagined. Surely like nothing he had imagined in his daydreams or seen in movies. There was the constant sound of gunshots, the roar of the jets, the screams of the dying, none of it was perceivable on its own. It all weaved together to form the music of warfare.

He jumped as Lucast crashed down beside him. The Ilmgralite's arm was extended towards the math's block roof. Tom saw the metal box that housed the air vents rattle before ripping off its brackets. It soared through the air and crushed several Murka's, including Mirkan, who had easily died no matter his rank.

"I'm here to get you out of here." Lucast demanded.

"No." Tom replied stubbornly, "These people will not die so I can run."

Lucast looked frustrated but he nodded, "Then maybe you can do better somewhere other than here." He grabbed Tom by the collar in a strong grip and began pulling him away. Both were flung backwards as the ground in front of them erupted in flame. Tom hit the floor with a dull thud, that knocked all the air from his lungs. His ears were ringing as he desperately tried to stand. His eyes found Price, who was

pointing towards the sky and yelling but Tom could not hear him, he could not hear anything but a high-pitched whine. His eyes went to the sky and his mouth fell open. Small ships were now soaring through the clouds. They had the same bird like shape as the dropships but they were smaller, nimbler and they flew directly at the school, missiles firing from their wings.
The sounds of battle slowly began to return to Tom's ears, but the new noise of the jets was now mingled with the sound of the battle. Everywhere Tom looked, explosions decimated parts of the school or the vehicles that soldiers took cover behind. His legs were like jelly, but he charged away from Lucast, tossing whatever pieces of debris he could find into the Murka line, but gun shots whizzed past him, making him cower again. He heard Lucast jump behind him and suddenly the Graul landed on a car in front of him. He felt static on his hand and watched as Lucast began diverting missiles back onto the Murka's line. None of the Murka's shots troubled him, each deflected by the electromagnetic field he flung around himself. Tom ducked as a bomber flew low over him and could only watch as its missile crashed into the English block, on the far side of the battlefield. The wall crumbled and He watched the silhouettes of people as they were covered in debris and flame.
"Dog is down." Tom heard a soldier say from somewhere nearby and his legs gave way. He

collapsed against the side of the jeep, desperately trying to catch his breath. *A whole team of Halves wiped out just to save me.* The soldier that had been speaking was standing over him now and he looked down at Tom, "We are go." He did not finish his sentence before a shot tore through him and he fell to the floor at Tom's feet.

His mind went blank in an instant. Numb, he scanned the battlefield. Every Agency soldier fought vigorously, their guns firing at the endless horde of Murka's while their wounded friends were carried off around them. Suddenly Tom felt twelve again and it seemed his friends were faring no better. Sophie was crying while Sam desperately tried to re-assure her, his eyes wet with tears as well. Price and Kat were cowering behind a jeep, determination still showing in their faces, but they were pinned down by too many of their enemy. Only Nicole was still making an impact, using the earth to crush any Murka's she could get to. Tom's eyes went back to Sophie, she was jumping at every noise. He needed to steel her, he needed to steel himself. This fight was for them and they could do nothing sat there like children. He stood up but stopped in his motion. Some Grignar were charging towards him, metal teeth already stained red with blood. Just as his hands ignited, they stopped, their eyes widening. Something round rolled into their midst and then exploded. He shielded his eyes and when he looked back, the Grignar were gone. To his left Susan and Luke from Fox team emerged. They were charging, creating a path between the Murka's. Tom went to join them when suddenly they vanished in a ball of red flame. The shockwave threatened to knock Tom off his feet, but the earth supported him. When the flame subsided all that remained of the two members of Fox was a crater in the ground. The shock of it should have broken Tom but instead he became as cold as ice, with Lucast's barriers as strong then as they ever were before. Thomas Lita, the knight of Earth, was ready for battle.

He charged towards Kat and Price, throwing up a shield of fire to cover his movement. His eyes fell to Kat, "We can stop this." He yelled.
"How?" She wasn't nervous but seemed frustrated at her lack of current impact.
He pointed behind him to the maths block, "The roof. We can see everything from there."
Kat and Price nodded so he turned to Nicole, "We are moving." He pointed at the Maths block and she immediately set off towards it. Kat and Price did the same, a great thorn bush cut off their foe and Kat electrocuted those it entangled.

Tom used that cover to get to Sam and Sophie. He tried to grab her, but she was limp in his arms. He came to her eye level. The redness of them extenuated the blue of her iris's but she seemed to be looking passed him to something else.

"We are moving." Suddenly her eyes flickered onto his and life seemed to return to her, "We need you Sophie."

She allowed herself to be lifted and moving seemed to reawaken something in her. She followed Tom closely and even killed a Murka with an instinctive flick of her wrist, that skewered it with one of her throwing knives.

It was the smell that first hit Tom as he stepped into the bottom floor of the maths block and the common room, they had slept in. It was a smell he knew from the Island, the smell of charred flesh and blood. The noise though was something new. A different sound to the battle outside but a much more heart-breaking melody. It was full of many layers, people screaming for help, words of comfort and prayer mingled with it. His eyes scanned the common room that was now filled with tables, school tables that Tom had used for study. Now none of them were being used for study. Nearly all were occupied by soldiers in different states of injury while medics desperately tried to treat them.

Two Halves stood in the centre of the room, one wind Halve, and a metal Halve. Both were in Southbrook doing their exams, but they had an important job here, supporting the roof against collapse and the constant barrage of bombers.

"I can help here." Nicole said swiftly and she moved away to go to an un-attended patient. Price, who seemed to have lost all his cocky demeanour, nodded as well, "So can I."
He ran off before anyone could protest and took the soldiers hand while Nicole worked to apply pressure to a wound on the man's leg. Tom gave his best friend a swift smile before leading the other three up the stairs. The walls rumbled as they climbed. On the second floor, Tom halted. The whole stairwell seemed to suddenly fill with smoke and orange light flickered from a nearby fire, "Sophie, Sam, deal with that." He ordered, "We don't need it getting any worse."
They left then, leaving Tom with Kat. No thought of the dark vision came to him as he climbed the last flight of stairs, he was simply happy for her company. The stairwell ended abruptly at a wall with a ladder attached. Tom climbed it without any worry and opened the hatch above his head. The noise of battle swiftly returned to him, but he paid little heed to it as he emerged into the fresh air.
Jets flew over their heads, but they stood brazenly, examining the battle. The Agency soldiers were dwindling, pushed back into little pockets. Only the Halves were holding back the approaching force, that had seemed to have landed in its entirety. The whole school field seemed to be filled by the brown shapes of Murka's that were constantly joining the battle.

The bombers were continuing to rain fire and So Tom and Kat set to work, Tom diverting the missiles while Kat launched bolts of electricity that detonated them while they were still at a safe distance from their soldiers.

His eyes stayed on a bomber as it turned in the air and flew towards them and he did not stop staring as the missile fired. His hand went outwards, his knuckles whitening under the strain. The missile began to twitch and then as he yelled, the nose lifted and the missile detonated in the air far above them. He did not though spot the other jet and he could not get his hands up in time as the next missile fired. Time seemed to slow. He was charging across the roof, shouting at Kat to stop but her hand was reaching outwards. He just got in front of her as the spark jolted the end of the missile. It exploded in front of them and Kat closed her eyes expecting to be caught in that whirlwind of flame but when nothing happened, she opened them slowly. Tom was screaming in front of her. His arms stretched out wide and the force of the explosion being contained within. Just as it looked like his strength was leaving him, he threw his arms forward and the explosion clattered against the ground below and the shockwave launched him backwards across the roof.

"TOM." Kat yelled just as he hit the roof tiles with a dull thud, she was by his side in a second, "Are you okay."

Vengeance of the Gods

His eyes widened, another bomber was approaching but as it sped towards them, something flew over their heads. The bomber lifted to avoid the oncoming missile and sped away. Seconds later and he was nearly deafened by the sudden roar of a jet as it sped over the school, shaking the building further. More jets followed, different flags showing on their tail wing. While a battle was fought for air supremacy, vehicles rolled onto the school field. Kat helped Tom up and together they watched the emerging military. Machine guns fired into the Murka line; the human line now thoroughly reinforced.

"How are you feeling?" Kat asked as she stared at the scorch marks on Tom's uniform.

He stretched out, feeling a sharp pain in his tricep where it had nearly been torn apart, "I've had worse." His eyes scanned the bombers, "We have done all we can up here."

Just then the roof hatch opened. Kat and Tom turned sharply, both of their powers showing in case of a threat but all that faced them was a blackened but smiling Sophie, "Lucast wants us." She said exhaustedly before immediately allowing herself to slide back down the ladder. Tom followed more slowly with Kat in the rear guard. Sam was waiting at the bottom stairs and he was coughing but Tom did notice a sudden lack of smoke filling the stairwell.

"Did he say why?" Tom asked as he charged around Sophie, using the adrenalin boost to numb his pains.

"He's gathering a strike force and he wants us in it." She replied without looking back.

The hospital was still just as busy, but Price and Nicole were hurriedly having a drink while they prepared themselves to go back outside.

They both held a distant look though and Nicole's eyes were red. He noticed a cover laying over the man they had both left them to help, "What now?" She asked, looking hard at Tom.

He gave her a smile, "We get back into the fight."

Chapter Fifteen- On the Front Line

The situation outside seemed more desperate than when they had left. Even with the introduction of the military, the human forces were still being pushed back further. The advance halted only by the Halves that still fought valiantly.

Lucast and David were in front of them, knelt behind a jeep, talking with one who made Tom's eyes widen. His hand reached out to Nicole, but he was too late, and she tore across the battlefield, heedless of anything but her boyfriend.

"Daniel!" She yelled, "What are you doing here?"

She stood in front of him, hands on her hips. Tom and the others arrived to hear his mumbled reply, "I came to make sure you were okay."

Nicole's cheeks were red all the way to her ears and Tom thought she was going to slap him but instead she threw her arms around his neck and squeezed him so tightly Tom was afraid he would snap, "You were meant to stay out of this."

David cut in front, "Tax called all Halve's sixteen or older to the fight and this idiot thought he would tag along." His words did not match the smile he held for Daniel.

"What is the problem?" Tom asked Lucast, who seemed exhausted and he was bleeding from a wound on his arm.

"The middle is holding but our left flank is about to crumble. I need to send our Halves there at once, but I think that may give us an advantage here. The Murka's forces are more spread out here, a strike force of Halves should be able to penetrate deep into the line and take a few strategic positions." He replied without waiting to take a breath.

"That could be suicide." Tom muttered.

Lucast shook his head, "We need to force Urgarak's hand. He has made a tactical error in not expecting a military response. The Murka's seem to be running short of ammunition."

David took over, "The drop ships weren't loaded and now we are targeting any that break cloud cover. We are receiving reports of Murka's that have pushed too far forward and are now entering hand to hand combat."

Lucast then continued, "That would suggest our victory is near but Urgarak still has his greatest weapon."

Sophie went white, "We need him to use the darkness."

Lucast nodded, "While we still have the strength and numbers to fight them. We must make him believe that his sentinels are all that can turn the tide in this fight. They will give strength to his troops but he will not use them until Tom shows what he is capable of."

Tom felt all their eyes on him, "How do we do that?"
David pointed around the car and several shots thudded against it but a lot less than would have when the battle had first started, "There are several strong Murka barricades up ahead that are using a machine gun to pepper our line. We are going to use the mobiles for cover and assault them from this side. Hopefully, that will force our enemy to divert forces towards us."
Tom looked at his friends, but they were all staring at him, waiting to find out what he was going to do. He quickly changed his cartridges before looking towards the mobiles. The Murka's who were tasked with watching this side, while their barricades focused on the middle, were surrounding the mobile classrooms, "Let's do it."
David gave him a warm smile, "On my mark." He burst round the jeep and lifted his hands to a smouldering ruin that had once been a Murka bomber. A huge piece of metal flew towards him, still glowing hot and he held it in front of him like a shield. He nodded and the others followed.
Tom and Lucast followed the closest behind, switching powers in any way to gain an advantage. Next came Price and Kat, who hurled her lightning bolts while Price called whatever plants he could to tangle around the Murka's. Next came Sophie and Sam, who worked together, launching balls of ice at any

Vengeance of the Gods

Murka's who were missed by Tom's barrage. Finally came the two earth Halves and they did the most damage, crumbling bits of earth to swallow Murka's or disrupt their advance. The strike team moved quickly, gaining fifty metres of ground in very little time. Suddenly David stopped them before a line of Murka's that fired pointlessly into the metal that quivered in David's arms, like it was held by a coiled spring. Then he released it and it charged at the Murka's line. Those who could not move quickly enough were crushed and those that did, suddenly found bolts of lightning striking from the heavens under Kat's barrage.

Sophie burst from around David and fired her water immediately. It crashed over several Murka's that were swept to the floor from the force and there they remained while Sam quickly froze it. So sudden of an onslaught did the strike team produce, that the Murka's almost seemed stunned into submission. Now they charged freely, all of them using their powers to crush what little defence remained to the Murka's here but to Tom it seemed like a small thing, a rock on the beach trying to fend off the coming tide. The distraction made him sloppy and he stumbled away from the others. He heard a gunshot and was forced to the floor as something crashed against his side. He winced, not daring to look down.

Tom thought he must have been shot; he was in pain but there did not seem to be enough pain.

Finally, he braved a look and sighed. A piece of metal was rested against his side, the dent of a bullet showing in it. His eyes scanned upwards to where David was watching him wide eyed. *A lucky and instinctive defence* Tom thought, knowing he would not get many more.

Tom got to his feet and removed his nerves by killing two Murka's with his flaming brand. As the Murka's fled from their powers, the strike team reached the relative safety of the first mobile.

"We need to split here." David said, his eyes were scanning the battle and Tom did the same. They were now in line with the first barricade but behind it, unseen from their vantage point behind the jeep, a munitions store was being erected, guarded by Murka and Grignar, "Kat, Price and Sam, you are with me. You will all be more use in the close quarters." He turned to the others, "The rest of you need to disrupt that weapon cache."

Lucast nodded, "We will see it done."

David again pulled the sheet of metal towards him and he left with three of Tom's closest friends, but he could not worry about them. Murka and Grignar had quickly caught sight of them and battle was soon to be joined again. Beside him Lucast hauled himself onto the mobile and he turned towards him, "Fire now."

Tom pressed his pressure bad and a huge swirl of flame appeared. This he threw to Lucast, who took control and It swang in a burning arc before crashing down onto the Murka's below. As they scrambled Tom and the others attacked, each using rubble to assault the Murka's, who blinded by rage and fearful of their munition stores, charged hopelessly at them with whatever melee weapons they could find.

Kat hid behind the metal, with Price on her heels and David in front of them. She was hobbling, desperately trying to ignore the pain to her calf. They were charging towards the first barricade. Price cut in front and launched one of his spikes into the ground. It erupted suddenly, huge twisting branches moving across the barricade with long and sharp thorns, gripping at metal and Murka alike.
David dropped the metal and charged first through the doorway of the second barricade. His power pulled fragments of metal towards him and these he used with deadly precision. Kat followed not far behind, her rods in her hand again and these she wielded like a girl possessed. Using them, she launched bolts of electricity and smacked them into her enemy. Sam was discreet, following behind slowly, ice forming in his hands, which he then hurled at any Murka's Kat downed to hold them steady. An uppercut from a hand covered in ice connected with a sickening thud into one of the aliens while a razor-sharp edge of ice sliced into another before Kat tasered it, causing it to

twitch uncontrollably on the floor.
With the initial structure conquered, Kat led the charge. One of the big brutes rounded on her, its swing she blocked with the rod in her right hand while the left went into the beast's stomach. She laughed as it flew across the room, knocking over the machine gunner and buying the human soldiers a valuable reprieve. Just two short minutes after the assault had started, only two Murka's remained. The rest were dead, dying, or incapacitated. Some by the clever work of Price, others by David's deadly precision and even a couple were crumpled by the force of Sam's gift but most had been taken down by Kat and she eyed the other two viciously, "Ice." She yelled.
Sam's hands flew forward, and the cold metal floor began to shimmer with the thin covering of Ice. Kat felt her feet lose balance, so she fell to her knee's in a dive and allowed her momentum to carry her forward. The Murka's tried to step toward her but their thick boots could find no grip and so they were falling as Kat approached. As she slid past, each felt the full force of one of her rods in the gut and the last two remaining Murka's fell. Kat stopped herself against the far wall and with careful feet she stood up.
"You know Sam. You didn't do bad for an amateur."
He didn't reply, he was staring down at a Murka at his feet, metal protruding from its neck. Its

lifeless eyes watching him. He had swang the punch that had left it easy pickings for David. The metal Halve placed a hand on Sam's shoulder, "We aren't done yet. Let us get back out there."

*

Lucast stood upon the roof of the mobile. His hands held towards it, trying to shift it upon its foundations while below him Nicole, Daniel, and Tom, battled against the gathering Grignar. Tom felt free, like he was finally back where he belonged. A fire brand was being thrown into his enemies, knocking them down and moving to the next, with just the subtlest movements of his body.
He could sense something though, a change in the air. The battlefield seemed to be growing darker with every enemy he threw down in front of him.
He turned as Lucast yelled, "The blocks." He pointed below him, "Break the blocks."
Tom threw fire into the charging Murka's, freeing up Nicole, who grabbed her boyfriend and the pair worked together, their hands held towards the great stone blocks that supported the temporary classroom.
Tom fought to keep the Murka's at bay. His fire brand fell away with the last puff of one of his cylinders, but earth came up in his defence. He pressed the button on his hand and let the

propane cylinder fall to the ground as he moved back from a charging Grignar. A battery came with him, his power over metal slotting it all into place so as the Grignar leapt towards him, a bolt of lightning shot from Tom's hands and sent it back to where it had come from. His hand reached towards the already black sky and bolts of lightning struck at the Murka's, who hid themselves beside the now rocking mobile, unaware of their coming doom.
Daniel and Nicole's face twisted with the strain of their powers, their knuckles turning white from the pressure. In an explosion of dust, both supports crumbled and with a lunge from Lucast, it toppled forward, crushing several and pushing others into Tom's path, who released such a charge that all flew backwards from him. Lucast landed nimbly at his side and the pair charged at the now retreating enemy. Nicole and Daniel's hands were raised in front of them and the abandoned weapon store was slowly swallowed by the earth.

The line of Murka's approached. Tom ducked under the swing of a first and pushed passed a second before holding his arm backwards. The Murka gave a yell of pain as two pieces of metal passed through it and came to a rest in Tom's hands. These he immediately threw into two more. The Ilmgralite's barriers stopping any remorse to come into the twelve-year olds head.

Lucast was close behind him. He struck one with his fist and pulled one of Tom's thrown shards of metal towards him as he did, slicing into a Murka who was ready to fire at Tom. A leaping Grignar managed to knock Lucast to the floor, his golden claws, tearing at the flesh on Lucast's arm. Tom gave a yell as he leapt over the Ilmgralite, a blade of fire appearing in his hand to slice down the Grignar's muzzle.
Murka's guns cocked in front of them, but even on the floor Lucast was not defenceless. His arm lifted and the ground beneath the Murka's cracked and crumbled, hurling them into a chasm created by Nicole and Daniel's burial of the weapon store. The sudden shift in the ground caused Tom to lose his balance and two Grignar charged into him but this time Lucast came to his aid. Rising like he was on strings, Lucast leapt over Tom and from his hand water began to swirl and the two Grignar were swept away in his torrent.
Tom was about to shout about victory when the whirl of engines roared in his ears. Their advance had been spotted and a jet whirled towards them. Just as the shots fired, Tom's vision was obscured by sudden leaves and a thud as the tree landed in front of him. Bark exploded from the gun fire but he ducked against it as the jet roared overhead.
He turned just as Price, Kat, Sam and David rounded on the uprooted tree.
"Nice of you to show up." He said, a smile

failing under the deep breaths of coming so close to death countless times that morning. The sound of battle, that had been distant while Tom's focused mind tackled his enemies, returned in an instant. Bombers were still falling from the heavens and they ducked as the math's block top floor exploded outwards. He guessed it could have been no more than half an hour since they were up there last. He prayed for those inside.

Price's finger jabbed Tom in his ribs, "Where were you when we were taking on the entire Murka army?"

Tom threw fire over the tree into another gathering force, "Oh you know. Just messing around."

His words faded as sound seemed to ebb away from the battlefield. All apart from the harsh cries of the Murka's who, seeing the gap in their flank, now swarmed towards the human line, desperate to make up ground while in the heavens the clouds darkened.

Chapter Sixteen- Sentinel's

Josh wandered through the school field aimlessly. The young wind Halve lived across the street and had emerged; mouth wide open when the first drop ships had landed. He out of all of those watching knew that this was what Tom had spoken of and the thought chilled him. He needed to help his friends, he had powers like they did, and he wanted to be of some use. He had slipped through the fence at the top edge of the field, but he soon wished that he had not. With the army and strike team Hawk, the Murka's had been pushed back here, leaving Josh to walk across the body strewn, crater filled battlefield. The maths block exploding made him jump into one of the craters where he lay panting, too scared to stay there, shaking legs stopping him from standing up. He covered his ears at the sound of gunfire, the roar of jets and the shouts of the military. Slowly, with great effort, he pulled himself from the crater. His eyes stared back at the world outside of the school fence, where the only evidence of the battle was one house burning, an RAF tail wing protruding from its roof.
He only made it two steps before a heavy body knocked him back to the floor, "Stay down." A familiar voice yelled.
A bomber flew overhead, launching a series of missiles into an army jeep that leapt into the air

in a ball of flame.
"What are you doing here?" The man asked as he hauled Josh back to his feet. Josh was watery eyed as he stared at Kevin, his wind instructor, and head of Hawk team.
"I want to help." He replied, hoping the quiver in his voice could not be heard.
"You are not safe here." Kevin grabbed Josh by his collar and pulled him, not towards the gate but to the new military line.
He fell against the cold metal of a Murka barricade. The sound of gunshots were deafening, and Josh held his ears closed. The smoke that seemed to constantly linger on the field, burnt at his eyes and he screamed in his discomfort. Then the noise stopped. Guns ceased and cries were enveloped by the stillness. It was un-nerving but more so when the Murka's began to chant with delight. Josh looked towards the soldiers. They had all stopped firing, their eyes searching the heavens. He found his eyes being drawn in the same way and his mouth fell open.
Six shadows were flying across the cloud layer, spinning, searching for something. Then suddenly they plunged to the ground. Two Josh lost to the far side. Three landed in intervals across the military line while the sixth landed behind the Murka's line and immediately they pressed onwards. Josh thought he must have been imagining things when smoke like figures began rising from the crowd, towering high

above the battlefield, and staring down at the soldiers with golden eyes that did not match the rest of the smoke like figures.
The soldiers opened fire at once but all in vain as the bullets passed through the sentinel's as though they really were made of smoke. The sentinel closest, returned itself to shadow and it passed through the metal barricade, filling Josh with dread and hopelessness as it did. When it emerged in the middle of the soldiers, a whip of its smoke like arm, ripped many of their guns from their grasps. Murka's poured through the breach, slaughtering any they could and only Hawk's protection kept them from Josh.
He could not focus on the Murka's though. His eyes watched as arms protruded from the smoke, reaching, and grasping at the soldiers with wispy feelers. The soldiers seemed to go strangely erect and then they collapsed, sobbing, and screaming, eyes shut as though reliving something truly terrible.
"Your fire Mark." Kevin yelled while his whirlwind swept through the Murka's, hurling them over. More human soldiers arrived and across their guns, Mark placed his fire. The sentinel, so intent on its writhing prey, did not see the guns or did not fear the primitive weapons of humanity. When the first shot fired it carried that flame with it. Josh shielded his ears from the high-pitched wail that followed.
"Fire now." Kevin yelled.
Gunshots sounded but they were drowned out

by the constant scream that continued until the fire in those munitions tore the sentinel to pieces. Enraged by its defeat, the Murka's poured through the barricade. Josh found himself being grabbed again, this time by a female Halve, with large and tattooed arms. "Pull back." Kevin yelled, his eyes watching another sentinel who had suddenly seemed to regard them with great interest, while at its feet, smoke tore at the bodies of those it had already killed.

They all leapt back from the tree as a shadow fell from the sky towards it. Price was the only one to hold his ground and branches grew to grapple at the now rising smoke but at every touch the tree withered and died. An arm went out reaching towards him but Lucast stepped forward and a shield of flame halted the sentinel's advance. Across the tree Grignar and Murka climbed, cutting them all off from eachother. Another shadow swept towards them, a smoking arm knocking Lucast away and the sentinel on the tree vanished into shadow. Price stared around searching for it, ignoring the Murka's that fought around him, waiting only for the end.

Tom ducked under a Murka blade, a sheet of metal protecting him from their gunshots. He had to reach the sentinels, had to be there to stop them before his friends could be hurt. He could no longer see Kat and Price through the bodies, but he knew Sophie and Sam were behind him, protecting his flank and stopping any Murka's who approached.

Tom drove fire into a Murka, parrying its blade while his eyes still scanned through the throng for a sign of the sentinel. Another shadow loomed over him but before a strike could come, he was showered in particles of ice and Tom looked down at the crumpled Grignar, an icicle, not dissimilar to those that ornamented his roof on Christmas day, sticking from its throat.

Over his head, water balls and ice balls flew, defending him but he could feel their strength wavering. The sound of a sentinel dying came across the battlefield, filling his heart.

"Stay close." He yelled to the pair behind him. He felt a tingle in his hand, a sudden surge of power. He charged with Sophie just behind him. Together they knocked more Murka's away, each coming narrowly close to death but all prevailing in the end. The power in Tom's hand, threatening to send all into oblivion.

A shadow charged at Price and he ducked just in time, but he could see the shadow rising into its smoke like form. An arm shot out ready to strike but it never connected. The smoke gave a scream and Price stopped. Kat's hand was shaking, her rod held into the middle of the entity. She gave a muffled moan, as an arm swept her away, launching her high into the air. She landed headfirst with a dull thud, metres away from Price.

Heedless of anything, Price ran towards her. He felt the sentinel coming for him, the wrongness of it prickling on his senses. It was like cold water had rushed through him as the sentinel passed and despair filled his senses. He collapsed at Kat's motionless form and stared at the blood mingled with her blonde hair. His eyes seemed to darken, like a filter of death had been placed over them. Grief took him, she was dead, he could feel it in his heart. Blackness and dire thoughts began to sweep through his mind, and he collapsed to the floor in the shadow of the sentinel, crying while in pain, Kat desperately tried to take his hand.

"Stop foul creature." Lucast yelled, standing in front of Price and the sentinel, the flame surrounding him only just touched the corners of Price's mind.

Sensing its doom, the sentinel withdrew after more easy prey.

Lucast crouched before the crying Price. Kat's eyes were looking at him, dazed but very much alive, she whispered, "What is wrong with him?"

"A darkness that will pass." Lucast said, two Murka's came to attack but fire ended that attempt briskly, "Daniel, David." He yelled and the two men charged over, "She needs help." He pointed at Kat while from a piece of metal,

he formed a stretcher for her to lay on.
"And him?" David asked.
"I will bring him back into the fight." Lucast deadpanned.
Ignoring all her pleas to stay there, David and Daniel lifted Kat onto the stretcher and then David lifted her towards the medical block. A swirl of fire surrounded Lucast and Price as the Ilmgralite pulled the young man's head towards him.
"She's dead." Price whispered, his cloudy eyes full of tears.
A blue light appeared in Lucast's hands and the black veil over Price's eyes lifted but Lucast did more than that. Thoughts of battle he formed in the boy's mind so that the eyes, that were once full of tears, became as hard as steel. The Sentinel was suddenly back in front of them and Lucast looked up at it, his golden eyes on fire,
"Find Tom." He ordered.
Price rolled away just as Lucast stood. He launched fireballs into the now charging sentinel who absorbed them, dying as it did but still it charged on.
"By the power of Drage, vassal of Livella, please give me the strength for this fight." A sword of flame appeared in his hand and he charged. Blind to all else he did not hear the gunshot. He screamed as the bullet tore through his ankle. One step and he was down, the flaming sword extinguished, and blood fell to the floor, blood of an Ilmgralite that seemed to make all the

world weep.
The sentinel loomed over Lucast's crouching form, who was so full of pain and so exhausted from the battle already, that he could not throw up a defence for himself.
"Fool." The smoke whispered, "The curse of Drage helped create us." Then it drove its smoke like hand through Lucast's chest and gun shots tore through the Graul's back. Lucast's head lulled forward and, on that battlefield, light years away from his planet, he gave back the gift he was bestowed. The first Ilmgralite to die on earth's soil for a hundred years.

Tom watched in horror as the Sentinel released Lucast, who fell to the floor and laid their rigidly. The yell of grief swept across the battlefield and many fled from the sound. Power surged through him, ghost like flames tickling across his arms. His pressure pad malfunctioned in his rage and bolts of lightning shot from him, striking the fleeing enemies. Tom felt his hands coming together and he fuelled his rage and grief into a single flame. White it burnt and as the Sentinel turned triumphantly towards him, the jet of fire shot towards it. The Sentinel screamed, consumed by the bright flame until it and the flame was gone. Tom fell to his knee's staring at Lucast's body, dead Murka's surrounding him but no new enemies dared to approach. Already they were wavering, two of their most powerful weapons had been defeated. Across the Murka line, the word retreat was starting to spread.

Josh heard the high-pitched scream of the sentinel as Tom poured his grief into it, but he could do nothing but cower beside the soldiers. Kevin was fighting and Josh tried to find courage through him, but his legs were like jelly and his power over the wind seemed a trifle thing compared to the might of an alien race. A jet fired at the Murka's line causing Josh to stand up, he was not cut out for this. One thought now fuelled his mind and adrenalin hardened his legs, *run.* He took one step and then suddenly the panic seemed to fill him. Before he could register it, he was ten metres away from the military line, but a sudden ball of flame sent him charging the other way, heedlessly running for any clear space. He stopped sharp. Five Murka's were watching him curiously, maybe shocked to see a child on the battlefield, or wondering if Josh was the one they sought.
"Please don't." He begged as guns were suddenly raised to his eyelevel, but a great wind swept them away swiftly. Kevin charged, hands towards them but the Murka's still managed a cry in their harsh language before another whirlwind swept them off their feet. The cry echoed across the battlefield and Josh watched one of the Sentinel's acknowledge it. An arm

suddenly seemed to stretch out from the figure and one black finger pointed in his direction. The sentinel suddenly swept into the air and charged into a nearby tree. The crows that had gathered to gorge on the dead suddenly flew into the air, smoke rising from their beaks with every call. The crows circled the battlefield, like they were governed by some will and Josh guessed the sentinel had taken them. The birds scouted the battlefield, passed where the cry had come, wheeling over the maths block, before focussing back onto them.

Kevin's arms came up in a sudden wind and part of that sent Josh spiralling away from him. The birds flew headlong into that whirlwind, the first few falling but more poured on, driven by the power of the sentinel. Kevin gave a cry as the black swarm enveloped him entirely. Josh screamed while the black birds pecked and tore until when they took flight again, he could not recognise his instructor.

His eyes swept upward. The birds, beaks still dripping red, were charging for him. His arms came up but not in defence of himself. The first thud he heard made him jump but it was followed by a series as each of the crows fell to the field where they lay lifeless, like a carpet of black wings. The darkness having finally consumed their fragile forms. Josh needed no other invitation, with his mind blank, he charged for the outer fence and the safety it provided.

Vengeance of the Gods

The battle had now turned completely. Leaderless and facing certain death or capture, many of the Murka's began to flee back to the heavens and several of these began to scatter. Most went back to their ship but Tom saw the odd few head for the distance, pursued by military jets.

The leading sentinel examined the battlefield menacingly, the other two sentinels came quickly towards it and absorbing into it they almost doubled its size. Tom grabbed the others swiftly, "We need to end this." He said to them. Nicole was sweating but she nodded. Price also looked determined and Sophie and Sam were already charging towards it. A group of arms burst from the sentinel, wrapping around the dead Murka's who suddenly began to rise clumsily as though they were puppets held by invisible strings.

"I will distract them." Tom yelled, flame surrounding him, "You get the sentinel."
Flame dispersed the dead Murka's and the others charged through the gap. The Murka's were on Tom in a second. He twisted around, doing all he could to block the blows. Two he dealt normally killing blows to but still they pressed on, no matter what limbs his burning brand severed.

Sam started the assault against the sentinel. A ball of ice he launched, to naive to realise the danger he was in. The darkness moved in time, but it had the desired effect. For just a second the dead Murka's stumbled, causing one to lose an arm, the blade that went to strike at Tom falling with it.

Sam flew backwards from the sudden smoky arm that struck him. He landed with a thud; all the air stolen from his lungs. Nicole charged by him, a huge slab of rock she launched, and the sentinel wailed as it struck but part broke away, turning to shadow and chasing her around the field before uprooting her so she joined Sam on the hard ground. The Sentinel though could not regroup before Price and Sophie launched their own attack. The sentinel turnt from side to side, doing all it could to dodge their many attacks. From his vantage point Sam saw it, a large beam that joined the sentinels to the Murka's. At his side he felt a Murka gun that he had landed beside, and prayed that it was loaded, "Tom." He yelled and he lifted the gun as Tom turned towards him, "Fire."

Tom's hand shot outwards and a bright flame shot from his hand. Sam pulled the trigger and the bullet passed through fire, carrying it as it collided with the smoky arm. The trail of the darkness erupted suddenly into flame and the long high-pitched wail filled the battlefield. The Murka's around Tom collapsed and in what seemed like pain, the sentinel began to rive violently.

Vengeance of the Gods

Price saw his chance, the last of his wooden rods he now grasped. He charged towards the sentinel and passed the shaft through one of Sophie's water balls before burying it deep inside the sentinel. A Smokey arm sent him flying but not before he began to sing. The spike erupted in a tree with thorns larger than any Price had seen. He sang as he fell, eyes never falling from the Sentinel. The tree began to tear at the smoke like body, ripping it apart and holding it in place. Slowly roots bore into it and the thorns lengthened and hardened until it ripped apart great chunks of smoke and then with a whimper the sentinel was consumed. The remaining Murka's surrendered and dropped their weapons. With the same whimper as the sentinel, the battle was over.

Chapter Seventeen- On board the Sira Mirta

Tom found himself beside Lucast, staring at his motionless form, wishing that he had been one of the Ilma so that his body was nothing more than a shell to be shed and re-grown. Some soldiers were cheering but many began to work, gathering prisoners or caring for the wounded. Tom turned at the sound of footsteps, but nothing could have prepared him for the arms that surrounded him. He caught Sophie's scent at once, under the sweat and the dirt it was there, and it was comforting. As she released him, Nicole came next and even the boys shared an embrace. Tom held Sam most tightly. He was quivering and Tom's touch seemed to make tears fall down his cheeks. He spoke only when Tom released him, "What do we do now?" He looked at the bodies that surrounded him and his pale face went green.
"We stay together." Sophie muttered as she took his hand, but it was too late. Sam turned around and hurled up whatever was in his stomach. Tom understood it, he was also coming down from the fight. He felt ashamed. Ashamed that he had been forced to kill, ashamed he had forced others to kill and ashamed most of all that people had died to protect him.

"It's over then." Nicole said slowly.
He looked to the still dark cloud, "Not just yet. Urgarak is still up there and who knows what else."
With that the five of them walked together in silence back towards the maths block, eyes on the floor to avoid the scenes in front of them. The ground floor was now nearly empty of wounded, a huge array of vehicles were parked in safety on the far side, blue lights flashing as the wounded were loaded into them.
There they found Kat; a bandage wrapped tightly around her head. To Tom's shock, Price burst into tears at the sight of her and he wrapped his arms around her like he was afraid she might soon melt away into nothingness.
"There you guys are." Said a female voice and Tom smiled at Ashley as she came over, hands on her hips, "We have been trying to find you."
"Is Tax here?" Tom asked instantly.
She shook her head violently, "He is trying to explain this mess to the world." Then she looked them over, "I am going to get you all a cup of tea, you look like you are about to pass out."
They did, Tom expected. He was feeling pained all over, the adrenalin boost in his palm doing nothing to keep his legs up. They were all leaning on something, probably aching in more places than they knew possible. Ashley left and returned moments later with six hot and highly sweetened cups of tea that they sipped silently

at.

"It is crazy is all I'm saying." They all shot up as two men passed. One was David, the other a small balding man who appeared to be bleeding.

"How many men from Hawk can you spare?" David asked as they disappeared into a classroom.

Tom sighed as he stood and gave his friends a reassuring smile, "I need to hear this."

He left without a word, moving slowly towards the classroom where David and the man were hurriedly talking.

"You can't expect us to take an entire ship." The bald man exclaimed.

"Listen." David said tiredly, "I have all the plans laid out, Lucast was very thorough in what he gave us. I don't like it either, but we have no other choice."

"David's right." Tom said to announce his presence as he stepped into the room, "With Urgarak still up there, this means nothing."

"Thank you Mr Lita." The acting leader of Hawk grunted, "But I will not risk my team going onto an enemy ship without any real intelligence."

"Now Mick." David said in a condescending tone before taking a deep breath, "Do you really think I don't know what I'm doing?" He pulled out several sheets of paper, all with crude notes and drawings, "The ship is called the Sira Mirta or Diamond heart. It is a troop carrier class two whatever that means but

Lucast explained that is nothing more than a simple first strike craft. It contains only enough troops and ships to begin a ground invasion. We must have got enough of the soldiers to make that ship nothing more than guards and crew. However, in case Urgarak decides that Tom's arrest is not what he seeks, it has enough fire power to destroy a small city."

Mick put his hands up in acceptance, "That's fine but how do we get aboard?"

David pointed to the ships bottom half, "The same way the bombers got out. This type of spaceship." He stared in disbelief that he was using the word, "Only has a small ground to air fleet, situated on its lower levels. The fly boys will mark strategic areas including the main doors for the launch area. We fire missiles to target these areas and hopefully force him into low flight to stabilise his pressure."

Mick thought for a second but there could be no argument about securing both Urgarak and the weapons he had stored, "It's crazy but we need to get that alien maniac." He quickly shook David's hands, "I better tell Hawk the good news."

David nodded triumphantly, "Gather whatever cartridges and weapons we can. We are going to need them. Halves only." Mick left the room with a small smile at Tom and David stared at him, "I know what you are going to say." He looked down, "You can come. We could use you, but your friends stay here. They are beaten up enough and I am not phoning their families to say why I let twelve years olds go on this mission."

Tom thought it was strange that he was comfortable phoning his parents and saying that but maybe he didn't see him like he saw the others. His actions never really gave him a reason to. Tom gave a swift nod; he knew he would be happier with them safe on Earth.

"Suit up." David ordered in a stern voice, "We will be leaving soon."

Tom cut out of the room and returned to his friends. They all looked exhausted; broken to the point that they would need a weeks' worth of sleep. When they spotted him, Price attempted to sit up sharply, "What is the plan?" He asked with a forced smile revealing his braces that were covered in blood.

"A team are going to assault the main ship." Tom replied bluntly, unable to look at them.

Price's smile faltered for a second, "When do we go?"

"We don't." He deadpanned, "Well I do. You guys need to stay here."

Sophie looked shocked, "But." She mumbled and Tom cut her off sharply, "David's orders, not mine."

He had expected more of a fight. Nicole and Price looked ready to, but his golden eyes stopped them, and they had sunk back down showing their exhaustion. Kat was pale, clearly in no state to fight and Sam was crying, not listening to the conversation. Sophie watched him with a blank expression, no argument on her lips which confused him.

"I don't want to go." He said, his eyes locked on hers, "But they will need me up there."

Sophie looked into his eyes, the Tempter's words of his death circulating in her mind but he was not going alone and he was not going to be a hero. Finally, she smiled and from her belt she pulled her two remaining cartridges and handed them to him, "You will need these." She whispered.

Tom took them and then three batteries off Kat. As soon as these were attached, David walked past him briskly, "It's time."

He nodded, "See you guys soon."

There were no hugs, no goodbyes. Those things would have to wait for when he returned, if he returned. He followed David without another word and was shocked to see that already the work was beginning. Weapons were being piled up, dead bodies laid together, both Murka's and human while prisoners sat in circles watched by armed guards. A helicopter was a new addition to the field, its engines running.

David was quickly handed a radio from a military soldier and Tom was close enough to hear his order, "Bring the rain."

his eyes went upwards to see the trail of missiles as they sped across the sky. Above the cloud layer they went, and great roaring booms soon echoed down to the ground.

Vengeance of the Gods

"We got him." David yelled triumphantly, "He's coming back down now."
Soon a noise cut out the sound of the Helicopter's engines. Tom's eyes went to the clouds that suddenly seemed to bulge before a great metal shape burst through. The ships engines slowly eased the spaceship down, creating a great swirl of air, that swept around all those working on the battlefield. It resembled in parts the drop ships, just of much greater size and even at that height he could make out the guns on its underside.
The whole school field soon came under the shadow of the great metal shape, that covered nearly the entirety of the town, bigger than four football stadiums.
David closed his mouth sharply and Tom realised his was hanging open also, "Let's move." His metal instructor ordered.
Tom ducked as he approached, even with the blades many feet above his head. Mick helped him in, and he hurriedly sat across from David and pulled his straps tight. He had been in a helicopter once before on the Island. Then he had been too tired to enjoy it. Now he was too nervous. Everyone else seemed just as cautious, apart from David who had his arms stretched out weirdly. The helicopter was soon racing into the air, the ship growing ever closer. Part of it was burning and a door opened into a wide hall. This, the helicopter soon passed into. Tom heard gunshots, but none seemed to hit the

surface of the helicopter and he suddenly
realised the reason for David's strange posture.
He was creating a shield around the craft.
The helicopter landed with a thud and the door
swept open. Callum Hart of Fox was first out
followed by a water Halve. While the water
Halve distracted them, Callum disarmed them
with a swipe of his hands. Many Murka fell
during that first onslaught in the hangar, the
power of the Halves proving too much for them.
They had lost one though, an old earth Halve
who had just been unlucky as a dying Murka
pulled the trigger as he fell.
Once the deck was cleared, they all looked hard
at eachother, "Where now?" Tom asked and
David shrugged, "We go up."

None of them could have really hoped to know
their way around the cramped ship. To Tom it
looked like something he had once seen on a
documentary about submarines. There was
little comfort, and everything was set low for
the Murka's hanging arm. They met little
resistance during their march. They climbed a
few decks and found themselves in a corridor
that must have stretched the whole width of
the ship, "Left or right sir?" Callum asked
without looking where he was going.
Pounced upon by Murka's, it took much of Tom
and David's strength to keep them from the
young man. Rage filled him, giving him a small
amount of strength to subdue the Murka,

whose thick arms gripped at Callum's neck. Many Murka's fled from his fire but one remained, surrounded in flame. David approached it gingerly, "Take us to Urgarak." It made a weird noise that none of them could understand. Callum, who was white with shock from his near-death experience gave a shrill laugh, "I don't think he speaks English boss." A shadow suddenly seemed to sweep across the corridor. The Murka went rigid, his eyes becoming black pools, "Follow me humans." It said in a voice clearly not its own.

It turned awkwardly and began to beckon for the humans to follow it down the long corridor. Tom stayed close to David, "This is bound to be a trap."

David smiled coolly, "I am counting on it."

The Murka led them into a large metal tube that he guessed to be a lift of some kind and he was proved right when it began to rise. The corrupted Murka did not seem to notice as David stepped behind it, or when he placed what looked like a metal tennis ball onto its belt, his finger hooked inside of an attached pin. The doors opened with a creak and Tom's heart sank. Murka's surrounded them, at least twelve with guns cocked and aimed straight into the metal tube. Behind them, standing tall, was Urgarak. His white scaled face was covered in many red scales, his golden eyes seemed to burn but there was what seemed to be a black film over them. Everyone seemed tense. The humans were barely breathing, the Murka's arms trembled and veins bulged in their thick arms.

Tom heard the pin be pulled.

"Grenade out." David yelled as he gave the Murka an almighty shove. It stumbled towards its kin before the grenade exploded.

Tom and David's arms shot out, stopping the shrapnel from shredding them and when the smoke cleared it was clear Urgarak had done the same and managed in doing so to shield several of his soldiers.

"Fools." Urgarak yelled and his arm shot up. A great trail of smoke charged towards David, knocking him backwards, taking down several Halves with him.

Tom launched the shrapnel back into the room and the Halves followed him into the bridge of the spaceship. Urgarak winced as a shard of metal sliced at his cheek but Tom's triumph turned to horror as no blood leaked from that wound, just the swirling black smoke of the darkness. Halves battled Murka then but Tom and Urgarak only had eyes for eachother.

The Graul of Uralese attacked first. A shadow charged towards him and he dived out of its way, flames coming up to protect him but that was when Tom felt it. He was exhausted, almost completely to the core. The radioactive element in his palm was sucked dry of energy and that last burst of flame had been the straw that broke the camel's back. His knees felt like giving way as all that had happened in the battle previously, fell onto him in an avalanche of unchecked emotion. He knew Urgarak could feel it. He looked around, desperate for support but more Murka's had been prepared in ambush and they charged forth now. None went for Tom, he was Urgarak's alone clearly and there was nothing he could do about it. A stream of darkness charged for him and only a flutter of flame came up to defend him. The stream quickly broke through and the darkness grabbed him, pulling him to the ground and surrounding him completely. His body became stiff and he felt as though a wave of ice-cold water had passed over him. He could not feel his toes or the tips of his fingers. All was becoming numb to him.

His mind began to pass from the world just as a film of blackness passed over his eyes. He could hear screams, pleading voices inside his head and he could put a face to every single one. They were the voices of the people who had never returned from Curamber and they were cursing him, blaming him as despair welled up in his heart. The darkness crept through his nose, into his lungs and slowly, like it really was water, he began to drown but his body could not move, would not move, to prevent it.

So intent on his prey, Urgarak paid now little heed to the battle unfolding around him. He was tearing at Tom's mind, unfolding it, filling it with dark thoughts so that it would submit willingly to his cause. Abgdon could not refuse him then and when this hero of earth was defeated, the rest would fall under his sway. Urgarak accounted little for the Halves fighting, the abominations of Ilmgral and that was where he was defeated.

Mick, blinded in his rage at seeing Tom near death, forgot about his powers while facing his enemy. The Murka who fell, fell from his own weapon, a knife of a strange metal. This Mick plunged deep into Urgarak's back. The Graul yelled in a deep wail of pain and the streams around Tom broke. A great swirl of wind knocked Mick back to the floor, but the knife had struck well. Urgarak clawed for breath and he tried to use his power to bring air into his lungs, but none came. Blood, black and boiling, burst from his mouth and knowing that his death was imminent, with no rebirth for him, he wept. He gave one last desperate whimper before falling beside Tom, who was now pale and lifeless. He stared at Tom as he died, sensing his failing heartbeat, and smiled that he might have achieved that.

As Urgarak died, the remaining darkness inside of him burst outwards. Passing through human and Murka, darkening their minds and driving them to despair.

A cry came from the Murka's and many surrendered then, kneeling before the humans as though they would to lords. Two halves had

been killed, one of Hawk's and Peter, of Fox, but all eyes were turned towards Tom. David was shaking, hands covered in blood, "Call in for reinforcements." He said sharply, eyes never straying from the motionless boy.
Mick crawled towards the twelve-year-old. His hand went to Tom's chest, and then to his ice-cold arm. He shook his head solemnly, the darkness forcing death into his mind.
David felt a lump form in his throat and rage filled him, "I will radio down and tell them he is here." He said coldly, "I can't be in here with him."

Tom listened to David's words and he tried desperately to open his mouth, to make any noise to indicate that he was still alive. Nothing was working though, even his breaths seemed to be coming once every minute and his heart was nothing more than a whisper. They were leaving, he could just about see their feet moving to the door. They would leave him, leave him to drown and to succumb to the voices and the un-relenting cold.
He searched inside himself, searched for any form of his own power still held inside his body. Then he felt it, a warmth in the tip of one of his fingers and through that he could feel the soft fabric of his trousers. Focussing, he channelled everything into that spot. Willing his mind, forcing his finger to move. A flutter, faint but there and then another. His whole finger soon

moved, and the horrible condemning voices were growing fainter. They had to see now, see before he lost this chance and any hope.

David stopped on the threshold of the lift and un-willingly he turned back into the room. His eyes widened, "Warmth." He yelled, "We need warmth."
He charged back towards Tom, his eyes resting on the moving finger. He took Tom's hand; it was cold but there was some life. When Tom gave a gentle grip, he nearly burst with joy. The others rushed over. Great balls of fire now circled Tom while soldiers removed clothes and covered his limbs with them.
"Tom." David whispered and he sighed as the corner of Tom's mouth twitched into a smile, "Let's lift him out of here."

They carried him then, the balls of fire still surrounding him. Soon Tom could move his arms and his legs, though they felt like he had run a marathon. When he was able, he absorbed the fire balls surrounding him and fire seemed to spread through his veins, clearing his mind and the last of the chill but now he felt bruised, as though he had been run over by a car.
"Did we finish it?" He asked now that he was able.
David seemed overjoyed to hear him speak, "Sure looks like it."

Vengeance of the Gods

Even though he protested, Tom was not allowed to stand on his own two feet until they had carried him all the way to the helicopter. He was glad of this because as soon as he did, his legs felt like buckling straight away and only his arms holding onto the seat kept him up. Several of the Halves strapped Tom into the helicopter but he was shocked to see that he was leaving on his own, "You are not coming?" David shook his head, "Not yet. There are still things we need to do here."
He gave Tom an affectionate grasp of his arm that made Tom wince before he disappeared. Tom's head rested against the metal boundary between the cabin and the cockpit. He felt like he could sleep for weeks but closing his eyes brought back the terrible voices and they shot open just as quickly as they had closed.
"You okay back there?" The Pilot said through a speaker by Tom's head. His numb arms reached for a microphone, "Never better. Let's get back down to home."

Tom's first step back onto the school field was difficult but he manage to keep himself up on his own two feet. The scene around him had changed. Vans were all over the school field, most bearing some logo of a news Agency. Tom could see that cameras were beginning to be focused on him, he turned his head away from them. The world would all be awake now, everyone had seen undeniable proof that aliens

existed. This would change humanity forever. Slowly Tom's hand lifted and knowing he was being watched, he called what little strength he had and a flame, small for what he was used to but still big enough to be seen by the news crews, floated in his hand. After a minute it vanished and the last of his strength was spent.
"Always a show man." He heard Price say from behind him. His legs gave way and he collapsed into Price's arms, "Are you okay?" Price asked just as the others arrived.
Tom allowed Price to lower him to the floor, "I'm just tired." He smiled at his best friend, "Sorry for stealing your limelight."
Price showed a bright smile, "I wouldn't worry. There is footage of us securing one of the barricades, that will be enough for me."
Soon Sophie, Nicole and Kat were hugging Tom while Sam stood nervously beside them. As soon as they had all squeezed him painfully, they took a seat on the ground by him, "We didn't think you were coming back." Kat said bluntly while Price held her hand, still looking shocked that she was there.
"I always come back." Tom tried to laugh but it failed him. He nearly had not, Urgarak had beaten him as easily as if he had been a Murka and that was a hard thing to process. He thanked all the gods that David and the other Halves were with him.
"Can I say it is over now?" Sophie asked innocently.

Vengeance of the Gods

Tom looked at the damage to the school and the camera's surrounding them, "It is far from being done. The world now knows we exist." He sighed and laid back against the ground, "I think our battles are just beginning.

Chapter Eighteen- A world that Knows

"Let me get this straight." The president of the United states stood as he addressed the emergency assembly of world leaders, "Are you telling us that you let them go?"

"I don't think anyone here would be happy if I kept advanced technology on my countries soil." The Prime minister of Great Britain answered coolly, "Or gave trial to an alien race that does not speak our language. At five thirty this morning, UK time, a delegation from the planet Ilmgral took control of the ship and escorted it off world."

The President did not seem convinced, "And what of those who died? Where is the justice for those people?"

"My people Mr President." The Prime Minister answered sourly.

"And what of these children?" The French president said then, "Why are their names not mentioned? it appears they were the ones that these creatures were after."

"They are children and therefore have a right to some form of legal ambiguity." The Prime minister replied, "Everyone here can deal with Halves in their own way and I shall do the same. Now if that is all, we have nations to address."

Tom watched as the screen changed and a news presenter filled the screen, "That was Prime

Minister Hardy, speaking last night at an emergency conference in New York. This morning we interviewed the Director for the Institute for detection and protection of Halves, Michael Warman." The screen changed to show Tax, earning a whoop from Kat and Price, "Many people have asked for the names of these Halves to be given out." The presenter said from off screen.

Tax gave a small smile, "The first reported Halve was over two hundred years ago." He began, "They have proved no more harm to the community at large than any ordinary people. It would be foolish to believe that they are now a threat, just because they are known to us."

"My viewers would be wondering what is stopping these people, with such amazing powers, from committing arson or robbing a bank"

"If you can tell me on instance when that has..." Tax was cut off by the presenter.

"Please answer the question Mr Warman."

"My organisation works to help Halves control their extraordinary abilities to the betterment of society. Imagine the world we could create where fire fighters could absorb flames or control water from the outside. A world where we did not need to use explosives in quarries or a world where Halves can grow food for people in starving countries. That is the world..." The screen went blank. Tom turned around and scowled at Tax just like Kat, Sophie, Sam, and

Price did.

"Enough of that." The Director said, "You will only get yourselves worked up."

"Any news on School?" Sophie asked innocently and Tax nodded his head, "We can't cram you all into the other schools in the area so a home-schooling programme is being set up for the remainder of the year."

At that the others all smiled but Tax looked sternly at them, "And I will make sure your new office is off limits during school hours so that you all actually do your work." He then smiled, "It seems you have found your way to my new office."

"It is incredible." Sophie said as she looked out of the seven-story window and stared over Southbrook.

"Let's go for a tour." Tax said, beckoning them all to follow him.

Tax's office stood at the top of the newly built Agency Hq. The seven-story block boasted state of the art facilities for the now leading department in earths defence, but its crowning glory was the vast and extremely powerful satellite that was housed above it.

Tom walked behind the others into Tax's private lift. He was now bruised all over and his limbs were a horrible shade of yellow from the battle a week earlier. The others though looked remarkably well, as though the battle had relieved some of the strain of Curamber, like it was the end of that hard chapter of their lives.

Tom though was more driven. He had been beaten, nearly killed. If he was meant to be a warrior for earth in the coming wars, then he needed to be stronger. When they stepped out of the lift, into a vast room with a padded floor, he saw the tools to do just that. The new training room was huge, with a station for every gift he could imagine.

"This is incredible." Tom exclaimed, "How much?"

Tax just laughed in reply and led them out of the training room and towards a flight of stairs. Tom took more time than the others to climb these, but they waited patiently for him. He was suddenly faced by a corridor with many rooms coming off it from either side. On the door's names were written and Tom whispered them as they passed, "Able, Boar, Crab, Dog, Echo and Fox." They passed doors that were bare but stopped at one at the far end, "Phoenix." Kat said aloud as she read the plack on the door, "Who came up with that?"

Tom smiled at them all, "I did. I thought it felt right."

Tax opened the door into a wide room. There were sofas, a ping pong table, at Price's request, and five desks. "There are two bedrooms just off their with showers and changing facilities." He eyed Price, "Male and female separate bedrooms." Price blushed and Tax continued, "When we send you out on assignment, you will operate out of here, but it is your room to study in and to relax after your training. We hope it is enough, we didn't know what to give our youngest strike team."

Kat, Sophie, and Sam dived onto the sofa's while Price ran over to the ping pong table. Nicole had refused to be there, and Tom knew why. Nicole wanted an end to all of this, and she had no intention of going back into a fight if she could help it.

Tom though went straight towards the lockers and found one with his name on it, "Uniforms?" He asked and Tax nodded.

"No weapons though Mr Lita. You will be given them when you need them."

Tax beckoned Tom to sit on one of the sofa's and he did it as quickly as his legs would carry him. Then he stood in front of them, "I'm not going to say life will be easy for you all after this. You were seen fighting in the battle, and I have no idea what people are going to think knowing you guys exist. All I do know is, you five are the future of this Agency and from everyone here I say this, welcome on-board phoenix team."

*

Captain Marcus was almost giving up on the flight through the heavy cloud. Below him it was snowing like it was never going to stop and he was not looking forward to landing on the private runway of one of Britain's richest people. The second-hand military jet flew like a dream, but it was his orders that frustrated the Captain.

Suddenly his radio burst into life, "Do you have a visual?" A deep voice asked.

Marcus almost did not reply but he pressed the joystick down slightly, breaking the cloud layer and found immediately his target just a few hundred meters away, "Affirmative." He said dryly, "I have a visual."

"Then take the shot." The deep voice ordered coldly.

Marcus looked at the wall of snow and the craft that was only visible because of the break it made in the blizzard, "I will never be able to get a visual of the crash site." Marcus explained but he still made sure to lock onto the Murka drop ship. He had followed it since the battle almost a week ago. That morning he had launched his assault, forcing the craft into the air and away from a civilian population. Now all he had to do was take the shot.

"Mr Christianson doesn't care about that; he wants it downed at once."

"Of course he does." Marcus whispered so the man would be unable to hear him, "And whatever Mr Christianson wants, he gets." He then spoke more clearly, "Taking the shot."

It was easy, Marcus watched the missile launch from his wing and knew at once it was a kill. At that range, the Murka craft wouldn't even know it was a target before it was hit. The back end of the craft exploded but was soon lost in the thick wall of white snow, "Target is down." Marcus said clearly, "I've lost visual and am returning to base. You better tell Mr Christianson to find it before the Agency does."

"He knows how to deal with them." The voice replied smoothly, causing a shiver to run down Marcus's spine. He knew that was not an understatement.

Marcus turned his plane around and set his course for his home base. Questions of his flight would be asked, and he would need to be far away when they were. He was looking forward to his Tongan beach holiday, far away from the blizzard that had enveloped Britain.

Vengeance of the Gods

Walking as a child they found him
*The secret knight of earth
Though the humans he called kin
Their skin they hid his birth
but he was of a greater kind
A power he had within
That only tragedy could find
in the mountains heart therein*

*And like a god he rose among the rest
and found the wicked heart
And they battled through a deadly test
that tore the stars apart.
A god fell from the sky
with the devil in his head
And the knight of earth saw him lie
with those of the Islands dead*

Part of the poem, The tragic knights of Earth.
Author Unknown.

The Knights of Earth Saga.

Book One:

THE ESCAPE FROM HUMANITY.

Thomas Lita is no ordinary child; his vivid dreams of a strange world and a people unlike those of Earth led him to the discovery of a power within himself which sets him apart from all others. He kept his ability to manipulate fire, water and more a secret, until his dreams led him to four others, each with a power of their own. When they find clues to the origin of their powers on a school trip, they unintentionally release an evil presence that threatens not just the island but the entire future of the universe. The friends must use their powers to defeat this threat, learning who and what they are in the process, unaware that what they will find will change them forever.

History of Ilmgral

Book One:

THE SUNDERING OF THE TWO MOONS.

From the creation of the Universe to the Sundering of the two moons of Ilmgral, read the most important tales from the earliest years of the Ilma. Set way before the curse fell upon them and before the Graul were raised to their equal, these stories detail how the chosen Ilma began to fall from the pedestal the Gods and their Vassal's set them upon.

Not much is known about the worlds beyond our solar system, the worlds that until recently we did not know existed. Chance has allowed me to study in the great libraries of Ilmgral, to see its vast history that Earth has now become a part of. For that reason, I have created this story, to show you the long tapestry of events that would one day bring universal war to Earth. In this volume I cover the early years of the Ilma, from the creation of the universe to the most tragic even of those ancient years. From the libraries of Dragor, I have translated these tales, so that we may better understand the role that has come to us.

Printed in Great Britain
by Amazon